A Season
for Martyrs

ALSO BY BINA SHAH

Slum Child

A Season *for* Martyrs

A NOVEL

Bina Shah

DELPHINIUM BOOKS

HARRISON, NEW YORK • ENCINO, CALIFORNIA

So here cometh
"Delphinium Books"
To recognize excellence in writing
And bring it to the attention
Of the careful reader
Being a book of the heart
Wherein is an attempt to body forth
Ideas and ideals for the betterment
Of men, eke women
Who are preparing for life
By living. . . .

(In the manner of Elbert Hubbard,
        "White Hyacinths," 1907)

A SEASON FOR MARTYRS

First Edition

Cover and interior design by Greg Mortimer

Library of Congress Cataloguing-in-Publication Data is available on request.

ISBN 978-1-88-328561-6

14 15 16 17 18 RRD 10 9 8 7 6 5 4 3 2 1

SINDH (also spelled Sind) is a province of southeastern Pakistan. It is bordered by the provinces of Balochistan on the west and north, Punjab on the northeast, the Indian states of Rajasthan and Gujarat to the east, and the Arabian Sea to the south. Sindh is essentially part of the Indus River delta and derives its name from that river, which is known also as the Sindhu River.

Geographically it is the third largest province of Pakistan. It is bounded by the Thar Desert to the East, the Kirthar Mountains to the west, and the Arabian sea in the south. In the center is a fertile plain around the Indus River. Sindhi is spoke by about 15 million people in the province of Sind. It is an Indo-European language, related to Urdu and other Indo-European languages prevalent in the region.

Karachi became capital of Sindh in 1936, in place of the traditional capitals of Hyderabad and Thatta.

—From "Sindh," in Wikipedia

Sindh, still a new country to us, is and will be an important portion of our Eastern empire, for two reasons. In the first place it may be made the common commercial depot of Central Asia; and secondly, it is an advanced line of posts thrown out to protect India from her natural enemies, the turbulent, war-like, and powerful trans-Indine nations.

—Sir Richard Burton, *Sindh & the Races That Inhabit the Valley of the Indus,* 1851

Oh God! May ever You on Sindh
bestow abundance rare;
Beloved! All the world let share
Thy grace, and fruitful be.

—Shah Abdul Latif Bhitai, Sufi scholar and saint (1689–1752)

Peccavi

The week after General Charles Napier defeated the last of the great Sindhi chieftains of Hyderabad, he sent a one-word telegram to the governor-general to inform him of the victory.

"*Peccavi*," he told his clerk, Jephson, a young man from Dorset who had only landed in Karachi three weeks before, and was suffering from a terrible case of dysentery.

"Sir?" said Jephson, wondering if he had misunderstood. The twinges in his stomach were crippling his concentration, and the army doctor had filled him up with so much castor oil and calomel that his head seemed to be swimming. His mother had warned him about the *mal aria*, about the typhoid, and about the heathen women (she was far too genteel to use the word "whores"), saying that each malady, taken singly or all together, could ruin a young man's life forever; but she had never told him that a simple flux could give him so much misery.

"Are you deaf, man?" said the general. He raised his chin and stared at Jephson; Napier was shortsighted and to glance down his high-bridged nose lengthened the distance between his face and the object of his vision, making it easier for him to focus his unsettling blue eyes on Jephson's quavering fingers. "Write it down. *Peccavi.* Oh, for Christ's—didn't you learn Latin at that damned hole you call a school?"

"Yes, sir," murmured poor Jephson, a sudden spasm twisting through him. He wrote down the word painstakingly and waited, pen poised above paper, for further instructions, massaging his stomach surreptitiously with his free hand.

Napier clenched his hand, then brought it down onto his table with such force that Jephson jumped in his seat. His face dark as the bark of a burnt tree, he proclaimed: "Six thousand dead at Miani. Five thousand at Dubba. I have Sindh, and for that I have been paid sixty thousand pieces of silver."

Only then did Napier's telegram make sense to Jephson— *peccavi* being the Latin phrase for "I have sinned."

Jephson looked up at the general, but the man was far away in his thoughts, mulling over his recent victories, no doubt. The persecution of Mir Rustam and his escape into the Thar Desert, pursued by Napier and a group of his very best English officers and native sepoys. The thousands of Sindhis marching into the battle of Miani Forest, falling to their knees as their bodies were blown apart by the English cannons. And the Talpur traitor, Ali Akhbar, who called off the Sindhi cavalry at the last minute during the battle at Dubba, his bribe money jingling in his pockets as he fled the hamlet on his dappled stallion, another gift from his grateful employer: Napier himself.

In truth, Napier was thinking about his wife and three daughters, who had all inherited their mother's dark Greek skin and Mediterranean temperament. He had betrayed Sindh for their sakes; the blood money given to him by the East India Company—whose directors he called "a parcel of shopkeepers"— would pay his daughters' dowries, *and* what was left would be used to appease his wife's formidable appetite for expensive clothes and ruthless entertaining. Not a moment too soon, because his youngest daughter was threatening to elope with a minor, disgraced aristocrat, and a suitable marriage had to be arranged quickly. And nothing was done quickly in this world without very great sums of money.

Napier, a career soldier, was haunted at night by dreams in which he was paraded through the streets of Calcutta with a sign hung around his neck, on which was painted a single word: MERCENARY.

And so the telegram was sent, and the company was very pleased, and General Napier was made commander in chief of India for a time, and his daughter married a captain in the Guides; and Jephson got over his dysentery but was struck down the next year by typhoid and buried in the military cemetery in Karachi, while his mother in her cottage in Dorset wept copious tears and embroidered countless cushion covers and pillowcases with his name.

For the next one hundred years, Sindh became a distant outpost of the Bombay Presidency. The British built railway lines and barrages, irrigating the fertile lands of the Indus basin until they blossomed into patchwork quilts of wheat, rice, cotton, and fruit orchards that stretched up and down the Indus River for a thousand miles. The British governed Sindh hand in hand with the local rulers, achieving their supremacy through a delicate balance of collaboration, bribery, and brutality pioneered by Napier and carried on by a proud line of governors-general with equally high-bridged noses and clerks of questionable education and dubious health.

But Sindh was the land of the Sufi saints, who wandered all

over South Asia, converting millions to Islam, that relentless religion that had roared out of the Arabian deserts with all the strength of an army of lions. With their gentle ways and their message of peace and love, the Sufi saints sang and composed poetry and bewitched the Sindhis into the worship of Allah and his Messenger, long before the British ever set foot on their shores.

The Sufi saints were buried in tombs all around the province; and over the centuries and generations their bones crumbled into the sand, imbuing all of Sindh with a peculiar strength that fired the souls of warriors, and would one day inspire them to throw off the yoke of British occupation. Then the Land of the Sufis would merge with the Land of the Five Rivers, the Land of the Pakhtoons, and the Land of the Baloch in 1947 to become a greater entity, a newly birthed country: the Land of the Pure.

The story of General Napier's telegram is only a rumor, originating from that famous cartoon in *Punch* that shows the general clutching a telegram in his hand that reads "Peccavi." But it is true that one hundred and sixty years after it was sent, the only tribute to the Conqueror of Sindh remains in the form of Napier Mole Road, an area in the Karachi ports famed for two things: the bridge that connects Karachi to Keamari, and its red-light district, where prostitutes hope to become movie stars, especially if they possess the light skin and blue eyes that may or may not have been gifted to them by some distant British ancestor.

October 18, 2007

Ali Sikandar sat at his desk, surfing the Web while fact-checking the special program his television channel was preparing for the arrival of Benazir Bhutto. She was to fly into Karachi tomorrow from Dubai after eight years of exile; Ameena Hai, Ali's producer, had just told Ali that not only did he have to write the copy for the background segments of the report, but he also had to go with the cameraman and sound technician to interview people at the airport for their reactions to Benazir's return.

"Dammit," Ali growled to Jehangir as soon as Ameena walked away. They worked as researchers for the television channel City24 News, where Ameena was well-known for taking particular delight in torturing her junior staff: making them rewrite copy, tearing to shreds what they'd already written, ordering them to stay in the office all night to work on a segment that was always cut from the final edit. Ali didn't have a choice: saying no to any of her demands would have cost him his job. Jehangir possessed a college degree from America and useful contacts all over the media industry, but Ali had only managed to finish a year of business studies at a university in Dubai before he had to return to Karachi to take care of his mother, and younger brother and sister. Now he attended evening classes at Bhutto University three days a week so he could look for a better job as soon as he had his BBA in hand.

So when Ameena leaned over the partition that divided the sweaty, cramped office into even more sweaty, cramped cubicles, placed her substantial arms on top of the partition in a way that emphasized her breasts, and informed Ali that he would travel to Jinnah Airport and follow Benazir's entourage into the city even if it took nine hours to crawl the twelve miles from the airport to Bilawal House, Ali had to agree to fulfill the assignment.

"Are you a Benazir supporter, Ali?" asked Ameena.

Ali returned her gaze coolly. "I'm not."

"Really? I thought all Sindhis loved Benazir. Bhutto's daughter, daughter of the soil . . ."

"My father was a supporter," said Ali. "I'm not that impressed." He noted with a sense of relief how much easier it was to speak of his father in the past tense. He no longer had to check himself, to make the mental effort to change from *is* to *was*. And he no longer had to deal with people's sympathetic glances, the hushed tones and the occasional *how-did-it-happen* that people cast in front of him like fishing lines, hoping to get some kind of drama or gossip on the end of the hook. Ali had already told his stories about his father's death, his widowed mother, the orphaned younger brother and sister, enough times that people's curiosity had been satisfied.

Now, when the occasional question came up, he knew exactly how to handle it: he simply said that his father, a Sindhi bureaucrat who worked in the taxation department, had died two years ago of a heart attack, leaving him, the eldest son of the Sikandar family, responsible for the family. Said with just the right amount of detachment, a sad smile, a tightening of the lips, he could change the subject quickly then, and nobody would be the wiser.

"Well, that's good," said Ameena. "At least you won't be too biased. Remember, no editorial comment, just the facts, when you file."

Jehangir stared at the blue-green veins traversing Ameena's cleavage and bombarded Ali with juvenile emails urging him to take a picture down her shirt and post it all over the Internet.

- *It's easy*, Jehangir wrote in his tenth overexcited email, an hour later, as Ali still sat and stared glumly at his Facebook page. *Just get a webcam, and then when she comes over, turn it in her direction while she isn't watching and then—*

- *That's sick*, Ali fired back, not bothering to read the rest. *But I can't believe she's sending me over to the airport! Two hundred thousand people are going to be showing up there. It's going to be a mess!*

- *Stop complaining*, wrote Jehangir. *Always complaining, Ali. You're going to get to see history in the making.*

- *History? I could care less about any of this.*

- *Wait, wait, wait. Wasn't your father a PPP man?*

- *He was. I'm not. I'm nobody's man.*

- *What about Sunita, aren't you her man?*

- *Shut up, loser.*

-*You first, jackass!*

The abusive nicknames were a constant running joke between them, a way to express affection, exasperation, and boredom in the office. But Ali was always careful to keep that one particular insult out of his repertoire—*fag!*—because Jehangir had recently confessed to him that he was, in fact, gay—or at least bi; he wasn't sure. In return for that particular confidence, Ali had told Jehangir about Sunita. Two young men, needing to appear invulnerable and in control most of the day, ended up telling each other a lot of secrets when they were the only people in the office at three o'clock in the morning, making sure that all the graphics were correct for a program that had to be aired in another four hours, bickering over McDonald's Big Macs delivered two hours ago, now stone-cold and tasting like congealed cardboard. Ali clicked back to the Wikipedia website, where he was pulling up information about Benazir Bhutto for the background report:

Benazir Bhutto (Sindhi: ب‍ينظري پ‍توٽ ;Urdu: ب‍ے‍نظري ب‍ه‍ٹو, pronounced [beːnəˈziːr ˈbʰʊʈʈoː]; 21 June 1953—) is a politician and stateswoman who served as the 11th Prime Minister of Pakistan in two non-consecutive terms from November 1988 until October 1990, and 1993 until her final dismissal on November 1996. She was the eldest daughter of Zulfikar Ali Bhutto, a former prime minister of Pakistan and the founder of the Pakistan People's Party (PPP), which she led.

In 1982, at age 29, Benazir Bhutto became the chairwoman of PPP—a centre-left, democratic socialist political party, making her the first woman in Pakistan to head a major political party. . . .

Benazir Bhutto's popularity waned amid recession, corruption, and high unemployment which later led to the dismissal of her government by conservative President Ghulam Ishaq Khan.

In 1993, Benazir Bhutto was re-elected for a second term after the 1993 parliamentary elections. . . .

In 1996, the charges of corruption levelled against her led to the final dismissal of her government by President Farooq Leghari. Benazir Bhutto conceded her defeat in the 1997 Parliamentary elections and went into self-imposed exile in Dubai, United Arab Emirates in 1998.

Ali skimmed the rest of the entry and picked out the important facts, cutting and pasting them into the Word document that was next to the DesiBeauties page that was open beneath the Wikipedia page. Education . . . family . . . marriage . . . Prime Minister . . . policies . . . policies for women . . . It was mindless work; Ali often thought a dog or a robot could do his job, but it was thirty thousand rupees a month—City24 paid that much to their researchers, hoping to lure them away from the older, more established rival channels—so Ali was not, despite Jehangir's accusations, complaining.

Ali stopped short at the part about all the corruption cases. Ameena had told him to stay away from too much controversy, to stick to the basic facts. "I'm not going to turn this into some kind of tabloid show just to get the ratings," she told Ali.

"Isn't that what this business is all about?" said Ali.

Ameena frowned. "We get pressure from the advertisers all the time to make things juicy. They keep saying the viewers need more *masala*. But I don't want to do that here. Someone has to try to show a little class."

Ali had a sudden memory of his father shouting that the accusations were all a pack of lies and that Benazir's father, Zulfikar Bhutto, was the greatest man that ever walked this earth. Ali thought that if Sikandar Hussein were to read the Wikipedia entry about the Dassault case and Surrey palace and Asif Zardari's polo ponies, he would become apoplectic. It was this image of his father, spluttering and red-faced, that Ali found he missed in an odd way now, even though it had upset the entire family whenever he had exploded like that in front of them.

Ali paused from his work to imagine a conversation with his father: Sikandar would bellow—he always thought that the loudest voice won the argument—that it was all cooked up by the army and the president, who didn't want Benazir to come back and win the election. Ali, certain that his father didn't know what he was talking about, would coolly argue that foreign courts wouldn't file false cases and there was enough evidence to convict a hundred times over. Sikandar would retort, in his raspy, cigarettes and whiskey-raw voice, that anything could be cooked up; even history could be rewritten if you put the right amount of money into the right palms. Just look at 9/11! What proof do we even have that they were actually Muslims? Anything can be made up, anything can be true or not true, depending on whose interests it serves.

Yes, Ali would answer. Just like the National Reconciliation Order the president had signed, which proclaimed all the politicians innocent of crimes of which they'd already been convicted. Even murders.

Then he'd say, "But Baba, we don't have to defend criminals just because they're Sindhis like us."

And Sikandar would have no answer to that.

The conversation would never really have happened: Sikandar would brook no argument about his beloved Benazir. Ali could still remember how his father boasted that he was one of the thousands who accompanied her on the procession when she'd first returned to Pakistan in the eighties. "She was standing on top of that truck for *eighteen hours,* smiling and waving to everyone, like a heroine—a princess. No, a queen. I swear she looked right at me and I started to shout, *Jiye, Bhutto* and everyone began to shout and then the whole crowd was shouting and it was like thunder, no, it was like the roaring of the sea. . . ."

As Ali grew up, his father kept telling the story over and over again, embellishing it and making it even more mythical with each retelling. "She is amazing. She is beautiful. She is our leader. She is so intelligent. She is . . ."

"He sounds like he's in love with her," Ali whispered once to

Haris, more than a little jealous and wishing the praise was being heaped on him instead of on Benazir. Haris signaled *Shut up* with his eyes, knowing that if their father heard him speak with such insolence, he'd get a slap, or more than one slap. And if their mother witnessed that, she would cry. Then his sister Jeandi would also cry, and his brother Haris would shut himself in his room and smoke a whole pack of cigarettes. Ali hated the weeping and the smoking even more than he hated his father's blows, so he'd controlled himself, even though he was sure that Sikandar had no idea how ridiculous he sounded. And now Ali could not show him that his precious idols had feet of clay, but at least there were no more tears in his household because Ali hadn't been able to hold his tongue.

Ali's father could not deny, though, that the leaders of Pakistan had left their country in a mess. A total mess.

As Ali drove his car through the Karachi streets, he had to avoid potholes and ditches because all the roads were dug up, as if land mines had exploded everywhere. He still stopped at red lights, but the rest of the traffic was generally so unruly that nobody even bothered to slow down at the intersections. Before leaving the house, Ali prayed that he wouldn't meet with an accident, because if you were in a bigger car than the poor bastard you knocked into, a crowd of excited hoodlums would gather around to beat you senseless in the name of vigilante justice. He often came home to a darkened house: the load-shedding guaranteed six, seven hours a day without electricity. He dreamt of being able to afford a generator that ran all their air conditioners, but they only had a UPS system that ran a few lights and fans for an hour, then shuddered and expired like an old ox that had suddenly decided to die in the middle of the road.

They'd just aired a special report at City24 over the weekend: how burglaries, kidnappings, and carjackings had become everyday affairs in the Pakistan of the twenty-first century. They'd opened the phone lines at the end of the show and the boards lit up with the scores of ordinary people calling to tell their stories: how gangs of men Ali's age or younger pushed a pistol into your face and forced you to give them your mobile phone. Sometimes they would pick you up and drive you around town for a couple of hours, stopping at an ATM machine, making you withdraw and hand over all your money to them. Everyone cursed the police, the administration, the mafia, but nobody held any hope that their laments would be heard by the authorities.

And in this last year, things had just gotten worse. The Supreme Court judges had been deposed; the country suddenly faced a wheat shortage—never before had Ali seen people standing in line behind trucks as bags of flour were thrown down to them, as if they had woken up in some famine-riddled African country. Suicide bombings everywhere, fanatics promising to take over the country, impose Shariah law, and conquer the entire world. *Newsweek* had recently featured Pakistan on its cover and awarded it the title of "The Most Dangerous Place on Earth"; only a fool would disagree with its verdict.

Just a few weeks ago, at a wedding, Ali was gossiping with a group of friends when one of them, Aziz, interrupted the conversation. "Have you heard what's been going on these days?"

"Now what?" said Ali, rolling his eyes.

"Well, you have to watch out for this guy. He'll stop you in the road and ask for a lift. When he sits down in your car, he just opens his vest and you can see that he's wired with enough explosives to blow you and your car to paradise."

"Oh my God," murmured Ali. The other people in their circle clutched at their drinks and bit their lips as Aziz went on.

"Oh God is right. Thing is, he doesn't look like a *jihadi,* just an ordinary, pleasant-looking guy. And you know what he says? *It's your lucky day. You're going to get to be a martyr.*"

"God, then what?"

"He gets in and makes you drive around for a couple of hours. But he isn't looking for an ATM, and he doesn't want your mobile phone. He wants you to drive until you find a military truck, or a bunch of policemen standing at a picket, and then he tells you to say your prayers and drive straight into them while he blows himself up."

"No!"

"I haven't heard of that happening!"

"It wasn't in the papers . . ."

"Well, you just have to be smart and drive around aimlessly and avoid anyone in uniform. After an hour or so the guy says, 'Drop me off here. You don't get to see paradise today. It's your unlucky day after all.'"

Ali looked at all their glum faces and said, "How's that for going out with a bang?" Everyone laughed in a shocked, guilty sort of way, but then a frightened silence descended upon them. Ali wondered out loud if the story was true or not, but Aziz swore that it happened to his friend's cousin's brother's friend, and the following week a newspaper carried the story, so urban legend and fact gelled into one quivering mass of fear and paranoia.

The Letters to the Editor columns in the newspapers were bursting with letters about Benazir's secret deal with the government and possibly America as well: *Make me prime minister and I'll let you come in and catch Osama bin Laden*. But the government insisted they couldn't ensure her safety, and with the top terrorists of the day promising to kill her on her return, the prospect of following the procession from the airport to her headquarters near Clifton Beach filled Ali with dread.

If he were Benazir, he would just have stayed in Dubai, enjoying the countless millions in the offshore bank accounts and the lavish mansion in Emirates Hills, and the occasional trip to America and Britain to deliver speeches about freedom and democracy.

Benazir claimed she was coming back here for the sake of freedom and democracy. Ali knew she was coming back to obtain the rest of what she had failed to steal last time. And tomorrow Ali would have to be there, doing his job for Ameena, terrorists or no terrorists, trouble or no trouble.

Tomorrow might just be Ali's lucky day.

* * *

"Ali, you are so stupid."

"Thanks a lot, Sunita." Ali pressed the mobile phone tight to his ear and closed his eyes in the darkness so that he could better concentrate on the smooth tones of his girlfriend's voice. "I love you, too."

"No, I'm serious, Ali." She blew a sigh down the phone that reached into Ali's ear and tickled his eardrums. "Don't you know how dangerous it's going to be there tomorrow?"

"I heard." Ali shifted in bed, twisting into the sheets so cool and comforting to his naked skin. He wondered for a moment whether she, too, was unclothed. Ali longed to ask her, but he lacked the courage, even though they had been going out for nearly two years now. There were some things you couldn't speak of to a girl even if she was your girlfriend and you wanted to marry her someday. Ali needed Sunita to know that he respected her, that he never thought of her as fast or loose or easy; he never even asked that she tell him about any boyfriends she might have had before him; he knew that a girl as good as her would not have let anyone else get as close to her as Ali was now.

Sunita Lalwani had long black hair that fell halfway down her waist, glowing skin just the color of warm sand, and almond-shaped eyes that she lined with heavy kohl even though in

Ali's opinion they needed no adornment. Whenever she walked by, men's hands would go to their balls before they could stop themselves. Ali saw it happen all the time, which was why he stood extra close to her when they were out together, sometimes putting his hand on her back or stroking her arm. A man had to show that a woman was under his protection if he didn't want others to leer or sidle up to her and misbehave with her.

They had met when Ali returned to Karachi after his year in Dubai: he was walking out of the university gates on the first day of class when he saw a petite girl, presumably another student, arguing with a six-foot-tall driver who wanted to force a large Land Cruiser into the precious parking spot occupied by her tiny Suzuki. Something about the way she held her ground against the driver caught Ali's attention, and then he realized that they were arguing in Sindhi. Intrigued, Ali walked over and asked Sunita if he could be of any help. "No, thank you," she said, in English so the driver, a grizzled man in a white *shalwar kameez* and a beaded Sindhi cap, wouldn't understand her. "I can take care of this myself."

Then she whispered something under her breath, and Ali was unsure whether she meant it for the driver or himself: "Birhna lussi!" The phrase was so vulgar and so unexpected coming from this beautiful girl's lips that Ali burst into scandalized laughter. Their eyes met: Sunita blinked once, then twice, and on the third blink Ali was hooked. Sunita suddenly relinquished her spot to the driver and allowed Ali to help her find another one; so he liked to think that she, too, had become enamored on that first day.

"They're saying there could be suicide attacks," Sunita now said to Ali. They were forced to talk in secret, late at night after everyone else was asleep, because Ali's mother would have a stroke if she knew of his Hindu girlfriend, and Sunita's brothers would murder her if they knew she had a Muslim boyfriend. They conversed in Sindhi, their mother tongue, which Ali's father always maintained was the sweetest language on earth. Ali always felt jubilant when he talked to Sunita: her voice made Ali taste *mithai* in his mouth, freshly made and smelling of rose water and sugar syrup, decorated with silver paper and packed into colored boxes for a great celebration.

"There won't be," Ali tried to reassure her, although he quaked inside thinking about it. Only today the news had come through the wires that Baitullah Mehsud himself threatened to have Benazir blown up the minute she set foot on Pakistani soil. "It'll be fine."

"And what about the crowds? Anything could happen," Sunita said.

"It'll be all right," Ali repeated, because he couldn't think of anything else to say. He decided to try to cheer her up a little. "I heard that she might get a helicopter to go from the airport to the mausoleum, at least."

Sunita snorted. "That'll be the day. No, it's going to be a big truck, a shipping container attached to it, and bulletproof screens."

"And bulletproof cars."

"And twenty thousand policemen."

"And bomb squads."

"And sniffer dogs."

They both began to laugh, because it all sounded so absurd, this spectacle — a real *tamasha*. The men and women were on the streets already, thronging the camps that were set up, their faces painted green, red, and black, the colors of the People's Party. They were pouring into Karachi by the truckloads and busloads all day, villagers from all the four corners of Sindh, celebrating and dancing to loud Sindhi music as if arriving for a wedding, or at least a *rukhsati*, the ceremony when the bride left her parents' house and came to live in the house of her groom. Benazir was married to Sindh forever, as some Sindhis said, but now she was staking her claim for her third prime ministership. Two hundred thousand people would be there tomorrow, ready to receive her and accompany her back to Bilawal House.

"The roads are going to be all blocked. How will I get to work?" Sunita said. She worked in a bank near the Hotel Metropole, and so traveled the length of Shahrae Faisal twice every day, but the traffic and the security cordons would make it useless to even leave the house tomorrow.

"Didn't they give you the day off?" Ali was incredulous.

"No. They expect us to be there on time. It's a British bank, you know. They have *standards*."

"Bastards."

Another sigh. "I need the job."

"Why do you think I can't say no to Ameena? I need the job, too."

"Oh, Ali . . ." sighed Sunita. "I'm so sorry."

"For what, darling?"

"If only . . . it's such a shame your father passed away while you were all still so young. You wouldn't have to work so hard if he were still . . ."

Ali felt the familiar shame suffusing his body that had driven him toward all the lies in the first place, coupled with the guilt he felt that he couldn't share the truth even with Sunita, whom he claimed to love more than anyone in the world. That his father was not really dead. But Ali always said he was dead because he had abandoned their family for a second wife, a much younger woman he had met and married five years ago, while he was still married to Ali's mother. And Ali had concocted this delicate tissue of lies about a dead father who had been a bureaucrat instead of a landowner because he was unable to face the derision of people around him, who jeered at the feudals and asserted that they were the root of all of Pakistan's problems.

Once, Ali had been in a conversation with colleagues at work; one of the women, a news producer in another department, had been railing about Sindhis: how illiterate they were, how lazy, how uncivilized. It turned out she was angry because her next-door neighbors, minor Sindhi feudals from the interior, had illegally taken over a plot of land next door and were using all their connections in the provincial government to lay claims to her rented house as well.

"Be careful," said one of Ali's friends to the producer. "Ali's a Sindhi."

The woman had the grace to blush, but then she lifted her chin defiantly and said, "I'm sorry, but I have to say, I don't like Sindhis at all."

"I don't like them, either," deadpanned Ali, and everyone laughed a little too loudly, the overexcited barking that ensues from an uncomfortable situation that nobody knows how to defuse. Ali had never forgotten the embarrassment of that conversation, and dozens of others like it, and the constant newspaper articles about the feudals being corrupt tax-avoiders with undue influence on the politicians, the calls for separating Karachi from the rest of Sindh, the television dramas depicting all Sindhis as bloodthirsty plantation owners who kept their poor peasants in chains and raped the village girls and chased down runaway bonded laborers with dogs.

He knew that he would never have gotten this job with City24 if they'd known he was the son of a Sindhi feudal. The media took it upon itself to expose the crimes of the landowners; they'd never want one of them in their midst. Far easier to tell people that his father was a bureaucrat no longer among them so nobody would ask him anything more about his family.

Even Sunita had to be kept ignorant of these facts of Ali's life, because she too would find them so distasteful that she would never have gone out with him in the first place. Sunita was already taking a big enough risk in getting involved with him because of the difference in their religions. To hear that Ali came from a family of feudal landowners, whom people looked down on in disgust, saying that they were dissolute and drunk, that they always had two wives and married their daughters to the Quran in order to keep the land in the family, would drive her away from him completely, and right now she was the only thing in his life keeping him afloat.

There was one more secret Ali was keeping from everyone for now: a letter of admission from Kansas State University lay in his desk drawer, and nobody knew about it yet, not even Sunita. He had an uncle and aunt who lived in Kansas; Ali had written to his uncle secretly last summer and was sent the admission forms. He'd been accepted for a degree course in business administration: a transfer, since he had completed a year of studies in Dubai and two here in Karachi, that required only three more semesters in America in order to graduate with a BBA.

He'd tried once to broach with his mother the subject of going away. "Why do you need to go to America?" his mother said. "You had a year in Dubai before you came back and looked after us—you *had to*, it was your duty. I know how difficult that was for you. But now you've got a good job, you're studying in one of the best universities in Pakistan. Aren't you happy here?"

"No," he said, simply. And he was astonished to realize how true it was. Nothing was making him happy here. *Nothing.* Not his job, not his studies, and if he was truly honest with himself, not even Sunita, as much as he loved her.

Life in Karachi every day was too much for him. Getting up to face the same family dramas every morning, his life never his own, having to arrange when to pick up and drop off Jeandi from school, Haris from university, his mother from her chores and appointments. Dealing with the no-water-no-electricity-no-driver-no-servant issues, day in and day out. The fear that anyone could break into their house and rob them, rape his sister, his mother. The stress of living in a city that did everything to grind you down and nothing to lift you up.

Ali had never even been to America, but he knew that over there he could be a different person: easygoing, happy, and free. He wouldn't have to give a single thought to what anyone else wanted, needed to do, had to have. He'd seen his uncle and cousins from Kansas when they came on their now-infrequent vacations to Karachi. They were bigger, stronger, more self-assured. Their English was impeccable, American and fast. They had wads of dollars in their wallets, rows of credit cards from foreign banks, driver's licenses that proved their legitimacy in that country. Ali wanted that supremacy so badly that he was willing to turn his back on the remains of his tired little family.

He'd never spoken of it again, after that first unsuccessful attempt. He filled out the forms and arranged for the admissions fees, all the while imagining how his mother would weep, and Jeandi would cower, and Haris would accuse Ali with the dark look in his eyes that said *How can you leave us here?* And Sunita . . . Ali didn't know what Sunita would say, nor did he want to imagine it. All he knew was that he had to go. He could be there for a couple of years, then send for Sunita, and nobody in America would care that he was a Muslim and she was a Hindu. They wouldn't know what a feudal was, or why everyone hated them so much.

No, Ali couldn't stand to stay here, in Karachi, in Pakistan, any longer; it would kill him one day or another, one way or another. And in this city, that could happen as soon as tomorrow, if it happened to be Ali's unlucky day.

The Old Man and the Sea

Even the most seasoned sailor must sometimes come ashore, and nobody felt he deserved shore leave more than Khawaja Khizr.

It was never easy being a Sufi saint, even if you were one of the *Panj Pir,* the Five Pirs. Even if you were regarded as the guardian of all waterways, oceans, seas, and rivers, and loved and worshipped by the people of Sindh—Hindu and Muslim alike—you could tire of riding a *palla* fish up and down the thousand miles of the Indus River, or become seasick at the sight of the blind Indus River dolphins leaping up and down to herald your arrival.

There were days when your bones ached, your eyes were rheumy, and an old man sometimes wanted nothing more than to lie down and have a long, dreamless nap, despite the glory and the excitement of Pir-hood. Never mind being mentioned in the Rig Vedas, the Quran, the romances of Alexander, and the Sumerian mysteries—and in this way, Khawaja Khizr thought that his other four compatriots, Zakaria Noor Gohri, Bahauddin

Zakaria, Syed Jalal Bukhari, and Lal Shahbaz, had it easy. Were they entrusted with access to the Fountain of Life and the Water of Youth? Had they guided countless eminent persons—Moses, Ilyas, even St. George—over the last eight thousand years to drink of those waters? Had they brought dead fish and dead kings to life as if they were tricks to be performed at a dinner party?

Of course not. Bahauddin Zakaria had only had to travel to Baghdad to be awarded the Khilafat—the head—of the Suhrawardia order; and that, too, after serving only seventeen days as the previous Sufi master's disciple!

Syed Jalal Bukhari had got involved in the mess up in Multan, with that foolish daughter of King Harichand who'd stolen their horses. Khawaja Khizr had counseled patience, but Jalal, always possessed of a hot temper, had rushed off and persuaded Lal Shahbaz to agree to his plan to destroy the city of Aabu, and all for what? The old king had still died of leprosy. That good-for-nothing tomboy princess had never returned the eighty-one horses and all the goods they were carrying. And worst of all, when the five Pirs' own wives arrived in Aabu in search of their husbands, Jalal was so furious that he'd cursed them all, so that they'd ended up buried under the earth.

Their screams, coming from beneath the dusty ground, still haunted Khawaja Khizr. Sometimes he woke up from nightmares in which he could hear them calling out, "Help us, oh please, Pir Saeen, please save us!" Salty tears running down his face and into his mouth, the blood pounding in his veins, his heart racing. Oh, Allah, why had he gone along with Jalal's madness? Why hadn't he revoked the curse and helped them out of the maw?

After that debacle, Zakaria Noor had approached Khawaja Khizr privately, on the island of Astola, in the Indian Ocean. "Let's go away," he told Khawaja Khizr, saddened by grief at the loss of his wife, who had been very young and pretty and much beloved by Zakaria Noor.

"Where to?" sighed Khawaja Khizr. He was resting in one of the caves in the cliffs off the south face of the island, his feet tucked underneath him. His green and brown robes surrounded him like lush foliage, but in reality there was no foliage on this strange, desolate isle, where he liked to come and offer his prayers sometimes when he needed a place to meditate and escape the vagaries of life. He'd sheltered there when Alexander's army had come marching through the mainland, and had decided through *istikhara*, the holy process of dream divination, that he should meet Alexander in the Land of Darkness and guide him to the Fountain of Life.

But that young man, also known as Sikandar and as hot-headed as young Jalal Bukhari, had refused to follow him at the fork of the path by the mountain pass, and so he had got lost, while Khawaja Khizr had followed the Pole Star and drunk from the fountain to become immortal. And Sikandar had gone on to try to conquer India but died in the attempt, a golden-haired child of thirty-two, while Khawaja was fated to live forever, patrolling the rivers of the Indus on his *palla* fish as his hair grew gray and then silver, and his whole being shone white in the luminous moonlight.

"I don't know," replied Zakaria Noor. "West, to Persia? Or east, to see the Yamuna and the Ganges?"

"I'd have to change my name to Varuna," replied Khawaja Khizr, shaking his head.

"Is that so bad? The Hindus love you as much as the Muslims. They pray to you as much, they light *diyas* in your honor, and feed the poor in your name. Don't you fancy a change?"

Khawaja Khizr gave it serious thought. It would be tempting to leave the Land of the Sindhu behind, with its crazy, lazy people, the fishermen who drowned in droves every year because they refused to learn to swim, the rulers and kings who thought nothing of going on sorties to plunder and pillage, as if proceeding to the river for a winter picnic. The truth was that, though Khawaja Khizr's message was one of peace, his devotees still struggled with their primal urges to possess and destroy. And it was tiring him out.

But in the end, he shook his shaggy white head and refused his friend. "I cannot leave them."

"Saeen, they don't value you!"

Khawaja Khizr smiled at Zakaria Noor, who was only a thousand years old, and still had the passions and ideas of a young boy. He put his hand on Zakaria's forehead, sweeping the hair away in a paternal gesture. "They may not value me, but they still need me."

"But that's not fair!"

The old man chuckled. "Fair? Not fair? It is not up to us to decide that."

So Zakaria Noor left Astola, alone. Khawaja Khizr stayed on at the island for a month, praying and meditating in the cave, coming out after the dawn prayer to watch the fishermen set off on their daily odyssey into the sea. He wandered among them, invisible, whispering *quls* into the ears of some, blowing Ayat-ul-Kursi onto the bodies of others. He waited on the cliff above the shore, praying for their safety, until their ships were seen again at noon on the horizon line. When they hauled their nets heavy with shining, slippery fish onto the sand, he offered *nafils* of gratitude to Allah Saeen, not just for the day's catch, but for the kindness of the sky, the generosity of the water.

And so it went on, for centuries. Eventually Khawaja Khizr returned to the Indus, stepped again onto the back of his faithful steed, the *palla* fish so beloved to the people of Sindh, who negotiated its thousand bones just for a taste of its sweet river flesh. He traversed the waterways of the Indus, blessed his devotees, oversaw the endless cycles of rain and drought, high and low tide. Summer, fall, winter, and spring, the farmers turned to him and begged for rain to water their crops, and when it came, they thronged his shrine at Bakar, that lovely island in the middle of the Indus. They set lighted lamps into scores of tiny boats floating on the waters, which always delighted Khawaja Khizr, and brought a rare smile to his weathered features.

The years passed. Khawaja Khizr was tired every day, the muscles in his legs hurt from balancing himself on the back of the tricky little fish, and the blind dolphins who accompanied him on his travels were growing fewer in number, poached as they were by greedy men. There was even talk that some monsters liked to use the dolphins as they would a woman, finding some perverse similarity in the genitals of both. Such talk broke Khawaja Khizr's heart, but still he continued with his work, asking Allah for strength and protection from the evil in men's souls.

In the later years of the twentieth century, another burden was placed on Khawaja Khizr's shoulders: to protect the land of the Indus from the war that had broken out between the Hindus and the Muslims. Khawaja Khizr could not understand how this had happened: the land had been one for millennia, and then suddenly he had woken for his prayers in the middle of the night, by an angel whispering in his ear that where there was once one country, now there were two. And worse than that: they went to war against each other, planting bombs in the ground, dropping them on each other's territory from airplanes overhead. Worst of all: the seas were no longer safe for the fishermen of both sides. Warships patrolled the waters, capturing innocent men who'd only sailed out to feed their families, throwing them into jails and branding them as spies.

Khawaja Khizr prayed nonstop for everyone, Hindu and Muslim, on either side of the arbitrary border that the British had drawn, and which was painted in the blood of millions in the mayhem that followed. He threw himself on the ground until his knees bled and dark marks appeared on his forehead and the palms of his hands from his prostrations. He stayed up for forty days and nights, reciting the Quran, performing the secret rituals known only to the Sufis, begging Allah Saeen to save these foolish people from themselves.

The effects of his prayers were subtle. On a night when Indian planes came out to drop bombs on Hyderabad, clouds suddenly gathered in the sky, blocking out the moonlight and forcing the planes to return to their base, their thirst for blood unfulfilled. Land mines scattered along the Rann of Kutch would not explode when stepped on. Prisoners somehow found their ties loosened, gates unlocked, guards asleep or otherwise occupied, and were able to escape and make their way safely to the border.

The war ended after three weeks. The people of the Indus had endured huge losses, but things could have been much worse. The worst of the fighting, in Kashmir, which was out of Khawaja Khizr's jurisdiction, had been contained; the land of Pakistan remained unconquered, although the generals were bloodied and ashamed. They would never admit it, and even stole a day out of the calendar to commemorate their "great victory."

And then war broke out again, hardly six years later. Khawaja Khizr returned to his prayer mat and redoubled his efforts, but this time in vain. Two countries became three: slaughtered students and pregnant women from Bangla came to Khawaja Khizr in his sleep and cried: "For what crime have we been killed? For what crime?"

Again and again. War, treason, corruption, and murder. After forty years of being raped by one government after the other, the people of the Indus lost faith. And Khawaja Khizr grew wearier than he could ever remember being, his every bone crying out for the relief of the grave. He wanted nothing more than to be reunited with his Beloved; he spent hours and days in solitude, in the cave at Astola, trying to achieve annihilation that never came.

Then, one day, Khawaja Khizr got off his prayer mat, lay down on the ground, and fell asleep. A long, deep, dreamless void, as if he were in the *aramgah*, the final resting place of the Sufi saints. He was not dead, but he could take no more. The weight of his years, the weakness of his body, caused him to curl into a fetal position and brought his heartbeat and breathing to an almost unobservable rate. He was somewhere between the worlds, traveling in the cosmos, his soul flown to heaven but still kept captive by his living body.

His absence began to tell almost immediately. The Indus gradually lost its volume, shrinking from a powerful flow to a thin trickle. Drought came more often than before and lasted longer, drying up plains that had been fertile and productive. Silt began to claim the best farmland; poorer farmers committed suicide when their lands were ruined by rising salt tables. The people began to wonder whether Khawaja Khizr had abandoned them, but they could not believe it, not yet.

It was only when the Red Tide came to the harbor that they knew something was terribly wrong. A young boy woke up early one morning on Bhit Island, just beyond Karachi, and ran down to the shore for his morning swim. He drew a shuddering gasp when he came upon thousands of fish lying belly up in the tides, dragged up and down the shoreline in fetid water the color of ancient rust. The boy ran screaming back to the huts and brought the men of the village with him to see. They knelt down and began to pray on the shore for Khawaja Khizr to end the Mara

Pani—the Deadly Water—as the bodies of the fish, in all shapes and sizes, ebbed between the branches of the mangroves and sent a powerful scent of death into the air.

Government officials claimed it was due to a type of poisonous algae whose pigment discolored the waters. The nongovernmental organizations stated it was due to the industrial pollution that came to the sea from the Lyari River. Unscrupulous traders gathered up the dead fish in their nets and tried to sell them at Empress Market to city dwellers who were too stupid to know better than to eat any fish found sick or dead.

But only the fishermen knew that it was because the people of the Indus had fallen out of favor with Khawaja Khizr, their protector and guardian. And disaster could only follow.

October 18, 2007 (ii)

Karachi was dressed up like a bride ready to receive her long-awaited groom. It was 10 p.m., and though night had fallen hours ago, the colored electric lights strung up on all the buildings were blinking frantically on and off, turning Shahrae Faisal into a brilliant outdoor disco: blaring pop music pulsed through the heat, and the smell of food and thousands of bodies rose into the air. Posters of Benazir Bhutto adorned every free wall, hanging from every bridge and lamppost; banners and flags turned the sky into a forest of red, green, and black. Men were dancing jubilantly, and someone had got hold of a can of silly string and was letting it off into the crowd, covering everyone in the foamy white strands.

Ali was trying to push his way through the crowd, looking for someone who wanted to talk to him and the camera. He was completely exhausted: his legs were shaking and he felt as though he'd been beaten by someone wielding a *lathi*. They'd been on the move now for fifteen hours, but "move" wasn't meant to be taken literally—the convoy had hardly traveled a few miles from

the airport since it arrived in the afternoon at quarter to two.
The team had already been waiting there—the cameraman, the
sound technician, and Ali—for two hours, having jostled and
pushed their way to the front of the crowds at Terminal 1.

Welcome, welcome, Benazir, welcome. The singsong chorus had
been blaring all day long from a loudspeaker right next to Ali's
ear. He told the cameraman to take a shot panning the crowd:
thousands of young men, some women here and there, a sea of
ajraks draped on shoulders and across chests and fashioned into
turbans to show the hospitality of Sindh welcoming its prodigal
daughter home.

When her vehicle emerged from the terminal—a huge, mech-
anized box placed on top of a truck, flanked by bulletproof cars
and armed escorts—the crowd sent up a roar of *"JIYE BHU-
TTO!"* It could have filled up three football stadiums with its
velocity, a greeting worthy of a rock star or the pope. Benazir,
a tall, proud-backed figure standing on the box, waved to the
crowds; she looked like the Pakistan flag: green *shalwar kameez,*
white headscarf, *imam zaman* tied around her arm, and prayer
beads clutched in her hand. Even from their distant vantage point
Ali could see the brilliant smile on her face.

The cameraman was busy filming the scene, but behind the
camera, Ali saw tears running down his cheeks.

"Haroon, are you okay?" Ali asked him. Haroon's hands
were shaking; Ameena would scream about that later, no doubt.
She wanted every shot to be perfect; she wouldn't want a wob-
bly frame. The news was not about honest emotion, but about
smooth edges and the right sound bite.

Haroon took one hand off his camera to wipe his eyes. "Oh,
Adda, I can't explain it, I can't explain it. She's home, and everything's going to be all right now."

He was such a young guy, Haroon: couldn't have been more

than twenty-two; a Sindhi like Ali, from Hyderabad. Barely old enough to remember the riots, the killings in 1990: when the MQM threatened to slaughter every Sindhi family who didn't pack up and leave their homes that very night. Haroon had to run to Qasimabad and take shelter in one of the shanties that were going up everywhere, haphazardly, surging with desolate, desperate men and women. His mother was sick in those days; she barely survived. Haroon was only seven or eight, but he had never forgotten.

Welcome, welcome, Benazir, welcome. The convoy set off and Ali and his team followed it—there was no space to drive a car; they had to make do with hopping on motorcycles all the way from the office and weaving their way slowly through the crowds that were heading to the same destination. They were all swept along in a powerful oceanic surge that reclaimed the land, inch by inch, for Benazir.

The open joy on people's faces, their smiles, shouts, whoops of laughter, were hard to resist. Ali tried to stay aloof from it all, neutral and observant, while directing Haroon to capture the best shots on the camera: a small boy with his face painted red, green, and black, dancing to an old Allan Fakir song; a group of Makranis from Lyari, breakdancing; old dignified men with white beards, the mirror work on their Sindhi caps catching the bright lights and flashing them around like shooting stars. Even after fifteen hours—more, these people had been coming to the city over the last few days, camping out on the streets at night—their enthusiasm was unabated.

Ali, though, was exhausted. Crushed. He'd been picking up little snacks from food stalls and roadside hotels all day but hadn't had a full meal; he'd even had to relieve himself against a wall in a tiny alley a few hours ago. He wanted nothing more than to go home and go to bed. Benazir or no Benazir. They had enough footage, he'd simply had enough. But they had to stick it out till she reached the Quaid's Mazaar, that peculiar landmark where Jinnah lay entombed, and which looked like the Taj Mahal stripped of its minarets. She was going to make a speech; at this rate they'd reach the Mazaar at four in the morning.

They had six or so interviews already—little clips of the man on the street, what did he think, all that bullshit—but they still had to do a few more. Ameena wanted to have a wide choice when she made her cuts in the editing booth. Ali spotted two men standing in the doorway of a cheap hotel, the Hotel Babar. One was a waiter, the other a doorman. A security guard stood beside them, toting a menacing shotgun; all three looked bemused at the circus passing before them.

This was a good opportunity, Ali decided. He beckoned Haroon and the sound technician, Ram, forward, and waved the microphone at the waiter. "Could you talk to us for a few minutes?"

The waiter saw that the three of them were from a TV station, straightened up, touched his cheap bow tie. "Certainly." The doorman looked affronted that he hadn't been asked, but Ali assured him they'd talk to him next. "And me?" said the security guard, clearly wanting to be part of the action. He was a Pathan from the north with a ferocious beard and sharp gray eyes. Take him out of his crisp blue uniform and replace his shotgun with a Kalashnikov, and he could easily have passed for a Taliban. "Of course," Ali replied.

Haroon focused the camera lens on the waiter and Ali, taking a few minutes to set up the shot. Ram held the boom above them, and Ali held up the microphone. He'd done this ten, twenty times already throughout the day. He rearranged his features into an expression that was the complete opposite of what he was feeling. "Ready, Haroon?"

"Yes, sir." Haroon nodded his head and Ram gave the thumbs-up.

"Right. What is your name, please?"

"Shahid Jokhio."

"And your thoughts on Benazir's return?" Ali knew he didn't have to be subtle, just quick. The guy was a Sindhi; he'd praise her to the skies.

"It's wonderful." The waiter wagged his head from side to side, a wide smile on his face.

"No, it's not," put in the doorman, unable to stop himself from participating. Haroon swiveled the camera so that they were both in the frame. It was impromptu, but it could be good.

Ali pointed the microphone at the doorman. "Why not?"

"She should have stayed away. What's the point? She was sent packing before. She's no good for the country."

"Your name?"

"Ahmed Rais."

The waiter was starting to fume, and he quickly inserted himself again into the picture. "That's nonsense; she had to come back. She's the only person who can get us back to democracy. We want her, we need her."

"She's not honest. She's corrupt. She's just going to do the same thing again!"

"She can change our country, our lives."

"She won't do anything except line her pockets and make us suffer."

"How dare you?"

"How dare I what?"

"Talk about her like that!"

"Who's going to stop me?"

Suddenly they were throwing punches. This is great! crowed Ali to himself: street theater unfolding right before your eyes, folks. The waiter and the doorman scuffled for a minute, Haroon capturing it all on film, the security guard standing and watching them with a grin on his face. "These two, they're always fighting," he said laconically to Ali.

"Politics, religion, economy. *Barey ustaad hain*. They think they're university professors but they know nothing."

"And you?" Ali asked. "What do you think about her return?"

He shrugged. It was enough of an answer for Ali, who happened to agree with him. "Thank you," Ali said. The waiter and doorman were still shoving each other, the Sindhi's bow tie askew, the doorman's hair flopped forward to reveal a bald pate.

Haroon put down the camera and called out to him, "Hey, uncle, that's a terrible toupee. Why don't you ask Nawaz Sharif to get you a hair transplant from his doctor?"

The doorman looked up, his face black with murder. Seizing the opportunity, the waiter landed a punch that sent the doorman stumbling into the arms of the security guard, who dropped his rifle right onto his own foot. He roared in pain. Ali, Haroon, and Ram backed away fast, and they were soon engulfed by the sheer mass of people, so the men couldn't come after them, even if they tried.

Once they were at a safe distance, Ali asked Haroon, "What was that for?"

Haroon grinned slyly. "He insulted Benazir. I couldn't let that go, could I?"

Ali smiled wryly and reached out to slap palms with Haroon. Okay, she was corrupt, but she was Sindhi, so . . . oh, how Sikandar would chuckle if he knew what Ali was thinking. Ram ducked his head, not wanting to meet their eyes, but he was grinning, too. He was shy, Ram. Ali always tried to include him in their jokes, the camaraderie that he and Haroon shared, but Ram

hung back, not comfortable enough to participate. Ali was sensitive to the fact that maybe other people at work gave Ram a hard
time because he was Hindu. Whenever he saw Ram hesitate like
that, he always thought of Sunita being discriminated against for
her faith, and he was astonished by the white heat of his sudden
fury.

The frenzy was unchecked, the crowds still going strong.
There were people hanging off every bridge, crammed onto the
tops of trucks and buses. In the apartment buildings that lined
both sides of the road, more people crowded the balconies,
watching the melee from above. The PPP had forecast that a
million people would be here tonight; the government was trying to downplay it, saying you could halve that number and then
halve it again. Ali calculated that there were at least seven hundred thousand people, a vast, incomprehensible number, all here
for this one woman, who might carry on her strong shoulders the
destiny of an entire nation.

They could still see her truck from where they were; she kept
going inside to rest, then coming out again onto the float every
forty-five minutes, standing on the platform, surrounded by her
aides and colleagues, both men and women of the PPP who had
been supporting her in the country while she was unable to be
here herself. Now she was back and their dreams were about to
come true. But what dreams? Visions of power, of money, of position and influence? It was like every time, in the alphabet soup
that made up Pakistani politics: PPP, PML, Q, N, F, ANP, BNP,
MQM—everyone jockeying for a piece of the very valuable pie.
And Benazir had helped herself to a very healthy slice the last
time she was in power. It was harrowing to think of what would
happen if she filled that seat again.

"Wow, she's got stamina," Ali muttered to himself. No matter what else he felt about her, he had to concede that much. She

had the strength of ten men, if she could stand all of this. She didn't just seem to be able to stand it; she seemed to relish it, drawing her strength from the devotion of the crowds swelling all around her, as if she were at once some kind of saint and queen and mother. Just maybe, he thought fleetingly, he was being un-fair to her, judging her so harshly because she was so tied to his memories of his father, good and bad, and the yearning for that man that ate at him like an ulcer in his stomach.

"Should we get something to eat?" said Haroon. It was just past midnight; they were crawling along near the Karsaz over-pass. Ali craned his neck but couldn't see any restaurants in the immediate vicinity, and it would take ages to go up the road and find the barbecue place next to the ice cream parlor.

"I'm starving, *yaar*," Ali said. "But we need to find some place that serves vegetarian food." And he indicated Ram with his raised eyebrows.

Haroon nodded. "We'll find something for him. Don't worry, Ram. Come on, I know a place down this way—"

The explosion hit them like tin drums to the chest. It lasered out Ali's mind and shattered his eardrums. A column of fire shot into the sky, illuminating the shocked faces of everyone around them. In that split second, everyone was frozen bare-limbed like winter trees, their shadows obliterated. Then they all dropped to the ground, some seeking to protect themselves, others felled by the blast, by flying shrapnel, by motorcycles being lifted into the air and falling down on their outstretched limbs.

Silence.

A shrieking started up, unholy, otherworldly. Smoke curled in the air; people were picking themselves up, dazed, others still lying on the ground. Ali came to life, too, moving his arms and legs and astonished to find them still attached to his body.

"What was that? What was that?" a man jabbered next to

him. "Did a tire burst? Has a tire burst?" Nobody answered him; people were too busy screaming, crying, howling to pay him any attention.

"Haroon!" Ali screamed. "Ram! Where are you?" He could hardly hear his own voice, the ringing in his ears was so great. "Here, here," Haroon replied from somewhere behind him. Ali blinked his eyes, astonished. Haroon had been just in front of Ali—how did he turn up ten feet away? And Ram was standing next to him. Their eyes were white and staring with fear through the soot and grime that covered their skin, streaks of sweat running cracks through the dark masks of their faces.

"Are you hurt?"

"No, I'm fine. We're fine."

They turned to look at the truck, where Benazir was supposed to be, but there was no way to see anything; it was sheer pandemonium. People milled about, confused and directionless, rushing forward to pick bodies up, trying to lift them into life. Guards and party workers surrounded the truck, but she was nowhere to be seen. Haroon said, "I think she went inside, just before it—"

Then, suddenly, another blast, a plume of searing light and fire, like a dragon's tongue unfurling, and this time people were running in panic away from the truck, not bothering to help their fallen brothers. Ali, too, fell to his knees with the impact. Ram sank from view.

Haroon screamed once, then fell silent; but instead of catching his comrade in his arms and dragging him away with him, Ali scrambled to his feet, put his hands over his ears to block out the pounding sound of the bomb, and ran. He wished that he too could die, just to escape from the sounds that couldn't possibly have come from human throats: moans and whimpers at once animalistic and raw, like the keening of scores of maddened, hysterical wolves.

The Seven Queens

S hah Abdul Latif came home one afternoon to a sight that
nearly stopped his heart: his wife, Bibi Sayedah, was sitting
at the kitchen table, her head buried between her folded arms, her
shoulders shaking with suppressed sobs. She sounded as though
she was keening for the dead, and this shocked Shah Latif so
much that he rushed to her side and shook her. "Khanum? Khanum, what is wrong? Has someone died?"

At first no words emerged from the quaking heap of headscarf
and sleeves, for that was all he could see of her. Shah Latif went
to the earthenware pot and drew out a glass of water, brought it
to the table, and set it down in front of Sayedah. "Drink, o wife,
and then I implore you to tell me what is wrong."

After a time, the weeping ceased, although Bibi Sayedah's
shoulders continued to shudder from time to time, like after-
shocks after the first earthquake has turned the earth loose. Shah
Latif sat down on a facing chair—there were only two in their
simple house—and took out his prayer beads, whispering some

of the ninety-nine names of God under his breath, slowing his breath and closing his eyes. He prayed for his wife: that Allah Saeen would restore her to her senses quickly and that no harm had befallen anyone they loved.

Ya-Majid,   Ya-Wajid,   Ya-Wahid,   Ya-Ahad,   Ya-Samad, Ya-Qadir, Ya-Malik, Ya-Rehman, Ya-Rahim.

Eventually his wife lifted her head and gazed at him with watery, swollen eyes. Shah Latif felt a heaviness descend upon him: she was still not much older than a girl, and he hated to see her cry. She had wept only once before: as she was leaving her parents' house to come into his as a bride. He still remembered the heavily shrouded figure, the *akhiyaan* over her face, wreaths of roses weighing down her slim shoulders, as she took step after tiny step in the wedding procession. Someone had brought a Quran and held it over her head for protection, and her fingers, painted with henna but lacking jewelry, were trembling as they clung to the edge of the veil over her head—for Shah Latif came from noble people, who could well afford to put the twisting gold *ver* on her ring finger and the *nath* through her nose; but Shah Latif himself had forsworn the riches of this world and wished his wife to follow the same path. She had agreed, but when he saw the tears sliding down from under the *akhiyaan* and onto her delicate throat, he wondered if she was weeping out of sadness or for fear of the life that he, already a well-known ascetic, would give her.

He owned next to nothing—a few bowls, a copy of the Quran and of Rumi's *Masnavi* his most prized possessions. But he was rich in mind: he could speak five languages, including Persian and Arabic; and rich in lineage, tracing his ancestry all the way back to the Prophet Muhammad, peace be upon him, which attracted the family of Bibi Sayedah, while his kindness of manner and gentleness of speech swayed Bibi Sayedah's own affections toward him.

When Bibi Sayedah had come to his house and they were left

alone on the night of their wedding, he had brought her a cup of milk flavored with honey and rose water, and bade her drink from his own hand. After she had her fill, he drank from the same cup, looking deep into her eyes, and she had lowered her face, unable to bear the intensity of his gaze. He tenderly laid his hand on her forehead and breathed a prayer over her head, then pulled her to his chest and kept her close there, wanting to imprint the very essence of her onto his heart.

Very quickly she became the love of his life, and he hers. She was a perfect companion to him: serene and contemplative, she moved through the house with utter calm. He even admired the thoughtful way she would put on her shoes, leaning against the wall with one hand supporting her weight, lifting her feet gracefully, first the right and then the left. He was a man of few words, preferring to save them for the pages of his poetry, but he couldn't help it if his poetry, spiritual and ethereal, became suffused with earthly love; even if his verse was meant to be an unending love song to the Beloved, he couldn't help but believe that what he felt for his wife was the perfect metaphor for what the Sufis had always felt for God. He'd absorbed their teachings, understood the beautiful symbolism of Sufi poetry, with its yearning and despair at the separation between the Beloved and His lovers, among whom he counted himself. But he had always thought that love would transport him to the heavens; he had never realized that it also sank down deep, into bone and blood, flesh and marrow— until he had married his wife.

And so he had written the tragic love stories of Sindh, putting down into verse the folk tales of that ancient land, inspired by the grace in his wife's smile, the welcoming presence that gave him his center, and helped him to face the hardship of travel.

The web of power grew in Sindh, trapping all within its silken skeins: the Pirs who were descendants of the Sufi saints and the guardians of their shrines arbitrated for the tribesmen in their conflicts large and small; the Kalhora kings recognized their power and used it to their advantage, gifting the Pirs with land and money in return for their political support and the allegiance of the tribes. Shah Latif ran from this juggernaut, and the jealousy of the Pirs and Mirs who feared that this man of God might approach the Kalhoras for a share of the power. Instead, he visited the four corners of Sindh and the outlying borderlands, roaming the plains, the rushing rivers, the flower-filled dales. He meditated at the Ganjo Hills, south of Hyderabad, spent days of contemplation at Hinglaj and the mountains of Lasbela in Balochistan. He visited his wife in some of his dreams, seeing her standing in the doorway of their house and waiting for him with a glass of sweetened *lassi* in her hands, or cooking him a simple meal infused with love.

He did not stop there; he went on to the foothills of the Himalayas, those sweet lands of Hinglay, Lakhpat, and Nani, and Sappar Sakhi, where he communed with yogis and *sanyasis;* to Junagardh and Jessalmir; joining in with Hindus and Buddhists and sun-worshippers and fire-worshippers, all in search of the Truth. He practiced yoga with a wizened yogi and compared the similarity of the *asanas* to the bowing and prostration of Muslim prayer, and observed that indeed there were many paths to achieving union with God. And furthermore, that wish to be one with the Lord was a universal desire; if one practiced the correct rituals, every cell would awaken and sing the praises of the Creator.

But no matter how far he traveled, his one secret desire was to be back in his home, under the same roof as his wife. The pious, virtuous Sayedah Begum, whose eyes remained downcast in prayer, who was hidden from the view of other men—for, like all women descended from the Prophet, peace be upon him, she practiced *purdah,* seclusion from the outside world—and who remained his hidden pearl, his treasure, his heart's dearest.

Shah Latif had always assumed that she had known how he felt about her. He thought she knew it from the way he woke in the middle of the night to cover her with their one threadbare quilt. He thought she knew it when he nursed her through her fevers and grippes. He had never thought of taking a second wife, ever, even though it was his right to take a second or a third or even a fourth.

So when she told him that day that he found her weeping at the kitchen table, why she was upset, he was completely stunned.

"I was waiting for Bibi Hanifah to bring me some *ghee* from the market. She said that she could find a better price for me if she went to the *dargah* of your grandfather, Shah Abdul Karim, as the *urs* is beginning and the farmers are bringing their goods to the shrine every day now.

"When she went to the shrine, she sat for a while to listen to the sacred songs, as the beating of the holy drums uplifts her a great deal on days she is tired from carrying her child. They began to sing the *sur* of Sassi-Pannu, in honor of the fact that you are Shah Karim's grandson, and the composition was a particularly melodious one, so she sat entranced for some time. And then she overheard two women talking behind her. They were saying . . . they were saying . . ."

"What were they saying?" said Shah Latif. He looked down at the floor, not wanting to reveal any emotion, but inside he was displeased that Bibi Hanifah was bringing back gossip from the *urs*. It was a festival meant to celebrate the saint's death—his marriage with God—but trust people to contaminate the sacred days with the vulgar and the venial. He prayed to God for patience, and waited for his wife to continue.

"They said . . ." Bibi Sayedah swallowed hard; he could see the gentle undulation in her throat. She was slim as a girl, the skin of her throat almost translucent, like fine rice paper. "They said that . . . that you love the Seven Queens more than you do your real wife. And that is the reason Allah has not yet blessed us with a child." She sank her head into her hands and began to weep anew.

Shah Latif stared at her, aghast. This was worse than he imagined: death was traumatic, but there was sweet succor in the thought that a true believer was finally achieving annihilation and would never again be parted from God. But this puerile village gossip . . .

He was no stranger to it; he sometimes walked disguised in the market and heard the whispers. Shah Latif was revered by many as a man of God but he was not without enemies who disliked his popularity among the tribesmen of Sindh. They spoke in hushed tones about how his wife was barren, how he was uninterested in affairs of the world, in having children like normal people. Why did he not take a second wife? Why did he not send his wife back to her people? Could there be something wrong with him? Was he like the Pathans, who, it was said, preferred young boys to women?

He had been able to bear it, but he had hoped that his wife, secluded in the home, would have been spared the wagging of their malicious tongues. But he had been wrong. It had reached his own doorstep, like a tide of sewage that raised a stink for miles around, and was impossible to wash away.

But to accuse him of loving the Seven Queens more than his own wife! It was outrageous. Blasphemous. The Seven Queens, the great heroines of Sindh, whom Shah Latif had immortalized in his poetry—Sassi, Marvi, Noori, Leela, Sohni, Heer, and Moomal—they were manifestations of love between God and man, lover and Beloved. They were not mortal women whose affections were to be competed for among men; they were not meant to be objects of lust. And they were never meant to be competition for his own beloved Sayedah Khanum.

In Marvi's loyalty to her true love, Khet, Shah Latif had secretly extolled his own wife's faithfulness to him. Sassi, who ran barefoot across the desert and died in search of her Beloved, made him wonder if his wife, too, would cross a desert to find him if he were lost and wandering. The tears Sohni wept on seeing the wound in her love's thigh brought to mind the tears of Bibi Sayedah on the night of their *rukhsati*. And as Rano had braved the eerie magnetic field that surrounded Moomal, Shah Latif too wished to penetrate the walls of his wife's heart, so that she would cast off her normal modesty for once and show him affection in her eyes, utter endearments more rare than diamonds and rubies.

Shah Latif rose from his chair. He went silently to the door, gathering up his long cloak and his walking stick. He did not need to tell his wife that he was setting out on a journey: she was used to him walking out of the door and returning later that evening, or after a month. It was one of her gifts to him, the ability to endure his absence without resentment. He did not know where he was going, but he knew he had to go; his soul was most elevated when his feet were moving. Sayedah Begum too got up and began to grind wheat for the evening meal. Already her face was composed again, her eyes large and gentle, fringed with lashes like the graceful chinkara that lived in the Thar Desert.

They did not exchange any words, any farewells or entreaties to take care, to go in safety. Her faith in God was absolute: she entrusted her husband to Him every second of every day, and so there was never a need to acknowledge the connection that could never be severed.

His two pups, Moti and Kheeno, leapt up when they saw him emerge from the door, but he did not reach down to pet them as he often did when going to the village. They whined and scrabbled in the dirt, then sat on their hind legs and watched him go.

After a time he came to the shrine of his grandfather, Shah

Abdul Karim. Its green flags fluttered in the wind; people were milling around, some with purpose, some aimlessly. The *urs* would be well under way tonight, with thousands joining in the celebrations, reciting poetry, listening to music, dancing in ecstasy. The market bustled with farmers and traders selling their wares; tables groaned under the weight of gold and silver, silks and embroidery, leather and brass amid the bleats and cries of goats, sheep, even camels in a small camp set up on the open field in front of the *dargah* where a man had come all the way from Thar to sell his precious beasts. The sound of santoor and tabla, reed flute and sarangi mingled with the scent of incense and roses, weaving a tapestry of aural and sensual pleasure that the Lovers would feast upon tonight.

A few *malangs* came up to Shah Latif, spotting him standing a small distance from the crowd. Dressed in their robes with begging bowls hung around their necks, they greeted him and sought blessings from him, a few lines of new verse to be sung at the festival tonight. But Shah Latif was silent, and soon they dropped away from him and melted back into the crowds. The truth was that his heart had been broken by the slanders, and he had nothing left to give to any of them.

He turned and walked away again, and as he walked, he recited the verse that he had written soon after his marriage, never telling anyone that he had written it for her:

The heart has but one beloved,
Many you should not seek:
Just give heart to one,
Even hundreds may seek;
Weasels they are called,
Who get betrothed at every door.

But the camel seller, the man from Thar, called out to him as he passed. "O great Shah! Where do you go?"

Shah Latif stopped, surprised that this man, a stranger, recognized him. "Peace be upon you, o Man of Thar. How do you know me?"

The man laughed. He was thin and dark, weather-beaten, and wore an *ajrak* wrapped into a turban on his head. "Who does not know the Shah of Bhit, whose *Risalo* has spread far and wide? As long as there are men in Sindh, you will be known. But why do you walk away from the *urs*, when most people are only just arriving?"

Shah Latif said, "I am called away on urgent business."

"But where do you go?"

"I do not know."

"Then that's urgent business indeed; God's business. When a man is called but knows not his destination, only the Creator knows what's needed. But He's told me to tell you where to go."

"Where is that, then, my friend?" Shah Latif leaned forward, curious and interested. He was not surprised that Allah Saeen had entrusted this simple desert man with such an important message. There were signs everywhere, if you only knew how to look.

"He bids you to go to my homeland, into the desert."

"So it shall be done. I thank you in His name." Without another word, Shah Latif turned and began walking east. The man from Thar stood watching him as he went, shading his eyes from the sun, the tall figure growing smaller and smaller as he vanished into the distance. Never had he seen someone so eager to obey God's word, the desert man thought to himself, before turning back to tend to his beloved camels.

Shah Latif walked and walked for many days and nights, sheltering under a tree at night, drinking from the river in the morning, eating a simple meal of flat bread, and taking a cup of goat's milk wherever it was offered to him. Some people knew who he was; some did not. But everywhere he went he could hear snatches of his verse being sung, recited, used as weight in arguments, admired, appreciated.

Beloved's separation kills me, friends. At His door, many like me, their knees bend . . .

. . . Countless pay homage and sing peace at his abode . . .

. . . Tell me the stories, oh thornbush, of the mighty merchants of the Indus, of the nights and days of the prosperous times . . .

Then one day he climbed a small hill and came down the other side onto a sand dune that ran parallel to the winds, rows of undulating ridges rubbed into the sand like the lines on the roof of his mouth. Nearby, he saw a group of women dressed in the bright colors of the desert, their arms covered in white bangles up to their elbows. They were cutting at a small scrub tree with hand-axes, and singing as they worked:

In deserts, wastes, and Jessalmir it has rained. Clouds and lightning have come to Thar's plains. Lone, needy women are now free from care, fragrant are the paths, happy herdsmen's wives all this share.

And when he recognized their song, he knew that he had arrived at his destination.

November 3, 2007

When Jehangir told Ali about the girls that went topless at French Beach, Ali laughed in his face. "I don't believe you."

"*Yaar*, I saw it for myself," drawled Jehangir. They were playing pool late one night in Masood's massive drawing room, in the self-contained portion of the house that his parents had allocated to Masood when he returned from university in the United Kingdom. They envisaged it as a flat where he would one day live with his wife and children; but since Masood showed no inclination to get married even at thirty-one, it had slowly metamorphosed into a bachelor pad where Jehangir, Ali, and various other friends hung out together, got drunk, and talked about all the great issues of life, such as what the Americans were doing to the Muslim world, which tycoons were cleaning up on the stock market and which were addicted to cocaine, and who were the sexiest and most available girls in town. Jehangir participated eagerly in all these conversations, pretending to all his friends as well as his family that he had a healthy interest in women. For someone who might be gay, though, he certainly knew a lot about the scandalous habits of the girls in Karachi.

"You're such a goddamn liar," guffawed Masood, as he aimed at a striped ball. He pulled the cue back and drove it forward with such force that the cue ball, instead of hitting its target, jumped right over it and bounced on the marble floor with a bone-jarring crash. "Bastard!" he shrieked.

"Are you calling the ball a bastard?" Jehangir said.

"No, I'm calling you a bastard," Masood retorted.

"Save your breath," said Jehangir. "I knew I was a bastard the day I was born. The doctor told my mother. 'Congratulations, Mrs. Mani, you've given birth to a bastard.'"

"Shut up and play!" Ali said. Masood bent over to retrieve the ball and an audible crack came from his spine, which made Ali and Jehangir both wince with pain.

"Ouch!" exclaimed Masood, straightening up and rubbing his spine. "I'm getting old." He followed this with a string of obscenities so vulgar that Jehangir burst out into shocked giggles.

"God, can you say anything without the help of a swear word?" Ali was disgusted with Masood, even though he was drinking the whiskey that Masood brought that evening in a plastic bag, a seven-thousand-rupee bottle of Johnnie Walker Black Label, guaranteed by Masood's bootlegger to be "the real thing." Ali felt that people used profanity because their vocabularies were weak, and Masood, with his father's fortune behind him and apartments in London, New York, and Dubai, had the vocabulary of a thirteen-year-old boy.

But he didn't mind drinking Masood's liquor, especially tonight, after a day during which thoughts of Haroon, the look on his face as he'd talked about Benazir, came unbidden to Ali's mind when he was in the middle of doing something completely unrelated to the story of the bombing. The glass of Black Label rested in Ali's palm, providing mellow inoculation against the memories of the explosion, the screams, the frantic search for Haroon, the slow-growing realization that they weren't going to find him, now or ever. He took another swallow of the whiskey to make everything move back into its rightful place. But there was nothing about that night that could be put right. Haroon had become another faceless, nameless victim of terrorism in Karachi, and soon nobody would even remember that he existed. His desk had been cleared away at work, his belongings given to his family. They'd stopped speaking his name even in the hushed tones reserved for the newly dead. There were a few attempts to put up a plaque in his honor, naming him as a *shaheed*, a martyr, but that would only happen if his friends pushed for it, and nobody was willing to do so, even Ali. It would be too much of a reminder about how any of them could have their names on a plaque the next time they went out in the field to film.

"Well, come and see for yourself," said Masood. "I'm having a party on Saturday at French Beach."

"It's too hot!" groaned Jehangir.

"Don't be stupid. Bring Sunita," Masood added for Ali's benefit. "And don't worry about the drinks. Plenty of *goray* coming as well. They always make sure we're well supplied."

Ali nodded. It didn't surprise him that Masood had found out about Sunita; Masood and Jehangir were close friends and, in Karachi, it was impossible to keep secrets forever. It didn't matter, as long as nobody said anything to his family, and Masood and Jehangir had no connection with them; they moved in more privileged, Westernized circles, lived in different worlds. Besides, Sunita would never come. She hated the sun and the salt water and the effect the wind had on her hair. Her mother was always going on at her about being too dark, even though Ali

thought her skin was beautiful. Dark brown, the color of teak-
wood warmed by summer sunlight. Dark like wet sand on the
beach, like milky tea. Ali hungered to know whether she was that
dark all over, or darker in some parts and lighter in others.

"'How will I get any good proposals if I'm dark,' she says.
God! I hate it," Sunita told Ali as they sat together at one of
their many café rendezvous, the only places in Karachi where
they could be together in relative privacy. She pursed her lips
around her cigarette, holding it between her finger and thumb.
Ali dreamt of her holding him just like that, and pursing her lips
around him and inhaling him the same way she was doing to
the cigarette. The thought made him weak at the knees and provided endless fodder for his fantasies many nights after. He took
another sip of his overpriced cappuccino and ignored the word
"proposals," even though it hung in the air like a sickeningly
sweet vapor all around them, reminding him of the impossibility
of their situation.

Sunita dreamt that they would get married one day. The only
way that could happen, Ali knew, would be if she converted to
Islam, and even that would not be enough to convince his mother
to accept Sunita as her daughter-in-law. *What will people say?*
she'd tell Ali. *Your father would never permit it. It would shame our
family.*

His father might not have allowed Sunita and Ali to get married, but it wouldn't have been out of shame. It would have been
because Ali's happiness, or that of his wife and other children,
hardly mattered to him. An ironic judgment coming from a man
who had acted so selfishly in the pursuit of his own pleasure,
thought Ali.

He knew very little about Shehla, his father's second wife, except that she was the thirty-four-year-old daughter of some bootlegger his father had befriended; he'd visit the man most evenings

to talk politics and drink whiskey. One day Ali thought he spotted her as she was coming home from her job—she worked in a bank, or maybe even a hotel as a "customer relations officer"—a euphemism for a high-class call girl, really, but nobody could say that in front of Ali's father and expect to leave the room alive.

Shehla must have been singularly beautiful; Ali's mother fervently believed she practiced black magic because, two months after meeting Shehla, Sikandar had embarked on an affair with the younger woman. The news was relayed to them by Shehla's father, who called Ali's mother one day and told her that they were married, and that Shehla was going to have a baby. Ali's father went to live with her somewhere in Defence, in a new house paid for by the bootlegger.

Ali sipped his coffee and let Sunita rest her head on his shoulder, her long black hair rubbing against his neck, thinking hard about all this. His father was never deliberately cruel to any of them, but then again, never was he purposefully kind. Ali caught himself: again, he was being unfair to his father. His father had done a million little things to please them as children: school pickups and drop-offs, trips to the beach where Sikandar sat behind them as they rode, screaming and shrieking, on the back of a swaying camel, and once, an exhilarating ride on a motorcycle around their neighborhood. There were regular comic books and candy, a weekly treat at the Holiday Inn where they could all order as much ice cream as they wanted. But then they'd all gotten older, their needs had gotten more complicated, and Sikandar withdrew, unsure and unable to cope with them in their growing emotional complexity.

Of course, he provided for his family; they lived a comfortable life and went to good schools and had a good car; they had a small house in Clifton. A family inheritance paid for Ali's education in Dubai, and there was money enough for Jeandi to have a decent married life when the time came. But Ali never truly believed the feeling that their father treasured his family, that their existence made his life any better than it would have been without them.

Maybe this was because they were the children of his second marriage; Ali was the only one of the children who knew his father had been married once before: his first wife had died in childbirth. Sikandar never talked about it, had never even mentioned it; Ali knew bits and pieces from his mother, and his imagination filled in the blanks with his own theories. Maybe his father's first wife was the love of his life, and when she died, he was too heartbroken to think of loving anyone else as much. Or maybe he had neglected her, too, and when she died, the guilt had poisoned him, so that he was unable to give his heart to his second wife or their children.

Ali fought long and hard to find excuses for Sikandar's indifference to them, but he failed to understand why it existed, in the end. He was always busy—he traveled often in the interior of Sindh for several weeks at a time. He'd return late at night, slotting back the next morning into the rhythm of their household as if he'd never been gone. He expected to be able to drift in and out of their lives like a minor player, instead of the most important person in their family.

And their mother? Ali's maternal grandfather, her father, was a member of his father's *biraderi,* the clan, and he'd proposed for her because he was close to her father by association, their lands neighboring each other just outside of Sukkur. But they were not related by blood, not even distantly. Sikandar showed no deliberate cruelty toward her; he treated her well, and with respect. But there were expectations: as long as meals appeared on the table, his clothes were laundered and ironed, his children born and raised, he was satisfied. Ali couldn't recall seeing his parents talk. They exchanged no smiles, no jokes; he rarely took her out with him, preferring to leave her at home like other Sindhi men did with their wives. She wavered somewhere in between elevated servant and tolerated spouse, but she was never an equal partner, companion, lover, or friend to Sikandar Hussein.

Ali never asked his father about his first wife. His mother once told him that the lady had died in childbirth along with her baby daughter, Ali's father's first child. He'd often searched his father's face for any trace of that tragedy marked in the lines around his nose and eyes. Sikandar's face was always inscrutable, the skin of his cheeks and forehead like seasoned, polished wood, but he'd never really opened his heart to any of them, the tragedy of his life showing not in his face, but in his actions. Ali guessed he'd married a second time because people around him urged him to marry and have children, and unlike a woman, a man could start a family at any age. He was already in his mid-forties, a distant, unreachable time in a man's life, when he became a father for the first time.

Ali's mother was an educated woman: she'd completed her matric degree and even done two years of college privately. Her family was too conservative to allow her to go to school so she studied at home and just went to her college to sit the intermediate exams, which she passed with above-average marks. She was interested in studying science; she might have even had dreams of going to university in Hyderabad and becoming a dentist, dreams that would never come true because her family would never let her have a career, let alone go to a medical college where boys and girls studied together. *It would have shamed the family.*

When she was eighteen, Ali's father's father came to her house—he was friends with her grandfather—and proposed on behalf of Ali's father. The proposal was accepted, his mother and father got married, and she moved out of the family home in Hyderabad to the small house in Karachi, and there they were today, his progeny, walking around on this earth like open wounds, hoping for someone to love them long after that someone had left them, first in spirit, then in body.

How many other houses in their sedate neighborhood, with its old houses built in the seventies, its overgrown trees lining the zigzag streets that flooded during every monsoon season, were like theirs: genteel on the outside, wasting away from neglect on the inside? How many other families lived like fractured glass, cracked but still holding up within the constraints of their frames?

The fear of losing Sunita through neglect, of becoming the same cold man that his father had been, pushed Ali in the opposite direction. He trusted the love between them, relied on it to keep him steady, keep him true. *If I ever have to get married to a woman I don't know and don't love,* Ali thought, *I will die.* Ali never wanted reenact the way his father had so carelessly squandered the love of his own wife and children. Nor did he want to come to Sunita because of lust, the way his father had approached the bootlegger's daughter. He had to be with her in honesty and honor, in order to be the opposite of what his father was.

He was convinced that the gap between them, the issue of their opposite faiths, was of no consequence: Muslims and Hindus had coexisted in Sindh for centuries; they even worshipped together at the Sufi shrines in the interior. All these issues could be worked out in time; the important thing was to believe in each other above all else.

Sunita had no idea how passionately Ali felt about it, and he hid it from her, worried it would scare her off if she knew how much he needed her, how deep his craving for her really was. It took shape in his incessant dreams of possessing her body, but in truth he wanted to eat and swallow her very being, the soul of her the only antidote to the emptiness he felt in himself.

So when she brought up how she feared her dark skin would dissuade her suitors, he did not tell her automatically that she never need worry because he would marry her even if she were as dark as tar. Instead, he drained the last sip from his cup and said, "I'll be really angry with you if you try to make your skin any lighter. None of that Fair and Lovely crap for you. Understand?"

He said it in a light, sarcastic way, while stroking her shoulder with his pale fingers, as if to reassure her that he would never let her go; but he couldn't help feel slightly excited by the look of fear in her eyes whenever he spoke that way to her. He knew Sunita had a complex about her dark skin; and her unspoken gratitude toward Ali for having chosen her above a whiter, paler girl—a Muslim girl—filled him with a power that he hated himself for feeling. Ali needed to keep her close to him, even while pushing her away—a delicate dance that lovers had been performing for centuries, one whose steps he was learning as he went along. He had learned, from his parents' marriage, that ambivalence was the opposite of indifference. And that love came with fear, because when you didn't fear the loss of your beloved, it meant you didn't really love them at all.

To Ali's surprise, Sunita agreed to come to the beach party, when he asked her the next day after Jehangir's pool night. They were taking a class break under the shade of a banyan tree in the university garden, sharing a packet of chili chips. "I'd love to!" Sunita said, when he told her about the invitation. "It's perfect weather, too. It'll be cool."

"Cool," Ali agreed. But nothing had been cool since October 18. Two weeks later Haroon was still missing, presumed dead, and Ali was having nightmares about the bombing that he didn't want to remember. Now he had two ghosts following him everywhere: Haroon and Sikandar. Maybe going to the beach would be a good break, a nice change. Maybe when Ali gazed upon the ocean, the calm blue water, and felt Sunita's hand in his, away from all the eyes that judged them, and the mouths that would condemn for being together, things would feel normal once again.

* * *

The day couldn't be any more alluring, a lazy, long Saturday that stretched out before Ali and Sunita like a gift that would take all day to unwrap. They were at Masood's beach house on French Beach, prettier and better constructed than most houses Ali had seen in Karachi: electricity and a generator, a flat-screen TV, and a huge glass-paneled lounge that made you feel like you were in a ship because you could only see the sea when you looked out of the windows. Servants were cooking barbecue on a grill in a pit outside—fresh fish, crabs, prawns—and Masood was plying the guests with all the liquor they could want. Sunita didn't drink, but Ali took an ice-cold beer and strolled outside to view the scene on the beach.

Masood was right: there were plenty of foreigners, which surprised Ali. You'd think they'd have all gone into hiding, given how bad things were in the city, but there were at least six or seven of them, men and women, the men clad in shorts and tropical shirts, the women in bathing suits. One of them, a Scottish woman in her thirties, the wife of the head of some multinational corporation, was even wearing a bikini, and although nobody was going topless, the sight of her in that daring outfit cheered Ali up a little. He felt sorry for them, could see they felt safe being here, far away from the city and its problems, protected by Masood's contingent of armed guards, who kept a respectful distance from the beach hut, ferocious with their Kalashnikovs clutched under their arms.

Besides the foreigners, there was a gathering of local guests:

Jehangir was there, Ahmed, Omer, Zulfi, and some of the girls that Masood knew: Leela, Zainab, Mishi. The guys were sprawled on the stairs that led down to the sea, the girls hiding from the sun except for Leela, who sunned herself boldly along with the *goris,* turning her palms up to tan along the insides of her arms.

French Beach was the best of Karachi's beaches; far better than Clifton Beach, where the sweaty hordes, as Jehangir called them, came to frolic on the weekends. Clifton Beach was purely for lower-class families, men in *shalwar kameezes,* women in bur-qas, six or seven children to each family arriving in Suzukis and vans and on the backs of motorcycles. They splashed in the water fully clothed, they ate freshly grilled corn and drank juice from roadside stalls, they ran around on the beach and flew kites; and nobody of any social standing or class ever went there, except for some of the residents of the Seaview apartments, who liked to take morning walks before the riffraff showed up.

Sandspit, the next beach up, lay beyond the city, flat and bor-ing like its name, and then came Hawkesbay, rockier and more desolate. The waves catapulted strongly against the rocks and there was a dangerous undercurrent in the summers; the best time to bathe there fell in the winter months, when the tides were calm and there were no jellyfish in the water. The entire coast of Sindh had been spared from the tsunami of 2004, the beaches left intact. Ali didn't like to imagine what would have happened to the fishermen who lived all along the coast in tiny villages. He was glad God had saved them from that kind of disaster.

And then there was the Rolls-Royce of Karachi beaches: French Beach, so named because in the seventies all the French people who were working in the city owned weekend huts here, leasing the land from the villagers on terms more favorable to the French than to the locals. And not just the French: Ameri-cans, Germans, Dutch, British people flocked here to windsurf, barbecue, tan, and drink, and you could hardly see a Pakistani anywhere on the beach. In those days the foreigners lived in Karachi without fear, their children went to international and local schools, and everyone loved having them around, hosting them at dinner parties and picnics.

These days the children weren't allowed to live in Karachi anymore; the few *goray* left moved around the city in cars with armed guards and blackened windows, scurrying from their heavily guarded homes to their work and back again.

It was not just the distance from the city that drew people to French Beach: it was strikingly beautiful, a natural cove enclosed in the hug of two rocky arms that extended out into the sea. You could climb the rocks and find crabs and small fish in the pools left there at low tide. The water sang deep blue, and beachgoers even snorkeled around the shallow reefs and windsurfed in the bay.

Sunita and Ali decided to go for a walk onto the rocks, away from the party. They rarely got to be together so openly in Karachi. As soon as they were clear of the huts, Ali took Sunita's hand and helped her to clamber up onto the craggy hill. They turned around and surveyed the stretch of golden sand, the huts that followed the gentle curve of beach, and far in the distance, the city buildings shimmering like mirages in the haze. Here there was no sound but the endless drone of waves breaking on the shore, the wind that soughed in harmony with the water.

They made their way carefully to the edge of the outcrop, and sat with their legs dangling over the side. The tide was gentle at this time in November; it sprayed a little water and foam onto their shins and covered their cheeks in a fine mist. The sun, too, warmed them rather than baking and broiling them as it did for most of the year.

Ali put his arm around Sunita and she leaned into him, and since there was nobody else around, he started to kiss her. She responded eagerly. Warm and accommodating, her mouth opened under his lips. Their tongues met, and they were both thrilled by the intimacy they were sharing under the open sky. Ali could feel her pressing close, wanting more; he would have loved nothing better than to push her back on the rocks and lie on top of her, take her right here, hiding their bodies in a rocky pool where nobody could see them. But he couldn't. As much as he loved her, she was not his to have as yet. Not like those two girls Jehangir found—while trying to decide for sure if he was gay. They'd claimed to be students at Karachi University but they must have come from Napier Mole Road; Jehangir went off with the taller one and Ali had the shorter one for an hour in that little apartment in Seaview that belonged to a friend of a friend of a friend. Sunita was different, and Ali owed her more than that, in return for all the love she'd given him.

The kiss ended and Sunita drew back with a little sigh. Ali leaned his head on her shoulder and she put her arm around him, stroking his wrist with her slender fingers. "Any news?"

Ali tightened his lips in an unseen grimace and pressed his eyes against her neck. "None yet."

"It's terrible!" she whispered.

"Two weeks. Can you imagine? Two weeks and not a word."

"The police?"

"They haven't been able to find anything. There were a lot of people missing," Ali said. One hundred and thirty-five dead, one hundred injured, at least thirty or forty people disappeared into thin air—no bodies found. Haroon was one of the missing. His father and brother came all the way from Hyderabad, turning up at the office one day last week to beg the station owner, Kazim Mazhar, to use his influence and help them find their missing son.

They talked to Ali, too, and he explained to them that he didn't remember much about that night, that after the first explosion Haroon was all right, but after the second one he disappeared and Ali didn't know what happened to him. They nodded at Ali, their liquid black eyes full of hurt and confusion. They were only simple men from Hyderabad, already scarred by the ethnic riots that they'd had to endure in the nineties. Haroon's father told Ali that he'd encouraged his son to move to Karachi, that he'd been thrilled when Haroon had been offered the job with the news channel. "I thought it would be a good change for him," he told Ali, in Sindhi. "I thought he'd be away from all the trouble in Hyderabad. Hyderabad is going nowhere and I wanted my son to go somewhere."

Ali clasped his hand and murmured polite words of commiseration, his heart aching for Haroon and for his brother, who looked as if he could be Haroon's twin. There were Sindhis who were die-hard PPP supporters, who would lay down their lives for Benazir and her father, but Haroon's family just wanted their son to get a good start, to make something of himself. They'd wanted to stay away from politics, live peaceful lives, earn a little honest bread. And now politics had robbed them of their precious son, and his family could not bury him because his body was nowhere to be found.

Benazir had appeared on television in the days after the bombing, talking about how it was a deliberate plot on the part of the government. She'd had no proper security, she claimed; the lights had been switched off just before the explosions and the government had refused to give them the electronic jammers that would stop any bombs from detonating near her cavalcade.

Ali didn't want to be anywhere near her image; he couldn't stand to hear her voice. It made him feel as though ants were crawling underneath his skin. But he couldn't avoid it; her face was everywhere, on the television, in the newspapers, on the posters that came up all over the city like mushrooms after a monsoon. Her voice, strident and demanding, boomed out from speakers everywhere, in people's cars, in restaurants, and most of all at the news station, where the programmers broadcast repeatedly the clips that they'd compiled from Ali's reports filed earlier in the day, before the explosion.

"Is it true?" Haris had asked Ali, as he sat on the couch with their mother and sister, watching the scene of the bombing repeated over and over again on all the channels. "Did they switch off the lights before the bomb went off?"

"Stop that, Haris!" exclaimed Ali's mother. "Don't you think he's been through enough already?" She'd nearly fainted when she'd seen the bombs on television. Ali called her on his mobile to tell her that he was fine, and she wept down the phone, uttering prayers for his safety and offering thanks that he was unharmed.

Ali didn't feel unharmed as he stood shaking in the chaos, people running around him, the ambulance sirens wailing, the smell of explosives and blood settled around him. The streetlights were flickering on and off. Broken glass from cars and nearby shops sparkled everywhere on the ground, and people who'd lost their shoes in the explosion were cutting themselves as they stumbled around, screaming out loud in pain and terror. Ali's heart was throbbing in his chest as though a strong fist were squeezing it unevenly, and for a minute he wondered if he was going to have a heart attack from fright.

He found Ram and they walked for a mile, away from the crush, holding hands. A doctor glanced at them as he ran by; they were covered in soot and grime but no blood, so he decided that they didn't need his help, even though Ali wanted to reach out and clutch at him as if he were a plank of wood and Ali a drowning man in the middle of a swirling river. Ali and Ram walked and walked, not saying a word, just wanting to put distance between them and the terrible thing they had just seen.

They didn't talk about Haroon, they didn't know what to do, because he had vanished and there was no way they could find him in the darkness and the confusion. In those moments they were as lost as he was; the only difference was that they would come back eventually and he never would.

"So did they, Adda?"

"Did they what?"

"Turn off the lights?"

Ali wanted to reach around and slap Haris. Instead, he frowned and reached for the remote, switching off the television, ignoring the shocked looks of his mother and sister, the openmouthed idiocy of Haris's face. "I don't know what she's talking about. They didn't turn off any lights. She's a bloody liar."

And now Benazir had gone to Dubai for a few days to see her mother, who they said was dying of Alzheimer's. It was only an hour and a half by plane; she could go and come in a day if she wanted to. Everyone was saying that she'd been frightened by the attempt on her life, that she wouldn't return. The president and his cronies were overjoyed with what they thought was their victory over her, contradicting all their statements that they'd had nothing to do with the bombings. They'd warned her not to come, they said. Something like this was bound to happen.

"And how would they know that unless they'd planned it themselves?" Sunita said to Ali, echoing what everyone was saying in the streets, in offices everywhere, in drawing rooms all over the country.

But Ali was tired of talking about it, of thinking about it. It was like being lectured nonstop by his father. He glanced back at the beach hut, thinking that they should probably get back, that people would wonder where they were and would think the worst, naturally. "We should get back—" He stopped in mid-sentence.

"What is it, Ali?" Sunita followed his line of vision, then gasped and took hold of his arm.

A crowd of men had surrounded the beach hut: fifteen or twenty men from the nearby village, dressed in shabby clothes, doing nothing but standing and staring twenty feet away from the area where the foreigners were lying on the sun loungers. The women were jumping up, grabbing towels to cover themselves, their husbands putting down their bottles of beer and trying to stand protectively in front of them. The fishermen were not approaching or retreating, just standing there and fixing them with their piercing eyes set deep in their weather-beaten faces.

Masood came out of the beach hut, gesticulating and shouting angrily at the men, but they were unmoved by his hysteria. He ran around to the front of the house, and returned a moment later with two security guards, who waved their guns and made menacing gestures at the crowd. Only then did they begin to disperse, streaming away from the hut like the tide drawing back from the shoreline, hissing and frothing as it receded.

Sunita and Ali waited till the men had completely disappeared before attempting to make their way back, Sunita walking behind him as they approached the hut. "What happened?" Ali called out to Masood, who was still standing outside, his face contorted with anger.

"*Yaar,* I don't know," he answered back in Urdu, so that the foreigners wouldn't understand him. "They were saying something about money, some kind of tax, they were saying, for using 'their' beach. Bastards."

"Did you pay them?"

"Of course not! What do you think I am? This beach doesn't belong to them. It's my hut; it's been my family's hut for twenty years. We got rid of them, though. My security is the best."

They glanced at the foreigners, who looked white and shaken.

Sunita, too, was scared. Her family had no idea she was out here with Ali; they'd been told she was spending the day with a girl-friend, the mall, a movie, having ice cream. It would be very bad for her to be caught up in any kind of scene. He wanted to hug her close, reassure her that he would look after her, but they never showed any physical affection in front of other people, whether friends or foreigners.

The tension began to dissipate; Masood handed beers around to everyone, clapping the men on the backs, assuring everyone that there was nothing to worry about, that they were just some pesky locals who'd wanted some money, and he'd taken care of things. The Pakistanis remained unfazed; nothing bothered them much, coddled as they were in the arms of affluence and laziness. The for-eigners, too, began to relax, taking their places on the sun loungers again. Sunita and Ali stayed outside, but decided not to wander too far away this time. They sat down on the stairs behind a little con-crete partition and looked out at the waves, trying to regain that feeling of peace they'd captured out on the rocks.

The Scottish woman in the bikini was already lying back on her beach chair, her face reddened from the sun, an unsightly constellation of freckles splashed across her chest. If she pulled the top of her bikini down, Ali knew he would see the freckles dotting her breasts. Next to her was an Englishwoman whom he recognized from a television show on a rival channel. She hosted some women's show, though Ali couldn't remember her name. "Well, that was a little boring, wasn't it?" the Englishwoman said laughing to nobody in particular; she was sitting up, tense, her arms crossed around her knees, glancing fearfully behind her; Ali guessed that she was afraid that the men were terrorists or religious fundamentalists out to kidnap and kill a few foreigners, even though that was hardly likely to happen here.

"Our host—what's his name?—said that they were from a

fishing village nearby," said an Italian woman, nodding in the direction of the dirt road and the settlements beyond.

"Och, don't worry about it. I've seen this before," replied the Scottish woman breezily. "Whenever we're out on the beach, the natives gather around to see what they can see." She shifted her hips and ran her fingers under her buttocks to loosen the fabric from the space between them, winking at her companions and jiggling a little to make her point.

Suddenly, a red-hot fire flared up in Ali. Before he knew what he was doing, he was on his feet lumbering toward them. Sunita pulled at his arm but he shrugged her off. The women glanced up as he stood in front of them, the bottle of beer clutched tight in his hand. Later they would say he was drunk, that he wasn't in control of himself, but at that moment Ali was the most sober he'd been in his entire life.

He said, very coldly, "Actually, they wanted to come and get a good look at your tits."

Their gasps were like the sound a pillow made when you hit it hard with the flat of your hand, the soft foam harboring pockets of air that could only be released with a physical blow.

"And your ass. Putting it on display for them like that, I'm not surprised."

The Scottish woman grabbed her towel once again and made to cover herself. Her husband, dozing on the chair next to her, shook himself awake. "What?"

"But you have to excuse them. They're only *natives,* they don't know any better, so when they see a white woman naked in front of them, what do you expect they're going to do?"

Ali threw the beer bottle onto the stairs. It shattered cruelly, spraying glass and foaming beer everywhere. Ignoring their cries, he stalked inside, Sunita following him, tearful horror written all over her face. Ali found Masood and told him that he was leaving, not bothering to answer any of his questions. He strode out to the car, got inside, and put the key in the ignition. Sunita climbed into the passenger seat, her shoulders shaking. Masood was standing in the door of the hut, staring at Ali as if he'd gone crazy. Maybe he had. Maybe when you were in a bombing and your friend died in front of your eyes, something shook loose inside you, never to be fixed again.

Ali punched the accelerator and backed out of the driveway. He turned on to the dirt road, where some of the fishermen who'd stalked Masood's beach hut lived in thatched cottages just across from the luxurious beach huts that cost more than they could earn in an entire lifetime. There was a small green shrine in the distance, its flags fluttering in tribute to some long-dead saint. Sunita cried softly beside him all the way home.

Ali dropped her off at her friend's house and drove home in the ugly traffic of a late Saturday night. Everything sickened him: the unruly lines of cars and buses, the beggars scrambling for a few rupees, the policemen doing nothing to control anybody, the smog hanging around the road like a thick orange blanket. His head was pounding from the sun and the beers. He wanted to go home and go to sleep.

When Ali reached his house, everyone was huddled on the couch in front of the television as usual, watching the news. His mother shushed him before he could even ask what was going on. He sat next to Jeandi at the end of the sofa and whispered in her ear, "What is it?"

Jeandi was twelve and idolized Ali. She put her arms around his neck and whispered back, "It's an emergency!" Her breath was fruity with some candy she'd been chewing on, orange or lemon boiled sweets from a tin. Ali hoped she couldn't smell the alcohol on his breath. He fixed his gaze on the screen and listened.

"If you're just joining us," said the woman on the BBC, "Pakistan's President Pervez Musharraf has declared emergency rule and suspended the country's constitution. Chief Justice Iftikhar Chaudhry has been replaced and the Supreme Court has been surrounded by troops, who have also entered state-run TV and radio stations. The moves come as the Supreme Court was due to rule on the legality of General Musharraf's October election victory."

Haris looked at Ali, clearly triumphant about knowing something before his older brother. "Benazir's coming back to Karachi."

"So what?" Ali stood up. "I don't care."

"Sit down," said his mother. "Musharraf's going to address the nation any minute."

"I don't care," he repeated. "I don't want to listen to what any of these bastards have to say. I'm going to bed."

To his surprise, his mother said, "Well, if you don't care about anything that's happening in our country, maybe that letter that came for you today will be more interesting to you."

She pointed to the bureau against the wall. Haris and Jeandi followed Ali with their eyes as he walked over to the bureau and saw the envelope with the official seal of the U.S. Embassy in Islamabad on it, addressed to him. The letter had already been opened, but it was useless to cry out about the violation of his privacy. There was no constitutional law that said your parents weren't allowed to open your mail; and even if there had ever been, it was suspended now, along with the rest of the constitution.

Ali took out the letter, affecting a nonchalance he did not feel. The letter informed him that his application for a U.S. student visa had been approved for the next stage: his interview at the U.S. Embassy was scheduled for Monday, November 12, 2007.

The Gift

Jeandal Shah recited the name of Allah that guaranteed victory over one's enemies: *Ya Fattah, Ya Fattah, Ya Fattah,* in time to the urgent gallop of his steed's hooves, as he raced down the bank of the Indus River. He only had a few moments to catch Alexander Burnes before the man sailed up the river in the galley that was anchored in the Indus Delta, ready to go all the way to Lahore. And if Jeandal Shah failed to do that, then all was lost, and Sindh was surely destroyed.

It had all started when the British political assistant in Sindh had claimed he was taking a gift of horses from his king, William IV, to Ranjeet Singh, the maharaja of the Punjab. The horses, he'd said, could not survive the journey overland and had to go by water. Burnes made his appeal through the official channels of the Talpur court, and if the Mir of Talpur had been paying full attention, he would never have permitted the British man to go ahead with his plan. But the Mir was distracted by his woes: trouble with his youngest wife, Raaniya Bibi. And, somehow,

Alexander Burnes—no doubt with the help of heavy bribes as well as honeyed words—was given permission to proceed up the river in March.

Unlike most of her contemporaries, Raaniya Bibi was educated, and could read and write Persian, Arabic, and Sindhi; nobody outside the Mir's family had laid eyes on her and yet tales of her beauty had spread far and wide across the land. She was fond, it was said, of alcohol, and this made her prone to laughing and joking, rather than behaving with the strict formality her position called for. And a courtier had whispered in the Mir's ear that she was having an affair with a member of the court: perhaps even Jeandal Shah himself, though this was surely a rumor designed only to remove Jeandal Shah from the list of the Mir's favored courtiers . . .

When Jeandal Shah heard that the ship had reached the Hujamree, one of the central mouths of the Indus, he knew that the horses were only a pretext; the real reason this British man and his band of spying, lying thieves had come to Sindh was to survey the Indus River. In this manner they would discover the forts all along the Indus and the numbers of men they contained, as well as their vulnerabilities, and the terrain that surrounded them. Then they would prepare their plans to invade Sindh, which the grasping and ambitious chairman of the East India Company, Lord Ellenborough, had decided was of enormous political and economic interest to their infidel empire.

Jeandal Shah had tried to alert the Mir, but the courtiers saw to it that he could not approach the *gaddi* that day, nor in the days that followed. Even though Jeandal Shah was Matiari's representative to the Talpur court and had been given a vast tract of land, paying the rightful amount of revenue and thus holding an important seat in the royal *darbar*.

"It's best you stay away from the presence of the Honored

King," said the bejeweled flunkey who barred Jeandal Shah's way into the *darbar*. "He is not in good temper, having been caught up in domestic strife, and he would not want to see anyone who might remind him of his displeasure with his queen. I suggest you go home today and try again tomorrow."

Jeandal Shah cursed at the man, but the flunky refused to grant him an audience with the Mir, and Jeandal Shah grew panicky, knowing that the British ship would soon move up the river and it would be too late to stop them. Jeandal Shah knew that he who controlled the waterways—its veins and arteries, pumping precious lifeblood through the land—controlled Sindh, and whoever controlled Sindh was halfway toward ruling the western areas of India; the Indus reached up like a jugular vein right into the heart of the Punjab, and once the British were allowed to contaminate those precious waters with their missionaries and merchants, troops and weapons were sure to follow.

Jeandal Shah could not bear to think of the foreigners traipsing all over Sindh, the English army boots treading the land that held the bones of innumerable scores of Sufi saints and holy men. They had no fear of Allah, nor any respect for the Prophet, peace be upon him. They would disturb with impunity the shrines where the saints rested, and destroy the source of the spiritual energy that shimmered over Sindh like a magnetic shield, protecting its people from harm.

When he was finally granted his audience with the Mir a few days later, he tried to present this line of argument to the king, who listened attentively to Jeandal Shah's words, but his abstracted look revealed that his thoughts were not with Sindh, but in the *haveli* where his queens lived. He was not worried about where Burnes wanted to go; instead, he feared who might be with Raaniya Bibi when his back was turned.

"Huzoor," said Jeandal Shah. "Sindh grows weak. The Pirs

who are entrusted with the spiritual affairs of this land are falling prey to greed and corruption."

The Mir rubbed his chin thoughtfully. "How so, Jeandal Shah?"

"The descendants of the saints have broken their vows of asceticism! They are far too interested in the vulgar affairs of daily living. They are accepting presents from the British political officers! The British know that all they have to do is have the Pirs in their pockets and we are their slaves!"

"Hmmm . . ." pondered the Mir.

"Huzoor, your generosity to the Pirs is unrivaled. Land, money to keep up the shrines, a seat in the *darbar* for their representatives—everyone knows you have been more than magnanimous with them, and astute in your knowledge of what will keep them loyal to you. But they are now weak and spoiled. Look at them, their white robes, their jeweled turbans! They are acting like kings in their own right!"

"Are they?" said the Mir, showing some interest for the first time in the conversation.

"The people of Sindh are simple folk, Huzoor. They just increase their tribute to the Pirs and promise them allegiance to the end of their days. But they worship false idols, who can be bought by the highest bidder! The British suspect this, and think that is the perfect time to gain a foothold into Sindh. They want to spy on our forts, to ferret out our weaknesses, and so destroy us!"

"You really think so?"

"Why else is this Burnes here, Huzoor?" Jeandal Shah bowed his head and waited for the king to see reason.

"Well, then. Why don't you go and receive him, and accompany him up for the first leg of his journey? That way you can make sure he's not up to any trickery."

"Huzoor, that's not good enough! He must be stopped—"

"Oh, Jeandal Shah, I'm sure you will think of something. I have more important matters to attend to, anyway. Now go, and do not fail me." And with that, the Mir clapped his hands. A courtier immediately rose to his feet and called out, "The *darbar* is finished for today!"

Jeandal Shah found himself being escorted out by the same flunky who had stopped him from seeing the Mir all the days before. He angrily shrugged off the man's hand on his elbow, and went to his rooms in the palace to try to figure out what to do. He paced up and down all evening, muttering to himself about the foolishness of men who were so deeply bewitched by a woman's charms that they could no longer think straight. Even kings could fall victim to female witchery; but the safety of Sindh was at stake, and men of honor could not sit idle and allow besotted kings to let its soil slip through their fingers like the grains of sand on a beach.

By the morning prayers before the first light of dawn, he decided that he would use his own initiative, so he raced to Thatta, near the Hujamree, to summon the help of his cousin, Sayed Sikandar Shah, a minor official at the Mir's court. It was a journey of some ninety miles; it took him nearly two days to reach Thatta, and by then Jeandal Shah was almost certain the British ship had already sailed up the river.

"Wake up, cousin, wake up!" shouted Jeandal Shah, pounding on the door of Sikandar Shah's chamber in his *haveli* in Thatta. It was all but impossible to rouse his cousin from one of his magnificent afternoon naps: Sikandar Shah was a hugely fat man, far too fond of mangos and *lassi* and huge fried breakfasts. His corpulence was the stuff of legend: no horse could carry him, so he had to move around in a specially built cart pulled by two mules, and his trousers were made from sixty *thaan* of finest cotton, instead of the usual forty.

"What? What is it?" said Sikandar Shah, appearing bleary-eyed at the door. "Is it dinnertime already?"

"Come with me. Immediately. It's an emergency!"

"But where?"

"There's no time! *Hurry!*"

Jeandal Shah had already had Sikandar Shah's peculiar means of transport readied, and he pushed, prodded, and bullied his cousin into getting dressed and taking his place onto the cart, glancing worriedly all the while at the sun as it moved across the sky. Finally the procession set off, the bad-tempered mules pulling the cart, Sikandar Shah groaning that his stomach hurt without at least a cup of tea and a *paratha* to fill it, while Jeandal Shah galloped ahead on his horse, his sword glinting under the afternoon sun as they hastened toward the mouth of the river.

By some miracle of God, the ship was still waiting at Hujam-ree, Burnes having been unable to find a pilot to take them across the bar. Furthermore, they'd taken the wrong route, ending up in the shallow mouth of the river rather than the deep water, stuck in mud as they'd attempted to plow up the channel.

"We're not too late, hurry, hurry!" shouted Jeandal Shah, as he dug his spurs into the flanks of his horse. He jumped down from his mount, but the unfortunate Sikandar Shah could not move as quickly, and had to be helped off the cart by two servants. The quick climb down to the riverbank elicited much moaning and groaning from Sikandar Shah, while Jeandal Shah danced impatiently around him, his sword half unsheathed; he was not sure whether he wanted to use it on the British interlopers, or on his own cousin, so slow was his progress.

Jeandal Shah could not see if Burnes himself was standing on the deck of the ship, a fine British galley with proud sails that were now unfurled and filled with wind. A second ship was moored behind them, and men clambered up and down the masts, across the decks, readying both vessels for the journey north. Jeandal Shah instructed one of his men to approach the ship and summon Burnes to the shore.

"Do you think he'll come himself? Or send a lesser man?" asked Sikandar Shah.

"He'll have to. We're here, aren't we? Protocol demands that he meet us himself," said Jeandal Shah. He'd brought his full cortege, including his drums and the official drum-beater, although he usually liked to leave them behind when making visits to his home. He was not a man who enjoyed the pomp and circumstance of royalty, preferring to keep a low profile and a simpler appearance when moving among his own people.

But this was a circumstance that demanded as much show as could be summoned up.

Sure enough, within fifteen minutes, Sir Alexander Burnes was on the shore, climbing up to meet them on the small path that led up from the bottom of the riverbank to the top of a dusty knoll. The British spy was a man of medium height and average appearance, and Jeandal Shah wondered how this ordinary-looking man could be the head of such an important operation. Sayed Sikandar Shah was at least three hundred pounds and Jeandal Shah himself was six foot, four inches tall; their magnificent stature, at least, announced their importance, while this man looked no more significant than a twig on the branch of some not-very-tall tree.

After the necessary courtesies were exchanged through an Indian interpreter whom Burnes had brought with him from the ship, Sikandar Shah stepped forward with a letter in his hand. "It is my duty as an officer of the government of the Mir of Hyderabad to inform you that you do not have permission to sail upriver. An embargo is laid upon all your vessels: you are confined to your boats, and urged by my master the Ameer to abandon this journey and take a land route instead. Here is a letter explaining all of this." He did not reveal that the letter had been written by Jeandal Shah that morning.

The British man spoke a few words to the interpreter, who translated, in Hindi, "We have come from Bombay bearing a gift of horses from our King William IV for His Highness the Maharaja Ranjeet Singh of Lahore . . . we have sent letters to the Ameer to request permission for this trip. . . ."

Jeandal Shah said, "We know all about this gift. Tell him he's to take them by land or not go at all. You've sent the letters, but they haven't arrived, and we're not fools."

The translator whispered, "Honored sirs, I can't say it that rudely!"

At the same time, Sikandar Shah spoke up. "If your agent desires, he can make an appeal to the Ameer in person, but that will require him to moor the ships and come to Thatta next week to discuss the ships' safe passage with the proper state ministers. Perhaps the ship will be allowed to sail, without yourselves on board, of course."

"His Highness the King will be very displeased to hear that his gift, offered in good faith, is being delayed in this manner, and will lodge a complaint with your leader the Mir. . . ."

"Tell him we'll take very good care of his gift!" said Sikandar Shah.

"He doesn't trust us?" Jeandal Shah growled, his hand on his sword.

"No, honored sirs, it's not that at all," stuttered the translator, a small, dark-skinned Goan who had no desire to return to Goa without his head. "It's just that he's concerned for the welfare of the horses; they are very fine steeds, they cannot take the heat; this is why they couldn't go by land, and he won't leave them alone, he says . . ."

All the while Alexander Burnes was examining the two Sindhis as if seeing them through the wrong end of a telescope. His eyes narrowed, and Jeandal Shah realized the British man thought they were lying, or at least bluffing, and that there was no real impediment to their plan of action. But he did not venture this opinion and instead nodded curtly, agreeing to come to Thatta to negotiate the terms of his ships' passage. Then he burst out in English, "How the bloody hell do you expect twenty horses to go up the river to Lahore by themselves?"

"What did he say?"

The translator, shivering, related this last sentence to the two men, while Burnes fixed them with a cold, angry stare. Jeandal Shah was getting ready to draw his sword, but after a pause, Sikandar Shah said earnestly, "Well, if they're such special horses, as you say, surely they must know how to sail a boat?"

Nobody spoke for a full minute. Then suddenly Jeandal Shah guffawed with laughter and slapped his cousin on the back. "That's a good one, cousin! That's a good one!" Then he bent forward and said to the translator in a low voice, "How many horses are there, really?"

The translator shivered. "One dray horse and four dray mares." At this, Jeandal Shah clanked his sword menacingly. The translator turned tail and ran, and Alexander Burnes cast one last furious glance at the two Sindhis before following him back to the ship.

Jeandal Shah and Sikandar Shah rode back to Matiari, congratulating themselves the whole way on having aborted the infidel British spying mission. Sikandar Shah celebrated by throwing a huge feast in which he gave several drums of *biryani* to the poor at the shrine of Shah Abdul Latif Bhitai, a distant ancestor of both men. The great Shah-Jo-Risalo was recited, with its grand verses telling the story of Marvi and her long captivity under Prince Umar Soomra; and as it was a Friday, two healthy young rams were brought to the *maidan* and made to fight. Everyone retired to their beds, full, happy, and suffused with a glow of patriotism. The honor of Sindh had been saved!

But only God knew what magic Alexander Burnes used on the Mir's ministers at Thatta, because in eleven days' time, Burnes received permission to travel up the Indus as originally planned.

Jeandal Shah had been appointed Burnes's official host or *mehmandar*, and he and another man of rank, Sayed Zulfikar Shah, were assigned specially to escort him out of Sindh by the Mir's head minister. But Burnes sweetly replied that he would neither return to the sea, nor go to Hyderabad to put his case before the Mir, since, he claimed, he already had permission to traverse the water route to Lahore. No amount of argument, cajoling, or appealing to the man's sense of decency or honor could make him change his mind. "I do not care if my honored host is a descendant of the Prophet," said Burnes, in fluent Hindi—another sign of witchcraft, thought Jeandal Shah to himself, smarting mightily from the insult to his lineage. Burnes continued: "I have been insulted, abused, starved, and twice turned out of the country by persons of low rank. But if you wish, I can go to the Mir and inform him that your detaining me has breached the treaty between the Sindh government and the government of Britain."

Sure enough, he appeared before the Mir, and in front of Jeandal Shah's disbelieving eyes, spoke with the tongue of a snake until the Mir agreed to let him use the water route beyond Hujamree.

Burnes departed from the court in triumph, back to his ships, and they sailed away, sails heavy with wind, the Union Jack proudly fluttering above. His parting shot to Jeandal Shah before he left: "We have entered, in the course of our voyages, *all* the mouths of the river, and we now have a map of them, and the land route of Thatta besides. I must thank you most sincerely for helping us to overcome our ignorance of Sindh. You are most definitely a friend of the British Empire." And he bowed low to Jeandal Shah, smiling a cold smile that did not reach his eyes.

* * *

"The Honored King requires your presence tomorrow morning in his private chambers to discuss important matters of state. Leave your cortege behind and present yourself at the Hyderabad Palace at seven."

When Jeandal Shah received this message, a month after the Burnes incident, he was puzzled. Everyone knew that the Mir had lost face in the episode, and Jeandal Shah himself feared that he had lost favor with the Mir, but perhaps the king had had time to reconsider and decided to take Jeandal Shah back into his fold. He said a prayer of thanksgiving to Almighty Allah, then went to his bed, leaving instructions to his servants to wake him just before the *fajr* prayers.

Jeandal Shah arrived before dawn at the palace in Hyderabad, where he was met by a servant who guided him to a darkened chamber and bid him wait. "But you are not to wear your sword in front of the Mir this early in the morning," the servant instructed him. "He is slightly unwell and the sight of your sword would disturb his harmony."

Jeandal Shah did not want to give up his sword, a beautiful steel blade inscribed with the names of his father and grandfathers; he was one of the few men allowed to wear his sword in the Mir's presence. But he was a man of honor, who had sworn obedience to the Mir when he'd joined his *darbar*. He relinquished his sword to the man, who promised to polish it and bring it back to him in even better condition than he had left it.

Jeandal Shah stepped into the chamber and realized that he was not alone. In the darkness, two eyes shone out at him, glowing like amber stones. And from outside he heard the voice of the servant man, who put his mouth to the keyhole of the door and said, "O Sayed Jeandal Shah, this is your reward, for daring to touch a Talpur woman! Now defend your honor or die trying!"

Jeandal Shah's heart nearly stopped. He knew exactly which woman they were referring to. It was no good pointing out that he had never laid eyes on her; he knew that the accusation was merely a pretext to get rid of him.

As the sun seeped into the chamber, Jeandal Shah could begin to make out the form of the creature locked in with him: the Mir's pet cheetah. The cat had been circling around in the dark, but now that it was growing light it could see him, too, and it began to lick its lips in anticipation of its next meal. *So this is what honor gets you,* thought Jeandal Shah to himself.

The cheetah hissed at Jeandal Shah, who flattened himself against the wall, cursing at the cheetah to stay back. The animal padded around the room and stared at Jeandal Shah with malevolent eyes, its fangs bared, its powerful muscles tensed underneath the silky yellow coat. It was the favorite plaything of the Mir, who kept it chained to his throne and threw it scraps of meat from his lavish meals. His courtiers liked to whisper that it was the reincarnated spirit of a great warrior, perhaps even one of the defeated Kalhora kings. It never went without meat for more than a few hours, but they'd starved it for two days before putting it in this bare room in the palace and then ushering Jeandal Shah in to face its wrath.

Jeandal Shah edged carefully away from it into a corner of the room, and looked wildly around for something to defend himself with: a chair, a picture frame, *anything*. But the room was completely bare.

The cheetah kept pacing back and forth, back and forth, its powerful shoulders rising and falling with each step. It lowered its head and sniffed the floor, catching the scent of its prey, then stopped and slowly turned to face Jeandal Shah. It lay down on its haunches, head raised, eyes fixed on the man, as if taking the measure of him before deciding when to pounce.

Jeandal Shah avoided looking into its eyes, knowing that a direct stare would be seen by the animal as a challenge. Nor would he call out for help to his enemies, who were standing just outside the door, waiting to enjoy themselves on his pleas for mercy. But he began to pray under his breath: "Allah Saeen, please help me, o Allah, save me from this disaster. Indeed, my lord! I am overcome, so help me . . ."

Then he looked down at his feet, and saw the means to his salvation: his enemies had left one thing behind in that room. A plain rug, a roughly woven *durree* approximately six feet long and four feet wide. It wasn't much, but it would have to do.

Jeandal Shah murmured one last prayer, then began to recite *Ya Fattah, Ya Fattah, Ya Fattah*, over and over again, growing in strength and volume until the whole room seemed to be filled with the holy name. In one fluid motion he scooped up the rug, then made a running lunge for the cheetah across the room, leaping high as he neared the great cat, who'd risen to its feet and was preparing to spring. But Jeandal Shah's height gave him the advantage: as he jumped, he unfurled the rug and brought it down onto the cheetah, trapping the animal in its folds. He landed on top of the cat, which struggled wildly to free itself from the rug, and used his enormous girth to pin the animal to the floor. The cat screamed and shrieked, but Jeandal Shah never stopped shouting "Ya Fattah! Ya Fattah!" as he held the cheetah down. And he caught the cheetah's neck in his bare hands and squeezed until the last breath left the cheetah's body with a mighty groan.

He was breathing heavily, great ragged gasps, sweating and trembling with the effort of having saved his own life. Only after a full ten minutes had passed did he dare move off the cheetah's body, which was still warm. But it was perfectly still: he pulled the rug away and saw its amber eyes staring back at him, glassy and unblinking. Then he sank to his knees and wept.

The men who were waiting outside began to tremble when they heard the great tumult coming from inside the locked chamber; they couldn't tell whether the piercing shrieks and screams were coming from the beast or the man. In the silence that followed, one of the courtiers reached for the lock and undid it, his hand shaking so badly that it took him several minutes to free the bolt. The door swung open, but they all shrank back, too terrified to witness the mayhem that lay behind it.

Suddenly, the cheetah's body fell out of the door and landed on the stone ground with a thud. And then Jeandal Shah stepped over the body and emerged into the light. His face and arms were scratched, his clothes were torn, and blood trickled from a wound on his head. But he was standing upright, in full possession of all his limbs. He looked at the courtiers and servants, all of whom were staring at him in terror, and spat at their feet.

"Here," he rasped, still breathing hard. "Here's the lover of your master's wife." And he prodded the cheetah's body with his foot. "Now bring me what belongs to me." The courtiers scurried off and ran in different directions, fearful of his revenge. But Jeandal Shah was not interested in revenge, only retreat. He took his sword back, and then he left the Mir's palace, never to return again.

He gladly gave up the riches and the power that came with a seat at the *darbar* of the Mir, and spent the rest of his life in his village of Matiari, overseeing his farmland and his fruit orchards, ensuring that his *haris* were well taken care of for the rest of his days. Perhaps he married and raised a family; perhaps he died a childless bachelor not long after defeating the cheetah. Either way, it was a far more peaceful pursuit in which to spend his life than dancing attendance in a palace where honor was a commodity to be bought and sold like a bushel of grain.

November 12, 2007

Ali was beginning to feel that the process for obtaining his US visa was going to be as painful, if not worse, than the root canal treatment he'd endured three years ago. It took five trips to the dentist and seven shots of Novocain, and he'd bled so much that he'd considered asking the dentist for a blood transfusion. "This just isn't normal," said the dentist, shaking his head, which shattered whatever little bit of confidence Ali had left in the man.

Having to come clean to his family about his plans to study in America was only the first part of the procedure. Looking back on that evening, after he'd turned off the television and had to face the accusing stares of his mother and brother, he could see now that it was not just the first, but the easiest part.

"Why didn't you tell me?" said his mother, for once her eyes dry as stones. Usually she wept easily, tears trickling down her face no matter where she was, in the middle of preparing dinner or going in a car on the way to a shopping plaza. She just wiped them away with whatever was handiest—the end of a *dupatta*, a tissue, the back of her hand—her tears as natural as digestion or breathing. To see her without the usual rain clouds surrounding her was strange for Ali, speaking to him of days before she'd been weakened by her demanding, larger-than-life husband and boisterous family.

"You know why I didn't tell you," Ali mumbled, squeezed into a corner of the sofa, his arms crossed mutinously across his chest. Jeandi had been sent to bed but Ali felt as though he'd taken her place as the youngest, not the eldest, child of the house. It was unnerving, this reversal of roles, with Haris now cast as the most obedient child and Ali himself the black sheep.

"Because you knew I would never agree."

No, because I knew you would harass me to death about it. This answer was only in Ali's imagination; he didn't dare say it out loud to his mother. The years of living with their father, tiptoeing around his volatile nature like stepping around shattered glass, had made Ali cautious about revealing his true feelings to anyone. It was safer to keep them hidden, even if they festered inside. Better to bear the discomfort of suppressed dreams and repressed hopes than to endure the storm of recriminations they would create, once brought into the light.

"But how could you do this without even asking me—consulting me?" said his mother.

Haris added nothing to the conversation; he just followed the words coming out of their mouths, his eyes moving from one face to the other as if he were watching a tennis match. Ali could see that a sense of grudging admiration for his brother's daring battled with the huge resentment that once again Ali was making plans to go away, plans that didn't include taking Haris with him. He'd suffered through that once before, when Ali had gone away to Dubai, and Ali knew well the chorus that would be replaying itself inside Haris's head right now: *Why does he always have to do this? He's so greedy, so selfish. Only thinking of himself. Never thinking about how we'll cope if he goes away.*

A similar chorus was playing in Ali's head, a sort of sibling telepathy between the two brothers. He'd whipped himself enough with the same thoughts for many years, knowing full well that as the eldest child, he was in the best position to claim life's privileges for himself. At first he'd never even thought about it, unconsciously accepting it as his birthright, but over the years his lack of awareness had given way to the realization that his good fortune left only scraps left behind for Haris and Jeandi—scraps of money, opportunity, his parents' attention and energies. He desperately didn't want his brother and sister to hate him for it. It wasn't his fault. But at the same time, he couldn't give up on his dream.

"When are you going to Islamabad?" said Haris, who hadn't looked at the letter; he'd only heard about its contents second-hand.

"The twelfth," said Ali.

"You should be careful," replied Haris, glancing at his mother, who had turned her back on both of them and was clearing up dishes from the dinner table. "There's going to be a lot of trouble up there now that the judges have been kicked out."

"It'll be fine."

Ali's mother whirled around from the sink and spoke up again. "And does your father know about this?"

It was the one question he hadn't expected from her. She barely mentioned his name anymore around them, seemed uninterested in the contact her children did or didn't have with him. But of course Sikandar Hussein didn't know about Ali's plans to escape this tired, claustrophobic existence that he'd been forced into. There was no question of permission being granted, blessings received. The day Sikandar had walked out from their lives, his authority over Ali's destiny had withered away, a tree blighted by a life-draining disease.

Ali rose from the sofa. "I don't want to discuss this anymore. I'm going to bed."

"Does he know?" repeated his mother. "You know he'll never agree to this."

Ali clenched his fists and muttered in a tight voice, "My father is dead!" It was the first time he'd spoken the lie in front of his family, and it gave him a dangerous, dizzying feeling to bring his two worlds so close together. He cursed his luck for having to split his existence in two, between the outside world where his father was a dead bureaucrat and the inside one where his father was very much alive, and a feudal to boot. For a moment he wondered what it might feel like to live in absolute truth, but he pushed away the fantasy like a gift he couldn't possibly afford.

"Don't say such things!" Ali's mother gave him a furious stare. For a moment Ali thought she might actually slap his face, the way she used to when he was younger and had said or done something unforgiveable—cheated on an exam, lied about being out late at night, smoked cigarettes. He found himself completely flummoxed by her reaction. After everything Sikandar had done to her, why should she care? A sudden feeling of betrayal stung him, made tears spring up unbidden in his eyes. He remembered how he'd had to console his mother through the long months after his father's abandonment, every month another nail in his father's imaginary coffin. Why did she harbor such loyalty to him now?

He dropped his hands, stared at the floor. He wanted to tell his mother he was sorry for upsetting her. But he couldn't make the words come out of his mouth. Defeated, he turned around and left the room, biting his lip hard so that he would not speak, tasting the blood in his mouth with an almost vicious sense of satisfaction.

Later, Ali admitted reluctantly to himself that Haris had a point: Islamabad had started to be rocked by the same violence that had convulsed Karachi for decades. Back in January, extremists in the Lal Masjid—the Red Mosque—had started making trouble, first occupying a children's library, then going into the city and raiding brothels, kidnapping the madams and exposing their clients. Soon they'd be attacking CD stores and women who weren't veiled; the city was in an uproar, demanding that something be done.

But the government had adopted a soft approach, hoping to appease them with talks and money. Negotiations hadn't worked, so a siege of the mosque followed; Ali's channel had covered the operation, a terrible, bloody night, with SSG commandos entering the mosque to capture those inside, waiting and armed to die in the name of God. Thousands of people tuned in to the station and Ali had to answer phone lines that were clogged with people hurling abuse against the government. Official numbers never revealed how many people had perished in there. But everyone knew that Abdul Rashid Ghazi, the imam heading the mosque, had been killed, along with women and children, and the repercussions had been terrible: suicide attacks on the army and the police in a city that had been so peaceful and calm, people said it wasn't a part of Pakistan at all.

The news broadcasts only added to the hysteria that the entire nation was already feeling. Ali had got into an argument with Ameena about it the day before the troops had stormed the building. "Do we really want to show this?" he said, in the middle of a team meeting where they were discussing how they'd cover it when the army finally made its move against the renegade mosque.

"What do you mean?" Ameena said, in a voice that said *I don't have time for your nonsense.*

"I mean, there are probably going to be a lot of people killed in this," said Ali, even though Jehangir was poking him under the table to shut up. "Do we really want to show dead bodies on television?"

"That's why they call it live television," said Ameena, completely without irony. And then she added, "Besides, can we afford not to?"

"But there's got to be some sort of international guidelines about this kind of thing," Ali said. "They don't show dead bodies abroad, or on the international channels."

"Well, this is Pakistan," snapped Ameena. "The advertisers are calling the shots, and they want action. I can't fight the entire system, especially not now. And if you've got a problem with that, you can go work for the BBC."

They'd jeered with laughter at him then, but now that the emergency had been imposed and the government had put drastic curbs on the media, they had to consider an even more draconian form of self-censorship than the one that Ali's protests had suggested. All the news channels were abruptly taken off the air on November 3, their producers instructed that they could no longer show current affairs programs or broadcast any of the protests against the sacking of the judges. Channels that agreed to the conditions were allowed back on, one after the other compromising and slowly flickering back into life; those that refused, like City24 News, were being threatened with permanent shutdown.

The programs were still being broadcast from the station in Dubai, but Kazim Mazhar was receiving telephone calls and visits from army personnel, pressuring him to back down. Ameena and the other senior producers and management disappeared into his smoke-filled office for daily meetings that lasted hours and produced no resolution. Ali, Jehangir, and the rest of the junior staffers performed their duties as usual, but everyone knew how high the stakes were; they'd seen other news stations come under attack by the police when they didn't do as they were told. There were rumors that someone might even try to plant a bomb in the building. Ali came home from work completely shattered, suffering from migraines and backaches that made studying for his evening BBA classes almost impossible. He'd had to grovel to Ameena to get even this one day off so that he could go to Islamabad for the precious visa interview.

Ali twisted his head left and right, seeking relief for his neck as he stood in line for a shuttle bus at the Convention Center, and wondered how long it would be before everything came crashing down around him. He'd flown into Islamabad the night before, checked into a cheap but clean guesthouse in F-4 and slept in a small bed with a lumpy, flat pillow that put a painful cramp in his neck. Now here he was at six in the morning, stripped of his mobile phone and most of his dignity as he went through the turnstiles at the center along with a group of several hundred other people seeking visas from the various embassies and high commissions in the Diplomatic Enclave.

His taxi driver had taken him through a long, circuitous route that went all the way up to the Margalla Road and around the new developments of the E block before swinging back to join the road that came in from Rawalpindi and the airport. It would have taken them five minutes had he been able to drive straight down Constitution Avenue, but the police had cordoned off all the approaches to the Supreme Court in anticipation of the lawyers' protests against the sacking of the Supreme Court judges.

"They've been here for a week," said the taxi driver, in Punjabi. "Standing in the roads, wearing their black coats, shouting slogans and raising their fists. Women, too! Can you believe it?"

Ali, who didn't understand Punjabi very well, mumbled a reply, too tired to make conversation with the driver. He was nervous about the interview; people loved to scare visa seekers about the US Embassy the same way he loved to scare others about getting root canal treatment. When he'd told Jehangir that he was going to apply for his student visa, Jehangir moaned dramatically, "Oh my God, I had to stand in forty-eight degrees Celsius heat for sixteen hours and when I got to the counter I had to take off my clothes and sing 'Yankee Doodle Dandy' while standing on one foot and then I had to promise my firstborn son to the visa officer and can you believe it: *they still didn't give it to me!!!*" Ali couldn't tell if he was serious or joking, until Jehangir grinned and confessed that he had an American passport.

Ali got out of the taxi and walked across the open-air parking lot, climbing over a concrete barrier to get to the ticket booth, where he was instructed to leave his mobile phone and bag at the collection booth. The only thing he was allowed to take with him was a plastic file with his papers and passport. Not even a bottle of water was allowed. He followed the people to the turnstiles and got into the line for the US Embassy bus, watching others separate into the lines for the UK High Commission, the Canadian and Australian outposts, and the various other diplomatic missions. His own bus also let people off at the Chinese, Korean, and Iranian embassies; a surprising grouping given the state of relations between all three countries and the United States.

A child somewhere in the line cried out, "Mama, this is just like when we were in line for the rides at Disney World!"

"Yeah," snorted a college student standing just behind Ali. "And now, kids, we'll all get strip-searched by Mickey Mouse."

Finally the bus arrived. The people clambered on, finding their seats in the rackety vehicle. There was no air-condition-ing, but the open windows let in the last of the cool morning air. Ali dreaded to think what the journey would be like at ten in the morning, when the sun was baking hot and there wasn't a whiff of breeze anywhere. He squeezed himself in between three young air force cadets, proud in their starched blue uniforms and smart caps, and watched as a few teenage girls tried to simper at them. The cadets hitched themselves up to full height and one turned to Ali with a friendly smile. "Where are you going?"

Ali said, "I'm trying to get my US visa. What about you?"

"We're being sent to China, on a training course. To Beijing!"

"What about you?" said the cadet to the college student.

"I lost my passport so I have to get my student visa reissued," said the student. Ali noticed the American twang to his accent for the first time. Would he start to sound like that, too, after a few years of living in America?

The bus set off, then stopped after a short distance. Ali and the other passengers watched as a man in *shalwar kameez* got onto the bus, holding a video camera. To their astonishment, he held it up to film the faces of each and every single person on the bus.

"What are they doing that for?" one of the cadets asked Ali.

"No idea," Ali shrugged.

The college student, sitting just behind them, said, "It's so that if somebody blows up the embassy they can identify the bomber . . ."

Ali frowned and edged as far forward in his seat as possible. He didn't want to be associated with anyone talking about bombings, even if the boy meant it as a joke. The three cadets, too, fell silent, their friendly demeanor replaced by stiff formality. The student shrank back into his seat and stared out the window.

The man with the camera finished filming and got off the bus, and then they were on their way again, slowly trundling through the gates of the Diplomatic Enclave. Ali felt disoriented: the area beyond the barriers was green and peaceful, full of streams and forests. A few bullocks bathed lazily in one of the streams in a dip beyond the road. Among the pastoral landscape, huge fortresslike embassies loomed up, surrounded by barbed wire and armed guards.

"Man, this is worse than being a Jew in a World War II movie. I feel like I'm being shipped to a concentration camp," muttered the college student to no one in particular. "Do you think they're going to take us and shoot us against a wall if we try to escape?"

"Will you shut up, you burger?" hissed Ali through clenched teeth.

The bus, basic as it was, came with one luxury: a conductor in the shape of a young Punjabi man who shouted out the names of the embassies as they passed by, announcing each stop. "Yas, yas, ladeez and gentleman, here is Australia embassy. Australia very nice, good day mate, yas. Okay ladeez and gentleman, here is Korea embassy. Very good thank you, how are you, *kim chi?*" He hopped off the bus at every stop, helping passengers off, guiding returning ones to empty seats, chirruping all the while like a mad myna bird. Ali tried with little success to tune out his running commentary until he heard the words "Here is US Embassy, George Bush, very good, thank you, goodbye."

He roused himself and quickly pushed to the front of the bus, mercifully leaving the college student behind. They'd been dropped on the other side of the road, so he and twenty other people had to dash across to the embassy gates, where they went through body searches, metal detectors, and the ubiquitous turnstiles. At last Ali found himself in an air-conditioned waiting room inside the embassy, along with ninety-nine other applicants packed onto rows of small chairs. The entire process, from Convention Center to embassy, had taken two hours: now all Ali had to do was wait until his turn was called, at 8:30 a.m. He went up to a booth to get electronically fingerprinted and registered before collecting a ticket, then sat down heavily in a chair and tried to nap a little before being called for his interview, his stupor disturbed every few minutes by the PA system crackling into life and announcing the name of the next candidate:

Riaz Samiuddin . . .

Karam ud-Din . . .

Ayla Haider . . .

On the front wall hung two photographs: one of George Bush and the other of Dick Cheney. Ali tried to not look at them, but it was impossible: their eyes followed you wherever you went in the room. Had either of them known what kinds of horror they were going to subject Pakistan to when they began the War on Terror? In the six years since 9/11, the country had fragmented, a civil war was going on in the northern area, fundamentalists were causing havoc everywhere. Was this what they had envisaged when they'd pressured Pakistan into taking sides?

Sarwar Patel . . .

Ali didn't know the answers to those questions; nobody in power had the answers either. The Pakistani president was firmly sticking to his position of supporting American policy in the Afghan war, which affected Pakistan much more than the war in Iraq, even though few people in Pakistan wanted to help the Western powers keep bombing the daylights out of the tribal belt. Nobody believed the claims of terrorist training camps the Americans and the Indians kept throwing at them . . .

Mohammed Hayat . . .

But the judges, who'd been all set to rule that the president's election was illegal, had been deposed on November 3, the day of the emergency; the chief justice and his supporters—senior judges and barristers—were placed under house arrest. And three thousand people or more had been arrested only a few

days after the emergency was declared: civil rights leaders, politicians, lawyers. The government had checkmated those who
would want to get rid of them through the courts in a masterful,
Machiavellian move—one that many people predicted would be
the undoing of the rulers.

And the so-called democratic forces, what were they doing to
try to make sense out of all of this? Nawaz Sharif was still exiled in
Saudi Arabia, although he was threatening to fly back to Pakistan
any day now. Ali didn't know if he would have the nerve to actually go through with it; nor whether he would boycott the upcom-
ing elections, which were scheduled for January. The word on the
street: all this chaos was being created on purpose so that elections
could be canceled. Elections, of course, that the West was forcing
on Pakistan in the first place. Democracy was a joke in Pakistan—
there was no point to any of it, that was the hideous irony. They'd
be rigged so that the president and his party could win. That was
how it always went in countries like Pakistan . . .

Toobia Khan . . .

Benazir Bhutto, away in Dubai during the emergency, flew
back immediately—a move Ali did not expect of her, but had to
grudgingly admit that he admired. Oh, Sikandar Hussein would
be laughing now! But it was true: if she'd wanted to run away,
that would have been her chance. Instead she had returned, determined to fight to victory in the January elections, and had
been put under house arrest four days earlier, when she'd tried to
lead a rally in Lahore. The death threats were still on her head.
The government declared that she was free to move the next day,
but that no heads of opposition parties were allowed to speak
at public gatherings. The rumors abounded that she'd enacted
some sort of deal with America, or the army, or both, in order to
eventually assume a seat of power, probably with the president
right by her side.

No wonder so many people were trying to get away from this ruined, broken country, to America and the United Kingdom and Australia and Canada and any other country that would have them. The waiting room was packed with them; there were hundreds more every day crammed into every diplomatic mission in the city. But if the West had done so much to make things bad for ordinary Pakistanis, why were they all so eager to abandon Pakistan and take up residence in Western countries?

Ali squirmed uncomfortably in his chair at this thought. He'd tried to avoid confronting it, even though he enjoyed participating in America-bashing as much as the next person. The United States of Hypocrisy, they'd said at City24, Ameena, Jehangir, all of them, and thought themselves so clever for having come up with the name.

And if that were true, then Ali would fit right in, when he went to Kansas and tried to become just like them, losing his accent, learning to love football and baseball, adopting their lifestyle as if he'd been born to it, so that nobody could accuse him of not fitting in.

Wasif Mahmood . . .

The circus of confusion went on in Ali's head, as the numbers were called and people shuffled to the booths in the back of the room to shout out their cases to the visa officers. There were all sorts of people in that room: educated members of the upper class who held themselves as if brushing against anyone else would give them a disease; middle-class families dressed in their best clothes, hoping to impress the visa officers; men in simple *shalwar kameez* and Peshawari sandals who could barely speak English. They spoke instead to local hires who translated for the American officers into the local languages of the area, Urdu and Punjabi, Pashto for the northerners.

Once called to their interviews, they all had to shout out

the intimate details of their lives through thick glass walls and microphones crackling with static. Ali heard each person's life story: where their children lived in the United States, how much they earned, whether or not they intended to stay in America for a short while or indefinitely, how they planned to support themselves. Babies cried and young married couples hushed them urgently; children played and ran up and down the narrow aisles, begging for water or chips from the tiny canteen set up outside. People were too scared to go to the toilet in case they missed their turn; one or two men rushed out of the toilet, hurriedly doing up their belts, cursing and grumbling but having to plaster smiles on their faces when their names were called. Ali watched as they faced the visa officers, who remained bland and polite in the face of the men who looked just like the tribals their army was fighting across the border.

Shams Siddiqui . . .

Ali could feel his hands beginning to curl into fists, clutching at the plastic file that contained all his documents: bank statements, acceptance letters, certificates of financial standing. Letters from his uncle and other relatives in America who promised they could guarantee financial support. Transcripts from the other universities he'd attended. Medical records. All proof of his good character, his good intentions. When, really, he shouldn't have had to prove anything to anyone.

He stood up. He took one step, then another, his legs shaking. People were staring at him—there was little else to do but stare at everyone else in the room. He was edging away, now, even as his number was being called and his name was reverberating on the PA system: *Ali Sikandar . . . Ali Sikandar . . . Ali Sikandar . . .*

He put a sweaty hand on the door handle and pushed it down. All eyes followed him, even the visa officers, the guards with their automatic weapons. He was terrified that they'd stop him, question him, take him away somewhere and ask him what he thought he was up to. He didn't know what they did to people who ran away before the interview. The siren call of America was still as seductive as it had ever been, amplified by all the people in the room, their hopes and their longing for the future so clearly on display. But he knew he couldn't face it. Not the way things stood now: with his family, with Sunita, with Pakistan.

Ali crept out the door just as the PA system clicked on again, and the next hopeful applicant's name was called.

Rahila Elahi . . . Rahila Elahi . . . Rahila Elahi . . .

He stumbled from the dark, cooled room into the blinding heat and made his way to the exit gate, breathing as heavily as if he'd just finished running a race. He promised himself that he would go to America, but now was not the time. Ali knew he could only make the move when the world swung back into balance again, when nobody had to feel like a criminal just because they wanted to cross borders, to gain an education or to be with the people they loved. America would have to wait until things were better, for Pakistan and for himself.

Outlaws

FROM THE DIARIES OF WILLIAM HENRY LUCAS,

DEPUTY DISTRICT COMMISSIONER, SINDH

Sukkur, Sindh, 1895
. . . the desert of Thar has one of the harshest climates ever seen by Man, for in addition to the extreme temperatures (more than 50 C during summertime) the soil is dry for much of the year & the sands are continually shifting (a mere 100–500 mm of precipitation in the short July–September southwest monsoon). Not many trees grow there, & those that do are very slow-growing: *acacia tortilis* may prove to be the most promising for desert afforestation; while *prosopis cineraria* provides fodder and wood for construction. The locals have a saying: that death will not visit a man if he has a *prosopis cineraria*, a goat, & a camel; for these will sustain a Man in even the most trying of conditions. . . .

There is fine hunting in Thar, despite harsh conditions: last Tuesday Williamson & his hunting party were led to a fine plain by their guides, pagans of the Bheel tribe who were hoping they would find a herd of wild boar & slaughter it & gift them the meat, which is tough and gristly and inedible, as payment for their assistance. The pagan tribes throughout Sindh enjoy the meat of that lowly animal, & make grand feasts out of the occasion, with much consumption of local liquor made from fermented crops. Williamson reported that he killed a chinkara in the early morning & saw blackbuck in the grasslands beyond the camp on the outskirts of Mithi; falcon-hunting will be great sport in the winter-time, as there are many migratory as well as resident birds in the desert.

I asked Williamson if he encountered any trouble along the way, disorder of any general sort; but specifically I wanted to know if he heard, from the villagers or any passing travelers, or had seen for himself any sign of the Hurs, those wretched outlaws who have been rampaging the districts of both Thar Parkar & some areas of Hyderabad; and whose existence poses a grave threat to the control which we have fought long & hard to establish in this savage Land.

England too has seen its share of outlaws, & one might make the mistake of comparing the tales of Robin Hood & his band of Merry Men, who roamed Sherwood Forest and "robbed from the rich to give to the poor," to the situation in Sindh. But those fictitious outlaws operated to right what they saw as the wrongs caused by an unjust and illegitimate king. & as soon as justice prevailed, the outlaws gave up their marauding ways & settled into a life of peace & tranquility. . . .

Sindh, on the other hand, is a land of intrigue and suspicion, where we have had to resort to a mix of influence & force in order to maintain law and order, a delicate balance which requires both an iron first & a stern heart. The outlaws which I speak of, the Hurs, are no genteel brigands with a code of honor to be strictly adhered to, as can be expected only from a country with principles & honor; but are in fact the worst sort of fanatics that I have ever had misfortune to come across.

It is also our misfortune that we are required to rely on the Pirs, those so-called descendants of Sufi saints who are imbued with tremendous influence over their followers, to help us maintain our control over Sindh. Were it up to me, I would eliminate them entirely from Sindhi society, & thus establish our writ directly, without need of these middlemen. But the truth is that they have become our collaborators in our rule over Sindh.

The system we have established since Sir Charles Napier first conquered Sindh has served us well; the Pirs command obedience from their followers, from the poor & uneducated simple man to the highest and wealthiest *Zamindar,* or land-owner, derived from the *murids'* religious devotion to the Pir, which gives him tremendous influence over all the residents of Sindh. In turn the Pirs deliver this obedience to us, along with their prayers for our continued well-being, which means nothing to us, being of a vastly superior faith, i.e. Christianity, but is of tremendous significance to those ignorant masses. . . .

Yet in order to maintain their economic & social power, they must keep up good relations with British authority. We may offer a friendly Pir a seat at our Durbar, or allow him leave from civil court appearances (a Humiliation they find too great to bear, we have discovered). A rebellious Pir receives treatment of a different sort: threatening to revoke his arms licenses, or even choosing to disallow him from touring his own territory robs him of that respect by which these savages live and die, by God! By a judicious use of reward & punishment, the Pirs keep themselves in our good books, so to speak, & we maintain a subtle but strong hold over this Godforsaken land.

But in the area of Thar Parkar, which is a district in the desert of Thar, the Pir of Pagaro treads a dangerous line, for his band of followers have been indulging in criminal activities of the worst sort, & he does precious little to rein them in, much to our dismay.

Almost forty years ago, the British Government made Pir-jo-Goth (the Pir's ancestral seat) part of the British directorate of Rohri, near Sukkur.

But, the present Pir of Pagaro seems to have forgotten our largesse, or that if he loses our approval, his own physical seat is in danger. For he overlooks the activities of the Hurs, & they roam up and down the countryside, enacting a reign of terror upon the hapless peasants, Hindu merchants, non-Hur *zamindars*, & anyone they perceive as a threat to their *Murshid*.

Last year, amongst conditions of drought & famine, the Hurs formed gangs to squeeze Hindu moneylenders & merchants, to show their own anger at God & His will—an illogical reaction indeed, but then the Sindhis are an illogical people & the Hurs— (but more on their nature later, as I must not get ahead of myself in this account). Before the difficult times they had attacked anyone they saw as a threat to the Pir of Pagaro, as well as anyone they proclaimed a spy or government informant, & those *zamindars* who were not followers of the Pir of Pagaro. They started to attack & murder police men. As further proof of their cowardice, they attacked women too & mutilated the bodies of their victims in a most vile & disgusting manner. They have even murdered non-Hur *khalifas*, who are the most high in status of the Pir of Pagaro's followers. . . .

A note here on the nature of the Hurs: they are the wildest & most intensely devoted to their *Murshid*, the Pir. The Hurs look down upon non-Hurs & will not even eat or drink with them. They organize themselves in a brotherhood known as the Hur Union; they are *fanatics with murder and revenge more to their heart than mere plunder,* as the District Magistrate of Hyderabad wrote in one of his police reports to the Commissioner of Sindh earlier this year. Clad in green clothes & a specially-tied turban, they salute nobody but the Pir by hand or voice; they flock to see him as if performing religious pilgrimage (men & women who go unveiled too, an unheard-of thing for a Mohammedan woman). He basks in their lavish gifts, their vast amounts of tribute in the form of land, cattle, & money.

What is vital to understanding the mentality of the Hurs is that they give their Pir a quasi-divine status that would shock most orthodox Mohammedans to know of. The majority of the Pir's followers, 200,000 of them, are known as the Salima Jamiat, and respect the relatives of the Pir; but the Hurs, only a small minority who call themselves the Farq Jamiat, revere no one but him. & defy *all other sources of authority.*

They have been compared to the followers of the Aga Khan, or perhaps the Hashashin of the Ismailees, & yet they are ready to sacrifice themselves on the altar of his faith in a way unrivalled by any other sect!

In return for this single-minded devotion which could only be seen as madness by a sane Englishman, the Pirs of Pagaro also begin to see themselves as something approaching royalty: they peacock about in long coats and even a crown, enjoying elephant riding, shooting, hunting & archery, & have built a huge shrine at Kingri, their residence in Thar Parkar. . . .

We decided at once to attack the problem directly, & on my orders, the number of both armed and mounted police was increased, with police posts being established in those villages and hamlets of Thar Parkar where Hurs lived, & where support & hospitality was given to the criminal Gangs. The locals bear the costs of the increased police presence: 50,000 Rupees in Thar Parkar District and a further 200,000 in Hyderabad district alone. We have also taken action against leading Hurs: our informants have helped us compile lists of terrorist sympathizers; we shall revoke guns licenses & sequester land, withhold canal water, & initiate legal action against them.

If this fails, there is always the incentive of a grand reward; late last year I authorized a great sum of 500 Rupees for information leading to the arrest & conviction of the leading Hurs. Perhaps this will sweeten the pot more than those wretched *lunghis* & *afrinnamas* written in gold & silver lettering which I secretly believe only the most foolish Sindhi would feel are of any merit whatsoever.

But no amount of monetary reward, I fear, will be able to counter the tremendous strengths of the Hurs. Firstly, to be a Hur, & moreso one involved in these sorts of nefarious activities, is considered a great honor: ballads are composed by wandering minstrels which sing of their being made martyrs, who go straight to Heaven without even facing the trials of judgment Day! The villagers vie for the honor of feeding & housing these criminals & even offer their daughters in marriage to the worst of the rascals.

When our troops enter their areas in strength, the Hurs flee into the Makhi Dand, a swamp in the wilds north of Sanghar, where the Hurs are to be found in greatest numbers. It can be imagined how well this covers anyone who wishes to disappear from the view of the authorities! Its shallow lakes, thick jungle cover, & trees (tamarisk & acacia) ensure that anyone who seeks refuge here will never be found, no matter how many times we order the grass to be cut or burnt down.

But there is hope for our situation, for we are making plans to ensure cooperation from the Pir; who will be told to ensure that his *Murids* quit their illegal activities. We have tried our usual methods on him, but he only gives us excuses; that he has already disowned those Hurs who continue to embarrass him & affect his honor in our eyes. But now we are tired of his excuses, & plan a more drastic way to ensure his cooperation in aiding us to bring law & order back to Sindh. . . .

He will be forbidden entrance to Thar Parkar or the affected parts of Hyderabad District. In this way he shall be cut off from his areas of greatest support, his tribute, or *nazrana*. & we shall leave the threat of the loss of his Darbar chair hanging over his head, like the Sword of Damocles, & warn him of what is to follow if he does not perform to our satisfaction.

I have already refused one of his gifts: a basket of fruit, which displeased him greatly. This has been as an earthquake throughout Sindh, & lowered his respect & damaged his *Izzat* greatly.

If he does not heed our warnings, then the next step shall be to disallow him an audience when the Commissioner visits upper Sindh at the end of this year. I shall make it known that the Queen of England is greatly displeased with him, & he shall be forced to convey this *in person to his followers*. For the Pir to have to approach his followers in an open audience in Hyderabad rather than await their pilgrimage to him in Kingri (another practice which we can forbid if we so wish) would be considered a greater shame than if Mohammed had refused to pay homage to Mecca and instead demanded that Mecca approach him instead!

Who knew that we could use the Sindhi love of honor as a tool against them, in order to coerce them into actions that are beneficial to our government? But any government that wishes to succeed in Sindh must always remember this point: that honor is equivalent, in their eyes, to power, & that even if that honor is symbolic, they will do anything to sustain it. *Anything.*

I am confident about my success in this endeavour, for this Hur Rebellion, as we have named it amongst our quarters, will ultimately fail. It is in the Pir of Pagaro's interest to effect a peaceful equilibrium with us, although he might be pushed from below by the needs & demands of his followers. This is because even though the Pir fancies that he holds his followers' lives in his hands as their godhead, we have, with God's grace, absorbed his *Gaddi*—his throne—into our own system of political control. Our power comes from the fact that we recognize no God but our own, the true Christian God, and we value nobody's honor but that which belongs to our own Beloved Queen Victoria, who is, after all, the true Empress of this land.

November 17, 2007

At first Ali didn't tell anyone about what he'd done. Not his family, not Jehangir, nobody at work, and certainly not Sunita, who hadn't known anything in the first place. He didn't want their questions, didn't want to supply them with explanations. They'd interrogate him: *Why did you do it? Why didn't you go through with it? What got into you?* And the inevitable conclusion that they would draw from his actions: *Well, if you let it go that easily, then it couldn't have been that important to you all along.*

But from the moment Ali had escaped from the embassy, he'd grown queasy with the fear that he'd made a terrible mistake. He'd waited for the bus to collect him on its way back from its rounds, and sweltered under the inadequate shade of a clump of trees planted over a rough shelter of benches and picnic tables. The people waiting with him were divided into two groups: those who were returning in triumph, and others who had been rejected and looked like they were going to commit suicide. Ali didn't know which group he belonged to, so he sat alone at a picnic bench and pretended to go through his papers, trying to hide his passport from view. Filled with nervousness and regret, he put his hand to his mouth and began to chew on one of his nails. By the time he reached Karachi, they were all bitten down to the quick.

His father would be the first one to jeer at him. "You've always been immature," he'd say, barely glancing up from his newspaper. "Always. You could never decide anything important for yourself: what you wanted to study, where you wanted to go."

"That's not fair," Ali always tried to argue back, feeling the ground shifting like quicksand beneath his feet.

"Maybe, but it's true. That's why I have to make the decisions for you. Because I know better."

Ali had a lot of conversations like these with his father, jumbled-up pieces of tapes that played in his head, based on real talks, imagined conversations, wishful arguments, discussions commenced but never completed. It was part of the legacy of having a parent who was no longer there. In all of them Ali argued his point with eloquence and intelligence, always persuaded his father to see his point of view. In reality he'd never been able to get his point across, never succeeded in feeling heard or understood. No matter how much he imagined talking to his father as an equal, though, he knew he could not rewrite history. His father had the upper hand on him, even in his own mind.

What always defeated him was that when it was time to make a choice, Ali's father made decisions only with his head, choosing what made the most sense and fitted in most practically with circumstances and chance. But there were many different types of decisions: those that you made with your head—what to study, where to go to university—were only a small part of the choices that presented themselves on any given day. What about those that were made by the heart, the body, the soul?

The decision to love, for example. It was something you decided with your heart, as Ali had with Sunita. He knew the pitfalls of getting involved with her, the chasm between their religions. But his heart had not allowed him to walk away from her. The decision not to sleep with her, even though his body was begging to take the lead like a rambunctious puppy that could only think of gamboling and chewing on everything in sight, was also made with his heart; because he loved her, he didn't want to sully her with his own base desires. And then there was the part of him, belonging to neither head nor heart, but some unnamed entity, more stubborn and less definable, that didn't want to be the unloving man that Sikandar Hussein had been to them all. He didn't want to be the lost man that went from marriage to marriage, unsatisfied with each subsequent reincarnation of the first, best love.

The choice to hate, even though it didn't feel like a choice, but something that just happened naturally, was also made by the heart. Ali loathed his father with a reflexive kind of hate, born out of the fear that his father did not care for him. Sikandar always told others how much he loved his family, his sons, even his daughter, though Jeandi as a girl was a second-class citizen in her father's eyes. But Ali couldn't sense it, nor could Haris. If Sikandar had been like other friends' parents, who quarreled with their children one minute and then in a tempestuous change of heart showered them with affection the next, Ali might have felt his sincerity. But Sikandar's departure from their house was the clear evidence pointing to the strength of his detachment.

And the decision to forgive—now that was a decision made by the soul. To forgive his father for his limitations, his weaknesses and vulnerabilities, his inability to show love was a step that Ali was not yet ready for. He could see it waiting for him as part of his future. Someday when he was married and had children of his own, when he lived through the stresses and pressures that a man had to go through in order to feed his family and still remained sane, he would understand, and then perhaps he would know compassion for his father's flaws. But for now, Ali wanted to run away from having to see his father as fully human.

To declare his father dead was a decision Ali made with heart, mind, and soul.

When Ali arrived home, they were all out of the house: Jeandi at her tuition center, Haris probably ferrying his mother to the supermarket or the doctor's. Relieved, Ali went to his room and shut the door. He didn't come out again until the next morning to go to work; he woke long before anyone else was stirring and didn't bother to eat breakfast before he went.

At the station, things had still not calmed down. Policemen stood menacingly outside the building, and Ali had to push through them to get to the door. They asked for his identification and press card, examined it with sneers, then thrust it back at him and waved him through. Ali noted that the policeman who'd looked at his papers held them upside down while he pretended to read them.

Ameena called him into her office later that morning. She was sitting at her desk and smoking, the ashtray next to her computer filled with cigarette butts from the previous night. The monitors on the wall flashed recent clips they'd filmed of the street protests that had repeatedly occurred since November 3. Ameena's hair, usually left open to fall around her face, was tied up in a tight ponytail, and she looked tired and grim as she glanced up at Ali from behind her computer screen.

"I want you to go film a lawyer's protest."

"When?"

"Saturday. Outside the High Court."

He hadn't gone on a film assignment since the bombing in October. He'd been given a week off to recover from the shock, then was restricted to desk work when he'd returned. Overseeing graphics, helping with editing, doing research, making phone calls—all soothing busywork to keep his mind off the void that had opened up in front of him on that night, and to stop him from thinking of Haroon. But Ali saw Haroon everywhere he turned: in the production booth he could see the man lurking in a darkened corner; when he sat down to lunch, Haroon was just leaving the cafeteria, his camera bag slung on his back. Ali once caught Haroon's face reflected in the bathroom mirror, two halves split by a large crack that had been there for years and that nobody had ever thought to repair.

"Are you up to it?" Ameena was asking him. Ali suddenly felt a rush of appreciation. She wasn't the hardhearted monster he'd always thought she was. He opened his mouth to tell her about how he was feeling, how Haroon's ghost was following him everywhere he went, feeding off his guilt and his shame, but she went on before he had a chance to speak. "Because nobody else thinks you are. And I have to say I tend to agree with them. But Kazim said to give you another chance."

She was acting as if it was his fault that the bombs had gone off! Ali gritted his teeth. "I can do it."

"All right." She reached for another cigarette and lit it without even having to shift her glance from the screen. "Don't get into trouble this time."

"Thank you."

Ali seethed through the entire day, stopping numerous times in his work to fire off emails to Jehangir about the webcam plan to humiliate Ameena, wishing he could tell the police that there were dangerous criminals being harbored inside the City24 building, longing to call up the American consulate and say Kazim Mazhar knew where Osama bin Laden was hiding. Jehangir was cautious in his replies; he'd kept his distance from Ali since that day at French Beach, informing him that Masood didn't want to see him again. "You embarrassed him in front of his guests, *yaar*," said Jehangir. "You can't put a man's *izzat* in the dirt and then expect him to still want to be your friend."

"The hell with *izzat*," was Ali's response.

Jehangir shook his head. "You've changed, Ali. You used to understand the way things work around here. Now it's like you don't even care."

"I don't."

"But you have to."

"No, I don't."

"You do."

"Shut up, man." Ali found himself too exhausted to call Jehangir anything more abusive, in their time-honored tradition. Too much had changed since the last time they'd traded their friendly insults.

Jehangir didn't retort with a curse, either. He just stared at Ali with wounded eyes and walked away. Ali swore at him as he disappeared into the conference room, but Jehangir was right: he *had* changed. He no longer wanted to play this game, take part in the etiquette of hypocrisy, where people met and exchanged all the right courtesies, then backstabbed each other with glee. He didn't want to meet an acquaintance at a wedding and greet him with "*Yaar*, how are you? It's been ages! We must meet up!" and then after a year, meet again at another wedding and do it all over again. He wanted to burn all the insincerity and showing off and meaninglessness out of his life until only what was true and meaningful was left. He didn't mind if he lost his so-called friends. As long as he had Sunita's support, he could start over again and befriend people whose lives he would be happy to live.

Ali reached the university in the evening with a few minutes to spare, an unusual event he took as a sign he was on the right path. Now that he'd dumped his plans to go to America, he'd have to take his studies more seriously, but he was ready for that, too.

Sunita was sitting on a bench under a banyan tree in the university garden. The tree had been hit by a bolt of lightning in a thunderstorm that sent it smashing straight through a classroom window. To everyone's astonishment, the tree hadn't died after the impact, but continued to grow sideways along the wall of the building instead of toward the sky. It was as much an institution in the university as the terrible canteen food and the draconian attendance rules. Countless romances had been conducted under its hunchbacked shade, and Ali had known he loved Sunita when they first sat together on that very bench where she was now waiting.

His heart contracted with pleasure to see her there, her long hair gently moving in the evening breeze, her stack of books set neatly to one side. She was eating an impossibly large samosa, stuffing it into her mouth; she had a small mouth that could open wide: when she was talking, laughing, kissing him. He wanted to laugh with joy at her enjoyment of such simple pleasure, and tell her that he loved every inch of her, seen and unseen, hidden or revealed. Did every pair of lovers in the world feel they were the only two who spoke the same language? No need for conventional greetings between them, just the truth, delivered with sincerity and a pure heart.

"You look beautiful." His smile faded as he realized she did not look up to meet his eyes. And the memory that he hadn't spoken to her since Saturday night—more than that, hadn't told her he was going to Islamabad—resurfaced in his mind, a corpse released from a watery grave that slowly bobbed into view.

Sunita swallowed down the samosa, then turned her eyes to him. "Where have you been?"

His options flicked through his mind. *Think, think. Think of something good. No, wait. Don't lie. That'll just make it worse. Tell her the truth.* "I . . . uh . . . look, I'm sorry. I was in Islamabad. And my phone was off for most of the time." He spread his hands out in front of her, palms up, in what he hoped was a conciliatory gesture.

"I know that. But why?"

"Because I couldn't have it on in the plane," he said lamely.

"That's not what I meant. Why were you in Islamabad?"

"Okay, Sunita, I don't want to argue about this, can we just discuss this in private?" Other students were milling around in the garden, not far from them, so they kept their voices down, their expressions neutral. So much of their relationship had to be conducted in public that they'd grown artful in protecting it under an umbrella of calm. But right now Sunita looked like she wanted to get up and stand on the bench, start screaming, maybe slap him, like the Bollywood movies his mother watched on cable television in the long, lonely nights after his father had gone.

"Why were you in Islamabad?" she repeated.

"Can I sit down?"

"No. Why were you in Islamabad?"

"Look, we're getting late for class—"

"Shut up and tell me right now or I swear to God I'll never talk to you again."

"I went to Islamabad so I could get a US visa."

Sunita's eyes widened. "Why?"

"Why do people get visas, Sunita, now can we please . . ." The patches of sweat were blossoming under his arms and on his back. He had a morbid fear of being like some men in his class who reeked of body odor and sweat, unaware that nobody wanted to sit next to them. He glanced around to see if anyone was already turning away from the guilty stink emanating from his body.

"Are you going to America?"

"Yes . . . I mean no . . ."

"Which is it?"

"I was going to, but then I changed my mind."

"For a holiday?"

"No."

"Then what?"

Everyone had gone now: class had begun. If they weren't in their seats in another five minutes, they would be marked absent in the class register. Three absences meant a failing grade: Ali already had two absences in the class, Business Communications. He took a deep breath and said, "I wanted to go study in America. I got into a university there, I needed the visa. That's why I went. But——"

Before he could tell her that he hadn't gotten the visa, that he had turned around and left, Sunita put up her hand in front of his mouth to stop him from talking more. Her face was naked with pain, as if someone had peeled back the topmost layer of her skin and exposed it to the sun. "When were you going to tell me about this?"

"I knew I would have to, if it all worked out. But I didn't know if it ever would."

"Really? Or would you have just gone off to America and told me once you were already there?"

"Sunita. I can explain. Please listen to me!"

"It's too late." She got up, swaying unsteadily, her hand pressed to her mouth.

"Are you all right?"

"I think I'm going to be sick." She pushed away Ali's arm and ran to the bathroom. He followed her, stood outside the bathroom, listening to the sounds of her retching, regrets and unformed apologies now joining his father's imaginary corpse floating in the rivers of his conscience.

The terrible sounds stopped, but minutes passed and no Sunita emerged. Ali began to worry. What if she'd fainted? He was afraid to check on her: anyone could get the wrong impression if they saw him going into the girls' bathroom. He could be in serious trouble, be accused of molesting someone. The guards would pull him out and beat him up in the street; the administration would inform his mother, and he might be suspended or even expelled.

His dilemma was solved when a girl came down the hall. He moved out of the way so that she could enter the bathroom, but as she was going in, he whispered, "Excuse me. My friend is in there. Could you just see if she's okay?" The girl studied him for a minute with suspicious eyes, then nodded her assent and went inside.

Ali leaned against the wall until the door opened again. The girl put her head around the door, her eyes filled with a mixture of pity and weariness. She looked as though this wasn't the first time she'd been asked to mediate a lovers' tiff on the campus grounds.

"She's okay. But she doesn't want to see you."

Ali nodded his thanks to her, and she returned to her class, her high heels tapping on the hard floor, ricocheting like gunshots in the empty hall. The fluorescent lights hummed eerily, one of them buzzing on and off, a fault somewhere in the wiring. Ali waited for Sunita to come out, and hoped that she would listen to him if he organized his thoughts more clearly, made his arguments more convincing, his entreaties more pathetic. But twenty minutes passed with no sign of her, and he finally realized that she would stay in the bathroom until he went away. He loved her, so he had to oblige. He climbed the stairs to his class but she never followed suit. Ali left the university at 11 p.m., knowing that Business Communications was not the only thing he had failed that night.

* * *

They were standing outside the Sindh High Court, a colonial building made of pink sandstone with graceful gardens and a stately driveway stretching out in front. Its long columns, sweeping staircase, and high windows spoke of the high hopes for justice in a time and place completely different from the battered city in which it stood today.

The gates to the court were locked in preparation for the protests, which had been taking place on an almost daily basis since November 3. Ali was there with the new cameraman, Arif, and another sound technician, Hassan. Ram had quit last month, too upset to deal with going back to work after what he'd witnessed on that humid October night. Ali didn't know the new men, but it was too serious a day to joke around and establish any kind of relationship beyond the professional.

Behind the gates, everything seemed tranquil, but in front hundreds of men and women gathered in the road that led to the court, marching around in large circles to show their displeasure with what had been happening all year. It wasn't just about November 3. That was just the straw that broke the camel's back, the final nail in the coffin—all the clichés that people used when they discussed the "state of the nation" on the current affairs programs, in the newspapers, in drawing rooms at fancy dinner parties. Only on the street had the clichés been put away and rhetoric channeled into action; nobody had witnessed anything like this in Pakistan ever before.

Most of the protestors were lawyers clad in black coats: some carried billboards with antigovernment slogans; others were shouting with their fists raised to the sky, "Go, Musharraf, go! Go, Musharraf, go!" as people clapped their hands and punched the air in time to the beat. Someone had even brought a drum, while others blew whistles in short, sharp bursts, creating a musical din that rose above the traffic from the busy downtown area. The sea of black coats, the grimness of their eyes made it look as though one large funeral were filling up the street.

Policemen and Rangers were lined up in rows, their mouths twisted into fierce scowls. The police carried *lathis* and riot gear, their bodies bulky in their bulletproof vests. The Rangers pointed automatic weapons at the demonstrators, who clutched handkerchiefs ready to wet with bottles of mineral water and tie on their faces in case the police decided to use tear gas.

Other citizens had come to support the lawyers: journalists, NGO workers, human rights activists, teachers, doctors. Ali had been interviewing some of them, recording their thoughts for the camera. A doctor agreed to speak to him, a young, handsome man wearing a black armband and carrying a placard that read *Democracy Now!* "We started our campaign for the restoration of the judges after the emergency was declared and the judges deposed, but really, our protests have been going on since May 12 all over the country, you know. Lahore, Pindi, Islamabad, all over Sindh . . ."

"Yes," Ali said. "The day the chief justice came to Karachi." The events of that horrible day were still fresh in everyone's minds: the chief justice was to participate in the anniversary celebrations of the Sindh High Court supported by the PPP and ANP, but threatened by the chief justice's power and popularity, the president instructed his own political party, the PML-Q, to hold a rally in Karachi at the same time to distract from the chief justice's arrival. Then, the MQM, also Musharraf's supporters in Karachi, decided to hold their own rally on that day, to show their loyalty to the president. What ensued was that first, bloody power struggle between the two factions, as MQM workers illegally blocked Karachi's main roads to prevent anyone from getting to the airport to meet the chief justice.

They'd held the city hostage: fifty people dead, bodies lying on the street, armed men shooting anyone who dared go to the airport. Both activists and ordinary people had to hide in their houses as if it were a siege, psychopathic teenagers taking shots at anyone passing underneath the bridges on Shahrae Faisal, the road that let to the airport. They called the people who'd died on that day the martyrs of May 12 . . .

"The government should hang its head in shame."

"So what do you hope to accomplish by these protests today?"

"We want the judges restored. We want those who were responsible for the violence on May twelfth to be brought to justice. And we want Musharraf to go."

"Do you think he'll listen?"

"He has to. It's what we want."

When the doctor rejoined the crowd, Ali watched him for a little while, chanting and walking with the others, until he lost sight of him among the black-coated lawyers. He calculated at least five hundred people were here. The tension weighed the air down, like humidity, making it hard to breathe and think. The day had its own momentum, barreling toward a conclusion that nobody seemed strong enough to prevent. The protestors were edging dangerously close to the police, shouting at them, insulting them. The police remained impassive, although Ali could see some of the Rangers' hands tightening on the barrels of their guns.

The politicians had been supporting these street protests; Benazir made statements every day that the people wanted democracy, that they wanted her, and that the demonstrations were proof of how desired she was. How convenient, Ali thought to himself, to fuse the two. Or confuse them. Who decided that she knew what the people wanted—and why should it be her? That was the problem here in Pakistan; everyone thought they knew what was good for the people of this country: a nuclear bomb; or Islamic law; or to join the War on Terror, because if they didn't, Pakistan would get bombed into the Stone Age.

Then the superpowers were telling them what was good for them: America told them they needed democracy. China said they needed military cooperation and warm-water ports. India said they needed to leave Kashmir alone. Afghanistan wanted Pakistan to leave them alone but take in all their refugees. Was it any wonder that the nation had become completely schizophrenic?

When was the last time someone actually cared about what the people wanted? Benazir's father, Zulfikar, thought he had it figured out: *roti, kapra, aur makan.* Food, clothing, housing. A socialist's dream, but the world was more complex than that, and so were people's desires. Back when Jinnah was alive, it was so simple: the people wanted their own country. And he gave it to them. But after that, what next? The leaders who came after him had their own vision about where the country should go. And their visions drove it straight to hell.

Ali's skull ached thinking about all of this, in the heat of the afternoon, seeing all those angry people, the barrels of all those guns. Benazir, Nawaz, Musharraf, Imran, the army: each one proclaiming himself the savior of this nation. Instead of having the answers, they thought they *were* the answer. And when you asked people to put their faith in a leader instead of in the institutions he or she was supposed to lead, you ended up with the country that they had today: Pakistan, going up in flames, falling apart at the cracks and the seams.

The shouting was getting louder, building into a crescendo that had lost its edges: instead of words, there was one long howl of fury, the sound of a people utterly frustrated, utterly betrayed. It made Ali want to cry. He didn't know where to go. Twenty-five years of age, and his father was dead to him, his love was gone, his dreams defeated.

Then, in the din, he could hear someone reciting poetry. *That's odd,* Ali thought, and turned around to see a man standing a few feet away in a lawyer's coat. He was middle-aged, probably the same age as Ali's father. Slightly receding hair, wrinkles around his eyes, two sharp lines etched from the sides of his nose to his mouth. His eyes were closed, and he was speaking Sindhi in a strong Larkana accent, half-reciting and half-singing some lines Ali recognized from Shah Abdul Latif's *Risalo*:

> *The birds in flocks fly;*
> *Comradeship they do not decry*
> *Behold, among the birds there is more loyalty*
> *Than among us, who call ourselves humanity!*

Ali stared at him. Could there be anything more absurd than someone standing here in front of the Sindh High Court during a protest march with rows of policemen ready to storm in at any minute, declaiming the lines of a classical Sindhi Sufi poet? It was surreal. And yet, completely fitting for this moment, this place— this country, which was like living in some surreal dream, or a nightmare from which it was impossible to wake up.

"Film him," he said to Arif. "Get him on camera."

There was a sharp beeping coming from his pocket. It took Ali a minute to realize that someone was calling him on his mobile phone. "Hello?"

"Ali," said the voice on the other end, so disembodied that Ali couldn't tell at first whether it was a man or a woman. "Come back to the station."

"Who is this?"

"It's Jehangir, Ali." *He always had a high-pitched voice,* Ali thought to himself.

"It's over."

"What's over? What are you talking about?"

"We've been shut down. Mazhar just announced it. We're off the air."

"Are you sure?"

"Yeah. Come back, Ali."

Ali switched off the phone. Hassan and Arif were staring at him. "What happened?" said Arif.

"We're off the air," Ali replied.

There was a moment of silence between them, while the crowd roared all around, a young lion testing the power of its new voice. The three men didn't know whether to rage or mourn. "I guess that's it, then," said Arif as he slowly put down his camera.

Hassan let the boom come to rest against his shoulder. "And I just got this job. How am I going to feed my family?"

Roti, kapra, aur makan.

Ali gave Hassan the microphone. "Take this."

"Where are you going?"

But he was already striding away from them, breaking into a run. He was only a few yards away from the protestors.

Now it was just a few feet.

Now he was in their midst.

Ali raised his fist and added his voice to theirs. "Go, Musharraf, go! Go, Musharraf, go!" He walked with them shoulder to shoulder. Men, women, old, young. The lines blurred, the boundaries between him and them dissolved. He was losing himself in the crowd, in their passion, their desire. Not even making love with Sunita could surpass this union, or the feeling of being raised to a level where he was but an instrument through which the plans of the world were realized. It was annihilation. What they wanted was what he wanted. What he wanted was what they wanted.

Maybe it was exactly how Benazir felt, when she was leading one of those rallies. If that was the case, then Ali could whole-heartedly understand.

Saeen

There were many important men who decided to attend the Khilafat Conference of February 1920; the dusty Sindh town of Larkana had to spruce itself up to receive so many men of such stature. Pir Turab Ali Shah Rashdi and Jan Mohammed Junejo, the organizers, personally traveled around the town in a bullock cart the week before the conference, issuing orders to their *murids* following on foot next to the cart as they bumped along the *kaccha* roads, inspecting lanes, walls, buildings, and open squares for any sign of garbage, dilapidation, or anything else that would bring shame to them in front of their honored guests.

Jan Mohammed Junejo clutched a telegram in his hand and shook it at Turab Ali Shah. "Look at this, Saeen! It's from Bombay. Gandhi is coming! Gandhi . . . Gandhi-ji. *Delighted to accept . . . look forward to convening with our Sindhi brethren . . . Hindu-Muslim unity tantamount to our goals . . .*"

"Gandhi? What interest would he have in seeing the Sultan

of Turkey restored to the Caliphate? It won't make the British change their minds about forbidding them to burn their wives on their funeral pyres . . . This is a Muslim movement, is it not?" said Turab Ali Shah.

"Gandhi-ji has been extremely supportive of the Khilafat Movement, Saeen. He told the conference in Delhi last year that they must start a noncooperation policy toward the British. He's always been in favor of Hindu-Muslim unity." Jan Mohammed struck a pose that he thought was reminiscent of the eminent lawyer. "'Unconditional help alone is the real help' . . ."

"He cares more for his precious cow than for our religious sentiments, Saeen. More bunting there, I think," said Turab Ali Shah, pointing at an area between two neem trees providing a rare patch of shade to an overheated square. A *murid* shouted "Ji Saeen!" and ran to instruct the village men who were struggling with a rope of white banners wound around their shoulders. Turab Ali Shah watched their efforts to tie the banner to the trees. "Higher," he called out to his *murid*. "No, higher—lower—higher—a bit lower . . ."

"And only yesterday I received the letter from the Sirhindis, and the Ali brothers, saying that they would be honored to attend. Honored! And our guest from Lucknow—Abdul Bari Farangi Mahali, Saeen, Abdul Bari himself! It's going to be a truly magnificent affair, Saeen. I can feel it in my bones."

"Let's hope the trains aren't delayed," said Turab Ali Shah. "No, fools! It's upside down!" The *murid* conveyed the message to the villagers, who fought valiantly with the banner until it was turned right side up again.

"Oh, don't say that, Saeen," cried Jan Mohammed. "I've been making *mannat* at Sehwan every month for the past year. If it goes well, I'll feed a hundred people. No, two hundred! Shahbaz Qalandar wouldn't let us down like that."

Turab Ali Shah frowned. "And if the trains aren't delayed, there might be rain."

"But there isn't a cloud in the sky!"

"Or the *angrez* will make some sort of mischief."

"They wouldn't dare!"

The two men argued like this, back and forth, for some time. They had been compatriots and friends for thirty years, but nobody could figure out how the friendship had endured, because they were as alike as night and day, or the sun and the moon: one always smiling, optimistic, the other dour and given to finding a flaw in every plan. Jan Mohammed was tall and thin, while Turab Ali Shah carried himself around like a billiard ball, portly and unable to move at any great speed. Squabbling like an old married couple, they continued on their tour of inspection: Jan Mohammed praised every flower and every fruit hanging from the trees, while Turab Ali Shah's face grew stormy with every heap of garbage he spotted from the height of his vehicle.

The mood in Sindh, in fact all of India, matched Turab Ali Shah's more than Jan Mohammed's, for scarcely a year had passed since General Dyer had instigated the massacre at Jallianwala Bagh in Amritsar, ordering his troops to fire upon a group of men, women, and children who were participating in the yearly Baisakhi festival. Only a coward and a tyrant could command men with Lee-Enfield rifles and *kukri* knives to shed the blood of innocent Punjabis who had gathered to celebrate a cultural and religious celebration. Although opinions were divided on whether or not the general had done the right thing—for talk of mutiny, as well as the assault of a British woman had been the match struck to the tinderbox of the general's emotions, and Dyer was called a murderer by some Indians and a hero by others—the massacre greatly strained the cords that tied the Indian nation to their British masters.

But that was not all. The Great War had seen Turkey lose its prominence as a world power, after the defeat of the Central Powers at the hands of the British, French, Russian, and American allies. Muslim leaders in India grew worried at this, and issued a call to their followers that Islam had to be defended at all costs. Turab Ali Shah watched in astonishment as the mullah made a fiery speech at the mosque after Friday prayers, crying out that the British were already encroaching on their schools and their laws, and their troops were desecrating the Holy Lands! He ripped up an English newspaper in front of the entire congregation to show his displeasure. Turab Ali Shah could not help but feel an answering cry in his own breast, one that seemed to encompass not just a protective feeling for the faith but a resentment against the British he did not even know he possessed.

The newspapers were printing the news from all corners of India and the trains were bringing them to Sindh from Quetta, from Bombay, from Calcutta; the message from Lucknow, Delhi, and Allahabad began to reach Sindhi ears: word of a great movement that would see the Sultan of Turkey restored to his rightful position as *khalifa* of the Muslim world.

The Pirs of Sindh began to tell their *murids*, in the Deobandi-influenced madrassas and mosques, and at the shrines where thousands of them flocked for festivals and pilgrimage, of this great new Khilafat movement. All Sindhi Muslims, conservatives, radical nationalists, Westernized secularists, rich Sindhi Memon businessmen, zamindars, the poor of the cities and the countryside were infected by a wave of agitation in support of the Pan-Islamic movement. Successful conferences in Delhi and Allahabad inspired Pir Turab Ali Shah and Jan Mohammed Junejo to organize a similar conference in the Larkana Town Hall, and it was this for which they were preparing with such zeal.

The two men finally arrived at the Town Hall for the final

walk-through, Jan Mohammed leaping down and extending a helping hand to Turab Ali Shah, who squeezed out of the bullock cart with difficulty.

The main hall was high-ceilinged, with long electric fans that rotated slowly, and in summer it grew unbearably warm. But this was February, a cool month, and there was no other place with sufficient gravitas for such an important event. Jan Mohammed pointed out that additional floor-standing fans could be brought in if the room became stuffy. "We'll have the walls sprinkled with water every half hour, to keep everyone cool." He turned to face the back wall. "We need more bunting here! The *Welcome* banners. Where are they? I had them specially printed, there's even one with Gandhi's name on it!" He whirled around to face Turab Ali Shah, his features twisted into a worried frown. "Oh, I do hope Allah Saeen ensures that we are not shamed in front of our guests—the honor of the Khilafat Committee is at stake . . ."

Turab Ali Shah allowed himself a small smile at his friend's sudden panic. Jan Mohammed worried about the oddest of things: Did animals have souls, and if so, was it *haram* to kill them for sport? Did women mind it when their husbands took second and third wives, and if it hurt their feelings, was it unlawful? When the Prophet, peace be upon him, had told Muslims to "seek knowledge, even if it means going as far as China," why were so many of the Pirs proudly illiterate? He lost sleep over these and a million other trivialities, sometimes he even forgot to eat his meals, and he walked for miles in the fields belonging to his family, pondering questions that had no logical answer.

Turab Ali Shah, on the other hand, had never been curious about anything; the tutors who had been engaged to come to his grand home in Larkana and teach him Sindhi and Persian had given up after six months, telling his father that the young Turab showed no interest in learning anything beyond the rudiments of reading and writing. Perhaps if he was sent to the madrassa, he might be inspired to do better in front of his peers?

"Out of the question!" his father had roared. "How can you expect the scion of this illustrious family to attend the village school with the children of *peasants?*" And so Turab Ali Shah had been relieved of any scholarly duties, leaving his mind free for the more important pursuits of hunting and falconry and meeting with other members of the *biraderi,* that extended family system that made brothers out of all *sayeds* from the same kin.

Heaven knows how Jan Mohammed Junejo had convinced him to participate in the Khilafat Committee, but once he'd given his word, he stuck to it, for loyalty was one of his strengths, even if learning was not. Jan Mohammed would never have been able to organize this conference on his own without Turab Ali Shah's solidity, both physical and moral. Besides, Turab Ali Shah liked the idea of a struggle: it gave him the chance to take out his many swords and ancient muskets and have them polished and oiled, and imagine himself a lieutenant in the Army of God that had been so enthusiastically put together a few years ago; it had seen no action, but you never knew. He had even gone without food for one day in October of last year, on National Khilafat Day, when the Muslims had prayed and fasted to show their solidarity with Muslims in Turkey and the Arab world. He had been mightily depressed that day, but Jan Mohammed cheered him by telling him he was a hero of Sindh for the sacrifice he was making.

"Inshallah, Saeen. Inshallah," Turab Ali Shah said to his friend, *inshallah* the one word that contained the world and everything destined to happen in it. This word was a great comfort to Turab Ali Shah; he employed it whenever there was a matter about which he knew he could do nothing. Jan Mohammed sighed and wrung his hands, cursing his own anxious nature and wishing that he could share his friend's stoic faith in God.

The other word that always gave Jan Mohammed solace was *Saeen*, the honorific that all Sindhi men used for one another. Whenever he called someone Saeen or someone called him by the same title, they were acknowledging each other as gentlemen, but more than that, as men of honor who could be trusted to uphold the principles of their world.

The days passed in a whirlwind of preparation until the morning of February 9. Jan Mohammed had been sick with nerves the night before and even vomited in the morning, refused to eat or drink anything but a glass of water, then rushed off to the Town Hall just after dawn. Turab Ali Shah woke at 6 a.m. and ate a full breakfast of fried sweetbreads, sweet paratha, fruit, and *lassi*. He bathed and dressed in his full Pir regalia of white robes and white turban, gilded waistcoat and handmade slippers. His *murids* were waiting outside on horseback, and he climbed majestically into his bullock cart to be escorted to the conference in style.

The Town Hall had been transformed from a sleepy little building into a hub of activity: men of importance bustled in and out of the doors, while peasants in their rough *lunghis* and *ajraks* milled around, pressing their faces at the windows to witness the proceedings inside. A troop of boy scouts from Hyderabad had even been assembled, and they ran hither and thither, directing visitors and guests to their seats. A trio of singers sang Sindhi folk songs and *surs* from Shah Abdul Latif's *Risalo* to the accompaniment of the musicians from Lal Shahbaz Qalandar's shrine in Sehwan. It was a cross between a *mela* and a court proceeding, and Larkana had never seen anything like it before.

Turab Ali Shah was nonplussed, thinking himself in good time for the opening ceremony, which was to consist of a long prayer recitation by the esteemed Maulana of Lucknow, and then the Address of Welcome by the chairman of the Reception Committee. But Turab Ali Shah realized with alarm that the speeches were already under way and now the president of the conference, the Pir of Jhando, was speaking to the audience from behind a long table set up on the stage. "My esteemed brothers, how many times have we heard that the British have a famous saying about us?"

The crowd murmured. They had heard the saying three thousand times before, but never tired of hearing it again.

"They say: *Respect the Baloch. Buy the Pashtuns. Oppress the Sindhis. Beat the Punjabis!*"

The crowd roared its displeasure.

"Look how they attempt to divide and conquer us! But we must not succumb! We must be united, not just with our Muslim brethren, but with our Hindu ones as well!" At this, he flung a hand out to acknowledge the presence of a small, dhoti-clad figure at the end of the table, who bowed in return and held his hands up in *namaste* to the Pir of Jhando.

The crowd clapped and cheered. "Marhaba, welcome, Gandhi-ji, *bhalley karein ayan!*"

Jan Mohammed glanced at Turab Ali Shah as he entered the room, his eyes shooting daggers at his friend's tardiness; Turab Ali Shah lifted his hands in apology to Jan Mohammed and began to squeeze his way past the chairs until he reached the front row, climbed heavily up the stairs, and took his place among the conference organizers and speakers at the table. He sat down heavily, recognizing Makhdoom Moenuddin of Khiyari in the front row of guests, but not the man on his right—and here he did a double take, for it was not a man that sat next to him, but a boy who couldn't have been more than fifteen years of age. The boy was slight, with dry, sallow skin, and a stiff, unrelaxed posture, as if he had just got out of bed after a long illness. Still, he was leaning forward in his seat, listening to the Pir of Jhando with great concentration. His face was shining, his eyes fixed upon the great men in their robes and turbans, and he kept straining out of his chair, as if he too wanted to jump up and make a speech in the gaps between the Pir of Jhando's words.

Turab Ali Shah gazed at the boy without curiosity—he must be one of the Makhdoom's sons, or any of the other guests here, who had brought the boy along to witness some history. He turned his attention back onto the stage, where the speakers were thumping their hands on the table in support of the Pir of Jhando's forceful rhetoric. The boy's face faded from his mind and Turab Ali Shah did not notice him again for the rest of the conference.

One by one the guests stood up and made their own speeches. Maulana Shaukat Ali spoke movingly about British troops in the holy places in Arabia. "Some say that there have been acts of desecration in the Jaqirat al-Arab," he said softly, bowing his head as if in prayer. "I have even heard reports that they had desecrated the tomb of the Prophet, peace be upon him—with the help of Sikh soldiers . . ." He raised his hands at the shocked outcry. "I know, I know, my brothers, it is shocking. It is an insult to Islam. We must stop it. We must work together to make the Khilafat strong. And cast out the British from India. Allah can only be pleased with our efforts to turn this Land of War back into a Land of Faith once again."

The conference went on for three days, and Pir Turab Ali Shah, it must be admitted, fell asleep during much of it. But even he was able to grasp the salient points: the pledging of large sums of money for the Khilafat, Angor, and Smyrna funds; the call to the Pirs to direct their *murids* to join the All-India Khilafat Movement and to consider emigrating to Afghanistan; the enjoinder to boycott government institutions and foreign goods. Gandhi's contribution was that Indians should wear only simple, homespun cloth, and Turab Ali Shah caught some of the Pirs looking at each other in horror at this. None of them would be willing to take off their fine silk robes and gold-woven coats in favor of dowdy *khaddar* cloth! Nor would they be willing to renounce the British-given honors and awards, or resign their places from government service, even if they were merely honorary.

This, Turab Ali Shah thought to himself, would be the sticking point in the Khilafat Movement—not the principles, which were mighty enough, but the question of whether the Pirs would be willing to give up the privileges with which British rule had endowed them. Pir Turab Ali Shah doubted very much that any man of standing would be willing to make such sacrifices. It was all right for Gandhi, who had never known the taste of meat and could give up anything else after that first step, but the Sindhi Pirs, descendants of the Prophets and the saints and mystics of Sindh? *Astaghfirullah!*

To his surprise, on the last day of the conference Turab Ali Shah found himself elected as an office-bearer in the Khilafat Committee, along with Pir Ali Anwar Shah, Taj Muhammed Amroti, and the Pir of Jhando. This pleased him greatly; Jan Mohammed told him that if this happened, he might become part of the All-India Congress Committee, and he began to entertain visions of himself traveling to Delhi, Bombay, and Calcutta, maybe even becoming one of its vice presidents . . .

"It's going well, isn't it, Saeen?" Jan Mohammed kept asking him, like a parrot begging for a cracker.

"Very well," said Turab Ali Shah, for once abandoning his usual pessimism, and for this he was rewarded with a flower of a smile from his friend.

At last, it was over, with fiery exhortations of Hindu-Muslim unity, promises to send thousands of *murids* on a journey of migration—a *hijra*—to Afghanistan, and the growing confidence that the Pirs of Sindh, although a small drop in the ocean of India itself, could in fact influence decision-making if they banded together and showed the nation the strength of their brotherhood.

Jan Mohammed took to his bed for a week to rest from his exertions, while Turab Ali Shah went hunting for a week in the Thar Desert, returning with a fine cache of blackbuck that he distributed to all his friends across upper Sindh. He was thinking of contracting another marriage with the daughter of a minor Pir in Hala, so he sent extra meat to that household, hoping that the man would give Turab Ali Shah his youngest daughter without worrying too much that she would be the Pir's third wife.

On his return from his hunting trip, he went over to see his friend Jan Mohammed, who had emerged from his seclusion and was sitting on the verandah of his *haveli* in Sindhri. The two men exchanged embraces and inquiries after each other's crops, children, and cattle. Tea and refreshments were offered and partaken of. Then, as Turab Ali Shah settled back in his chair, enjoying the early morning weather, the fine dry air and a breeze as gentle as a mother's caress, Jan Mohammed said, "Saeen, have you seen this?" He held out an invitation card for Turab Ali Shah to inspect; it was written in Sindhi on one side and a flowing Persian script on the other.

Turab Ali Shah gave it a cursory glance. He didn't usually read his invitations; he had an assistant, a *munshi* whose education he had paid for, to look over all his correspondence, read him important articles from the newspaper, and take care of his household accounts. "I haven't been back to my house," said Turab Ali Shah offhandedly. "So I haven't been able to see my social invitations as yet. What does it say?"

Jan Mohammed read out loud from the card.

Bismillah hir Rahman ur-Rahim
You are cordially invited to the Khilafat Conference in Sann on March 17, 1920.
The honorable Hakim Fateh Mohammed Sehwani is to preside.

The speakers who have graciously consented to grace this occasion:

Shaikh Abdul Majid Sindhi, Dr. Nur Mohammed, Shaikh Abdul Aziz, and Shaikh Abdul Salam (editor of *Al-Wahid* newspaper).

Your attendance will be a great honor for our beloved Khilafat Movement.

Jeay Sindh!

Ghulam Murtaza Shah Sayed

"Ghulam Murtaza Shah? Who is that?" said Turab Ali Shah.

"I don't know. Isn't he in your *biraderi*?"

"If he is, I've never heard of him."

"Me neither." Jan Mohammed pulled his lips in a puzzled grimace. "It's very odd, isn't it, Saeen? I mean, the Khilafat Conference we organized . . . I don't mean to brag, but people were saying it was truly a momentous occasion. All thanks to his grace, of course. But the committee has a reputation to uphold. We can't have just any upstart deciding he wants to host a conference . . . there are standards to maintain . . ."

Turab Ali Shah realized, with a shock, that his friend was jealous. *Jealous!* What a womanish emotion. Men did not feel jealousy; of all men on this earth, Pirs least of all. Who could compare to any of them, in stature, reputation, position? But then Jan Mohammed had always been a sensitive one . . .

"Well, I suppose we'll find out when we get there," said Turab Ali Shah, and that settled the matter.

But Jan Mohammed was not content to let things rest there. He found out through his network of friends and relatives that this Ghulam Murtaza Shah was from a noble but poor Sayed family who faced many financial problems after his father had been murdered in a long-standing feud. Their land had been under the

Court of Wards since 1906, and their agents and house servants had abandoned them when their fixed income from the courts proved insufficient to run a grand household in keeping with the style of the *sayeds* of Sindh.

This Ghulam Murtaza Shah had been homeschooled and kept in relative isolation because his mother and aunts feared that his father's enemies were planning to kill him, too, so little was known about his character or his activities. But he had established an organization for the Sindhi Muslims of Sann, along the lines of the Hindu *panchayat,* which dealt with the community's issues, and persuaded them to settle their matters amicably rather than lodging a thousand and one complaints at the police station over the pettiest of conflicts. And he had managed to persuade people to stop spending quite so lavishly on their children's weddings, another pet habit of the Sindhis, who were essentially simple people but loved to show off to one another.

"If he could manage that, then he's someone to be reckoned with," Jan Mohammed reported to Turab Ali Shah. "Look at who he's persuaded to come speak at this conference! I'm beginning to worry about all of this. No, don't ask me why. I just have a bad feeling."

"How old do you think he is?"

"Must be in his twenties? No older than that."

Jan Mohammed sniffed virtuously. "The arrogance of youth!"

"You were young once, Jan Mohammed," chided Turab Ali Shah.

"Maybe," said Jan Mohammed, as if this too were a fact that could be disputed. "But I always knew my place!"

The two men traveled together to Sann the following week. Turab Ali Shah watched the world go by from the vantage point of his bullock cart, while Jan Mohammed sat on a gentle gray mare and clopped along beside him. They rode through acres of fields: wheat stalks swollen and heavy, ready for threshing; rice paddies shining under the March sun; mango orchards pregnant with the budding babies of fruit that would be perfumed and ripe by summertime. The canals snaked through the lands like ribbons of silver, and in the distance herdsmen drove their cattle into the shallow waters, where the animals drank and bathed like kings, lowing and grunting with pleasure. Turab Ali Shah breathed in the air that was rich with manure, silt, and heavy moisture, and knew that he was in a place where his forefathers had been buried, where he would be buried, where his sons would be buried when they died. No matter what happened in the world around them, this would never change.

But his heavy complacency was shaken when they alighted at Sann and went to the conference, which was held at the mausoleum of Makhdoom Bilawal. They passed through the pistachio-green walls of the shrine and walked through to the courtyard, where the tables had been set up and the guests sat in neat rows in front of it. Where their own conference had been noisy and messy, this one was organized and controlled; no sounds of tinny music, no shouts from passersby, no announcements to interrupt the speeches of the participants. The audience was filled with the familiar faces of the Khilafat Movement in Sindh, and the men were paying attention as they never had in their classrooms or mosques. As Turab Ali Shah and Jan Mohammed focused their eyes on the speakers' table at the front, they recognized the various Maulanas, the editor of the *Al-Wahid* newspaper, and Hakim Sehwani with a baton in his hand, as if he were going to conduct an orchestra through a magnificent piece of music, a quiet hush of seriousness and dignity surrounding them all.

And along with all the eminent faces, in the chair of the convener of the conference sat a boy. Not just any boy—the same fifteen-year-old that Turab Ali Shah had seen at Larkana, sitting next to Makhdoom Moenuddin!

Both Turab Ali Shah and Jan Mohammed watched with dropped jaws and bulging eyes as the young boy clambered up onto the table and began to address the audience. To a burst of applause he modestly lowered his head, while Hakim Sehwani held his hands up to stop them, and then, failing that, banged his baton on the table.

"Let him speak! Please, let our esteemed Sayed Ghulam Murtaza Shah speak!"

Turab Ali Shah and Jan Mohammed were paralyzed. So this was Ghulam Murtaza Shah! They had expected a young man and instead they'd found a child—a pup! And this pup had dared to organize this meeting under the mighty auspices of the Khilafat Conference!

"It's an outrage!" hissed Jan Mohammed, through clenched teeth.

"Hmph," grunted Turab Ali Shah. "What's he doing on that table?"

"He's too short to be seen otherwise!"

The youngster, who'd recovered some of his color since the meeting in Larkana, stood straight and proud in front of them and began to speak, in a high, excited tone. "Bismillah hir Rahman ur Rahim. My fellow Sindhis, my older brothers, Saeens . . ." Turab Ali Shah groaned to himself. The boy's voice hadn't even broken! Why, he wasn't even old enough to shave his whiskers! Turab Ali Shah considered walking up to the table and telling Hakim Sehwani that this was highly out of order. But then the boy continued, and reluctantly Turab Ali Shah forced himself to listen.

"You must know, my brothers, that two days ago, the commissioner in Sindh summoned me to Kotri and warned me that the Khilafat Movement is an anti-British campaign . . ." Boos filled the courtyard. "He told me that if I did not end my participation, they would halt the monthly income that has been given to me by the Court of Wards; and the commissioner requested that I cancel this conference. But I told him that all the arrangements had been finalized and that there was no stopping the conference now. And I say to you that, indeed, there is no stopping this movement now!"

"Wah, wah, wah!" cheered the audience.

"My great ancestor, Sayed Hyder Shah, came to me in a dream. He told me that no one could be allowed in his court without prior preparation. I asked him what that preparation was. He said, 'He who keeps on serving his homeland Sindh and its people without any discrimination shall be instructed further with the passage of time.' My brothers, I offer myself to Sindh in her service forever!"

"Jeay Sindh!" came a cry from someone's lips. Jan Mohammed turned sharply to stare at Turab Ali Shah, who was himself surprised to find that his mouth was the offender. Finding that he liked the taste of the words on his tongue, he shouted it again. "Jeay Sindh!"

The crowd took it up and carried it on. *Jeay Sindh! Jeay Sindh! Jeay Sindh!* Long live Sindh! Forever and ever!

"The welfare and security of Sindh and her people is dependent upon our taking care of those sublime souls and the places where they reside: Shah Hyder in Sann, Sayed Khairuddin at Sukkur, Lal Shahbaz Qalandar in Sehwan Sharif, Shah Abdul Latif at Bhit Shah . . . the list goes on. We must protect them until we die."

"Jeay Sindh!"

"I have decided to serve Sindh by choosing the paths of political and social welfare of my people. Therefore I have called upon men far greater than I to speak at this conference, and for its success and the success of the Khilafat Movement, I appeal to Almighty Allah for his help and blessings and guidance."

"Ameen!" shouted the Maulanas from the stage.

"And so I say to you, we must put our faith in the Khilafat Movement. For it is only when the Muslim world is free, and the British have quit India, that Sindh will reap the benefits for a thousand years or more. I know too well that some of our compatriots hate independence and love enslavement. But it is a trap that we must avoid at all costs. We must never accept oppression in our beloved Sindh, no matter who the oppressors are or where they come from."

People murmured to each other, naming those Pirs who everyone knew supported the British and had refused to take part in the Khilafat Movement, remaining loyal to the government instead. Ghulam Murtaza Shah paused for a moment as he wiped the sweat from his forehead. "I would like to quote the lines of our beloved Shah Abdul Latif, whose shrine I visit every month with willing devotion:

> Oh God! May ever You on Sindh
> bestow abundance rare;
> Beloved! All the world let share
> Thy grace, and fruitful be.

"I thank you, my brothers, I thank you, Saeens, I thank you for coming here today and giving me your support. May Allah Saeen bestow upon us not just abundance, but victory!"

"*Jeay Sindh!*"

The boy quickly climbed off the table and sank back into his seat, his chest heaving with effort and emotion.

Turab Ali Shah couldn't wait until there was a break, at which he heaved himself out of his chair and shot off toward the stage as fast as his legs could carry him. Jan Mohammed clutched at his sleeve, but Turab Ali Shah charged the table like an overexcited bull and went up to Ghulam Murtaza Shah, his hands outstretched.

"Well done, by God, well done!"

Ghulam Murtaza rose from the table, glowing at the praise. He bent downward to touch Pir Turab Ali Shah's feet, then they *salaamed* each other with the *namaste* and embraced. Turab Ali Shah clapped the boy on the back so hard that he coughed and his glasses almost flew off his head.

"Do you really think it was good?" Ghulam Murtaza said shyly, and it was only at that moment that Turab Ali Shah realized how young the boy really was.

"Saeen," said Turab Ali Shah. And that one word was enough.

Ghulam Murtaza flushed again. "Do you know," he said, in a hoarse voice, so low that Pir Turab Ali Shah had to strain forward to hear him, "I have been an orphan since I was sixteen months old. I always thought I was unlucky to never have known my father. But I see today that it is not true."

"How do you mean, Saeen?"

"Just look . . ." The boy gazed in wonder at the rows of men that had come here from all corners of Sindh, Pirs, *waderas*, zamindars, men of learning, men of the lands, men of menial work, and men of intellect. "Sindh may be my mother, but it seems today that I have many fathers. And if they are half as proud of me as you are, then my Baba, may God rest his soul, does not have to worry."

Then Turab Ali Shah turned away so that Ghulam Murtaza would not see the tears glistening in his eyes.

November 23, 2007

Ali put down the phone and stared at it as if it were a loathsome creature: a cockroach or a rat, instead of a combination of plastic and computer chips. He had been calling Sunita every day for the past week, but her phone was always switched off. *The number you have dialed is not responding at the moment: please try again later.* That meant she'd changed her number—it was easy enough to do in Karachi, with cheap SIMs available at every corner shop and market in the city. Her inaccessibility made him panicky; he found himself without appetite, lacking in confidence. He couldn't even bring himself to entertain his many sexual fantasies; at night, instead of lying on his back and thinking about her in bed with him, he just slipped into unconsciousness.

He had a recurring dream during these nights: he was standing at a shrine somewhere in the interior of Sindh—he couldn't tell which one—while worshippers and pilgrims passed by, ringing the bell at the doorway before stepping across the threshold and going to the saint's tomb to offer prayers and make their promises to him: *Grant my prayer, O blessed Saeen, o offspring of the Prophet, peace be upon him, intercede with God on my behalf and I will feed sixty poor people every Friday for the rest of my life.*

. . . Get my daughters married . . .

. . . Cure my father's illness . . .

. . . Please let me have a child . . .

But instead of joining them in their adoration, he stood paralyzed on the fringes of worship. He tried to raise his hands in prayer, and found he could not remember the words. And then Sunita suddenly marched past him, dressed in a sari with a *bindi* on her forehead, carrying a tray of little pots with spices and a small blazing *diya*. She went up to the saint's bier, which was covered with a green cloth and heaped with roses, set her tray on the floor, then put her hands together in *namaste* and bowed her head, praying softly. He would wake from these dreams and quickly check his phone to see if she'd texted him, but no message ever waited for him.

Ali still saw her in class, but she refused to look at him or respond to his attempts to speak with her. She surrounded herself with girlfriends and pretended she couldn't hear him when he called out to her. She was blanking him as effectively as if she'd disappeared. Every time he saw her, his heart jumped to his mouth with the hope that today might be the day she ended the ostracism. But when she turned away from him, dashing his hopes, he grew more and more dejected, leaving him with the realization that he simply didn't know how to fix the gap that had opened up between them.

Still, he emailed her every morning. At first he wrote her the story of what happened at the embassy, how he'd left just as his name was being called, how he'd thought the moment would have terrified him but all he could feel was an exhilaration and the strange confidence that he was doing exactly the right thing. Then he worried that she would find him still selfishly centered only on his own life, so he wrote to tell her something that would make her soften her heart toward him: nothing pleading or apologetic, just the little details of his day in the hopes that some phrase or memory would resonate with her, and draw her back to him.

He told her about how the channel had been shut down and while they were still going to work, the station was like a graveyard, with little to do except look at each other's strained faces and play solitaire endlessly on the computer. He told her how he'd arranged a small fund for Haroon at the office, one of the accomplishments he was most proud of at City24. He wrote about how the electioneering was making him sick with the sight of all the banners going up with politicians' faces sneering down at him from every lamppost and wall. He didn't bother to mention that Haris and his mother were barely talking to him after the US visa debacle. He'd explained to them again and again that he hadn't gone through with the interview, that he'd changed his mind about going to America—but it seemed that his desire to go in the first place was betrayal enough to them.

Ali accepted their wrath meekly after a time, finding himself too exhausted to explain his motivations or actions any further. In his more contemplative moments, he wondered if they weren't substituting him for his father, punishing him for Sikandar's abandonment all those years before. It seemed as if years of pent-up wrath were being released now, as if Ali had torn the skin off wounds that had seemed to heal but were in fact still raw under the surface.

The only person who gave him any affection these days was Jeandi, too young to understand why her eldest brother had done such a bad thing by wanting to go and study in America.

"Adda, when you go to America, will you take me with you?"

Jeandi asked Ali one day when they were having breakfast together. He was chewing on a piece of toast and watching a cricket
match on television while she played with a bowl of chocolate-
flavored cereal that was turning the milk brown as she stirred the
soggy flakes over and over with her spoon.

Ali almost began to tell her that he wasn't going, but the look
on Jeandi's face, hesitantly hopeful, touched something soft inside his heart and he decided to indulge her in the fantasy. "Of
course I'll take you with me."

Jeandi did a double take, as if she hadn't been expecting him
to agree. "Will you take me to the mall there? I've heard they're
really big and they have everything in them!" She spoke quickly,
worried that the offer might be rescinded if she didn't secure it
fast enough.

"Yes, of course."

"And will you teach me how to drive?"

"I can do that here, Jeandi."

"No, Adda, Amma says it's too dangerous for girls to drive.
She says they can get kidnapped or worse. What's worse than
being kidnapped, Adda? I don't want to have that happen to me.
I'll wait until we get to America and then I'll learn there."

Ali's eyes watered suddenly. "That sounds great. And I'll buy
you a car, too."

"Really, Adda?" She pulled the spoon out of the chocolatey
mess and sucked on it happily.

"Yes, anything you like."

"Thanks, Adda!" She jumped up from her seat and came
around to give him a hug. He patted her arms as she wound them
around his neck and rubbed her cheek against his. She'd been
so young when their father had gone; people always said that it
was difficult for boys to grow up without their fathers, but Ali
suspected that Jeandi was suffering the loss of her father in her

own way. It was up to him to take his father's place, to show this child that there was still a man whom she could turn to under any circumstances, who would love her even when she believed that she was unlovable. It was the only gift he wished his father had given him when he'd been that young.

After breakfast he sat down at the computer to write Sunita his daily email. *I'm going to a meeting of the People's Resistance Movement tonight at nine. It's at the Second Floor. I met them when I was at the lawyers' protest last week; they're just ordinary citizens, not politicians or anything, and they're organizing ways that we can get involved. I just thought I should check it out. Maybe it's something we could do a story on. If—I mean when—we come back on the air!* He paused, then added, *Maybe you could come, too. It sounds really interesting.*

Ali stopped, reread what he'd written, and deleted the last two sentences before pressing SEND. He couldn't say anything that would pressure her to meet him. If she wanted to come, she knew where he'd be at nine o'clock that evening. He'd keep telling her every day where he was going to be; it would keep the bond alive between them until she was ready to forgive him for having sinned.

* * *

The Second Floor was a coffeehouse that had opened only six months earlier, but Karachi's intelligentsia flocked to its poetry readings, musical concerts, lectures, and workshops. People who had returned from America, Canada, or Great Britain, looking for a place to help them forget that they were in Karachi, came to browse the tiny bookshop and try out the mouthwatering iMacs and MacBook laptops on display. Artists exhibited their graphic designs and oil paintings and watercolors on the brick walls, while a colorful mural on the opposite side of the room created lively debate among the customers about its surrealism: shirtless men painted in tones of sepia clasped each other as they walked among bright green fields, other similarly shirtless men performing manual labor in the shadow of an oversized tractor and a red-fronted truck.

As Ali walked into the coffeehouse, two women were standing in front, arguing.

"I think it's vibrant," said one. "Who's the artist?"

"Someone called Asim Butt. I don't understand it!" replied the other.

A fluttering movement from above caught Ali's eye and he looked up: from a beam in the ceiling dangled a copy of the Pakistan constitution with a single word scrawled in black marker across its front: SUSPENDED.

He found a seat in the back row, making sure he had a good view of the projection screen set up in a corner of the room. The chairs quickly filled up with people, eager, nervous students, *khaddar*-clad NGO types, journalists from various newspapers and magazines, teachers, and professors. Ali recognized a few of them; most were his age, while some were in their forties and fifties. He nodded to familiar faces, counted the black armbands on their arms, and reached and took a sticker from a pile on a nearby table. Printed on the sticker were the words *Restore Democracy Now!* and a black palm print with a red thumbprint.

At a quarter after nine, two young men and a woman got up to the front of the room and introduced themselves as the organizers of the movement: Imran, Bilal, and Ferzana, activists who held day jobs in a law office, a school, and a newspaper group. Ferzana pressed a button on the laptop and the overhead projector began to beam images and words onto the screen. Bilal, the lawyer, explained them, waving his hands in elegant circles to emphasize his points.

"As you know, the Supreme Court dismissed all the petitions challenging Musharraf's eligibility to contest the elections on November nineteenth. And on the twenty-first, the president handed down the order that amended the Constitution—"

"The suspended Constitution," called a man, pointing at the ceiling, as the audience snickered.

Bilal grinned. "Yes, the suspended Constitution. And what the PCO said was basically that all actions taken during this emergency are legal."

The audience muttered their disapproval, shaking their heads and rolling their eyes.

"Pakistan was suspended from the Commonwealth yesterday. The Western countries are putting pressure on Musharraf to hold fair elections. But the United States is reluctant to get rid of a ruler who is so willing to do their bidding when it comes to the War on Terror. That's why this People's Resistance Movement is so crucial. We need to show that we won't accept the undemocratic actions of this government, no matter what the West says."

"Quite right. Quite right."

"The judges have already been deposed, and now they're under house arrest: Munir Malik is seriously ill and in need of dialysis, but they won't let him go for treatment to the hospital. Same thing with our prominent human rights people—Asma Jehangir, Hina Jilani, Iqbal Haider, I. A. Rahman all under house arrest. And it's not just well-known figures, but thousands of people who have been illegally detained or who are missing, in the Frontier, in Balochistan, in Sindh and Punjab. All their lives are in danger."

Imran spoke up at this point. "The suspension of the Constitution has given Musharraf unchecked powers to do what he likes, without regard to human rights violations. Here, have a look at your rights that have been taken away."

A new slide appeared on the screen:

Suspended Rights:
Article 9 (Security of Person)
Article 10 (Safeguards to Arrest and Detention)
Article 15 (Freedom of Movement)
Article 16 (Freedom of Assembly)
Article 17 (Freedom of Association)
Article 19 (Freedom of Speech)
Article 25 (Equality of Citizens)

Ali murmured along with everyone else, wondering which fact was more depressing: that these rights had been snatched from them or that he hadn't even known he possessed them in the first place.

"And now, today," continued Bilal, "the Supreme Court—"

"The false Supreme Court!"

"The illegal Supreme Court!"

"The bastards!" A roar of laughter followed this last cry.

"The Supreme Court has handed out a clean chit to Musharraf. They've validated the emergency, the PCO. And criticized the deposed judges for standing in the way of law and order."

Amid the rumbling, a girl said, "So how can we help?"

"Yes, what can we do?" Ali said. He and the girl looked at each other. She wore boxy spectacles, the kind that pretty girls used to look extremely intellectual. Her long, golden-brown hair was done up in a messy chignon. He smiled at her and she nodded in reply. This was the kind of girl who wouldn't give him a second glance on the street. If democracy could get him this kind of action, then he was all for it! Then Ali remembered Sunita and quickly turned his attention back to the front of the room.

Ferzana took the microphone from Imran. "Believe me, we all know the feeling of helplessness. It's been like this for the last thirty years, the citizens at the mercy of the army. But we're determined to show the world that the people of Pakistan do not want dictatorship. We're going to make sure our voices are heard."

"How?"

"Protests. Marches. Vigils. Blogs. Keeping in contact with the outside world no matter how many media restrictions are in place and how many times they bring down the Internet. We'll make sure that the international media, human rights watchdogs, Amnesty International all know about what's going on in Pakistan. We'll pass around a clipboard; please leave your cell phone number and email address, because that's the way we'll contact you to let you know when something's going to happen where you can participate. Our idea is to be smart protestors, because we know that the army and the establishment are out to get us. You can imagine why we won't want to announce our events in the newspaper." As laughter burst out once more, Ali took the clipboard from his neighbor and hesitated only a moment before writing down his telephone number. Then he quickly wrote down Sunita's cell phone number and email address just beneath his.

Ferzana leaned forward and stabbed at the computer with her finger. The screen dissolved into a new image: protestors on the ground, bruised and bloodied; police above them, beating them with long wooden rods. People in the audience gasped out loud. Ferzana let the image linger for a few silent minutes, then she clicked the keyboard again and the picture was replaced by one last slide:

Our Aims:
Support the civil rights organizations
Demand the suspension of financial and military aid to Pakistan

Restore the Constitution
Release political prisoners
Restore the judiciary
End media curbs
Musharraf should step down as head of the army
Free and fair elections

They left this up on the screen so that even after the meeting was over and people were breaking up into small groups to drink coffee and discuss what they'd heard, everyone would remember what they were fighting for. The journalists in the audience clicked off their digital recorders, while students copied the list of aims into notebooks with bright cartoon figures dancing on the covers. Ali wandered around, ordered a cup of coffee from the bar, then sat down with a group that included Ferzana, a few journalists, and the girl with the square-rimmed glasses.

"Free and fair elections is all very well," said one of the journalists. "But who are our choices? The same damned crooks that stole everything from us the last time around?"

Ferzana nodded. "I know what you mean. But things have changed since eight years ago. Pakistan's changed. There's bound to be new faces. We have to participate in the election process; we can't just let the army go on throwing their weight around because there's no alternative. That's their line, isn't it? All along they've said that democracy doesn't work. We have to show them that it can and it will."

"Who are you going to vote for?" asked the girl with the glasses. Ali leaned in closely to hear the answer.

"Benazir, definitely."

"What? Why her?" Ali blurted out loud. As all eyes turned to him, he swallowed nervously. They were watching him, politely waiting for his input. For a moment Ali was speechless. He couldn't tell these people that he mistrusted Benazir because his father had loved her so much. But he recalled that this was precisely the reason he did resent her: she was the child his father had wished for, instead of the son he had actually gotten. The pride that his father should have invested in him, in Haris, in Jeandi, had been diverted to an icon to which none of them could ever measure up. And if Ali's father had tried to escape the dissatisfaction he'd felt with his own family by obsessing on Benazir, then Ali had done exactly the same thing—except where Ali's father had heaped all his admiration and hopes on Benazir's shoulders, Ali had laid all the frustration and rejection he felt from his father at Benazir's feet.

"I just think she's a Western tool," Ali said lamely, while his mind clambered around all these fleeting thoughts.

"It's not about being a Western tool," said Ferzana. "She speaks their language. She's a woman. She's Westernized, secular, intelligent, articulate. They feel they can trust her. That's important—as much as the West has interfered in our affairs since God knows when, we still need to work with them."

"Besides," added Salma, the girl with the glasses, "isn't Benazir a great symbol for how we want our country to be? We don't want to be ruled by the Taliban, or the mullahs. She's the exact opposite of them. That's why the fundos don't like her. She makes them nervous."

"But she's a feudal," said the journalist.

Ali cringed. How many times had someone said the only way to solve Pakistan's problems was to eliminate the feudals, enact land reforms, destroy their power base? "We need a revolution!" they said. "Kill the feudals. Redistribute their land. Get them out of parliament and government. End this tyranny once and for all!" Then, when they found out that Ali himself was a Sindhi, they'd halfheartedly apologize, thinking that he, too, was one of them. "We don't mean you. We know you're not like that."

"I'm not a feudal," was always Ali's answer. If he said it often enough, he told himself, it would stop feeling like he was trying to claim his brown eyes as blue, or his blood type as O when it was really A. But unlike the lie he always told about his father, this one had yet to feel true.

He held his breath and waited to see how Ferzana and Salma would respond now.

Ferzana said, "Maybe that's where she came from, but that's not where she's going. She's educated. She has a different outlook on things. She values justice, democracy. Religious freedom. Women's rights. That's what Pakistan needs. That's what Pakistan wants."

"She did nothing for women when she was last in government!" said the second journalist, a woman.

"She couldn't. Her hands were tied," said Ferzana. "The army was still calling the shots. And she was only thirty-five years old when she became prime minister. Think about that. Could you have run an entire nation at that age?"

"And the money that she stole?" said Ali, at last.

"She should give it all back if she cares so much for this country," said the woman journalist, nodding in agreement with Ali.

"I saw a great cartoon in the newspaper," said Salma, putting her hand over her mouth to stop the giggle that was already trying to escape. "There was this poster on the wall, right? And it had a picture of Asif Zardari and it said, *Asif not to return to Pakistan*. And there was one of his polo ponies standing in front of the poster, weeping."

Laughter broke out all around. Ferzana guffawed so hard that tears squeezed out of her eyes. The two journalists slapped palms; it was their newspaper in which the cartoon had been printed. Ali smiled at Salma, and she winked back at him

"Look, I'm not saying that Benazir is perfect. She made a lot of mistakes. There was a lot of wrongdoing in her government. But she's paid her dues. She's been in exile for eight years. Her husband went to jail for ten. I think she's changed," said Ferzana.

"Maybe," added Salma, "she deserves a second chance."

Ali sat at the table after everyone had left, pondering what Ferzana and Salma had said. Plenty of people said that Benazir's first term had been all about revenge: for the death of her father at the hands of the military. That was why she had allowed her husband to ride roughshod over the country's coffers with such impunity. Could she possibly be back for a different reason this time? To make amends? To seek redemption? Ali nursed his cup of coffee late into the night and thought about redemption and second chances until the waiters began to clean the tables and put away the chairs. Only when they turned off the lights did he leave, driving home so deep in thought that he almost missed the turn to his house.

* * *

So Ali found himself pulled into the world of smart protesting. It was as if someone had given him a shot of adrenaline. Each morning, on waking he immediately grabbed his cell phone, but he wasn't checking only for Sunita's messages anymore: there might be a text waiting for him to say that there'd be a flash protest in three hours outside Agha's Supermarket, or the Press Club, or the Sindh Secretariat. He'd reach there and meet the other protestors with grim smiles and tight nods, and someone would hand him a placard. They'd stand there, not saying anything, just holding up their signs while photographers took pictures and the video cameras from press agencies rolled. After fifteen minutes they'd put down their placards and silently melt away.

An email asked for volunteers to go on the Save Pakistan

Graffiti campaign, so Ali volunteered for that, too: they met at four in the morning and went around the city, stamping the image of an army boot with an X marked through it under the tutelage of the young artist Asim Butt, who taught them how to use stencils and spray paint under the cover of darkness. In the morning people woke up to see their handiwork and, the next day, photographs of the crossed-out army boot appeared in all the newspapers. The graffiti was painted over by the end of the week but the protestors had made their point.

Ali went to candlelight vigils at night, joined protests during the day outside the City24 News building condemning the block on the Pakistani private media. These were noisier affairs, with protestors shouting slogans and defying the police to stop them. "Down with PEMRA, down with censorship!" they screamed, shaking their fists in the policemen's faces. Ali was astonished at the many people that showed up for these events: as well as the usual journalists, NGO activists, and students, he saw housewives who brought their children, accountants, artists, and musicians. All kinds of people, it seemed, realized how precarious the future was and were tired of the endless cycle of victimhood that being a Pakistani had meant for the last sixty years.

Bilal, Imran, and Ferzana were at each event; Salma was a medical student at the Aga Khan University, so her time was limited, but she came to as many protests as she could. Ali worried about her the way he'd worry about his sister; the three leaders could take care of themselves, but Salma was just a kid, and her parents would take her out of medical school if they found out what she'd been up to while she was supposed to be studying chemistry and anatomy.

Ali told no one in his family about his growing involvement with the People's Resistance. There had been a gradual thawing of relations since Ali had returned from Islamabad; things had almost gone back to normal between him and his brother, while his mother, still hurt by Ali's secretiveness, talked to him about harmless household matters; the everyday discourse gave a semblance of normality to their home life. He didn't want to do anything to upset that recovering balance, so he merely said that he was away on work when he had to slip out at midnight or in the early hours of the morning. They didn't question him, either; Ali could see that they were frightened by the way he could draw shutters down and keep them out of his private world.

Talking to Sunita was out of the question. She hadn't bothered returning any of his texts or emails. She'd even changed some of her class periods, so now he only caught glimpses of her as she hurried out of the university gates, and at a distance he couldn't even be sure it was her. She had faded away from him, like a desert mirage that weakens as you approach and finally disappears under the sun when you run toward it.

The only place Ali felt free to discuss his new activities was at work, which relieved some of the boredom and the tension created by that boredom. Nobody at City24 knew what was going to happen: the channel was still off the air, both here and overseas, since the government had pressured the Gulf nation from where they'd been broadcasting to stop their transmissions "for the sake of law and order." They were continuing to record programs, make documentaries, but they were banned indefinitely from reporting the news day by day, hour by hour.

Now, instead of disappearing inside her office for six hours at a time, Ameena lingered by the news desks. Ali expected to be snapped at, or told about some assignment he'd have to run and cover, so when she sat down at his desk and looked at him expectantly, he didn't realize at first that he was actually supposed to have a conversation with her.

"So, Ali," Ameena said, fixing him with her narrowed gray

eyes. "I hear you've been going to some of these citizens' protests. I hear they're quite revolutionary."

Ali was alarmed. How did she know? But then, this was a television station. And other news stations, those that had bowed to government pressure and promised to stop airing controversial footage, were back on the air. Ameena had contacts in all those places; she had spies in a hundred different parts of Karachi. Kazim Mazhar had his own contacts in the government and in Islamabad. It was the only way to run any kind of business in Pakistan: things got done according to what you knew and who you had to pay to find it out.

Jehangir was at the next desk and though he continued to sort through the papers in his file cabinet, Ali knew he was listening carefully to the conversation between them. Ali had tried to talk to Jehangir about the protests, to persuade him to join them at the next protest at the Press Club that Friday. But Jehangir just rolled his eyes. "*Yaar,* that's not my scene. I'm going to Underground that night anyway."

"Underground?"

"Oh, *yaar,* don't tell me you've become so boring you don't remember how to have any fun. Underground. Café. In Zamzama?"

"I know where it is, Jehangir."

"Of course you know where it is because I took you there. So why don't you forget all this resistance bullshit and come with me? Arty's coming, Lila, Xeneb, some of the other girls. Don't you want to find a new girlfriend now that you and Sunita are—"

"No, I don't. And I don't like that place. Too many media types there."

Jehangir laughed. "What does that make us? Come on, *yaar.* Good scene. Plenty of booze and other fun ways to pass your time. Know what I mean?"

"I'm not into that shit, J." Ali didn't want to get into the discussion on why he didn't try hard drugs, why trying hash a few times had been enough for him, why Jehangir seemed to get such a kick out of pills and lines of coke. He couldn't even remember when Jehangir had started indulging; it seemed like he'd been involved with it for a long time now. But Ali knew his own life was complicated enough without drugs. They were a distraction for people who didn't have the sort of problems that he had.

Jehangir had tried to convince him, then shrugged his shoulders. Ali was thinking about what Jehangir said, about Sunita and he being . . . were they? They'd had no contact for two weeks, but it felt like two years. He put the thought away under the section in his mind marked *To be answered later.*

He turned to Ameena and said, "Yeah, actually it is really exciting. The protests are amazing. So many people there from so many different backgrounds, working together for one cause. And it's not just protests. They're doing really cool things, too. There's going to be a car rally next week, can you believe that? A car rally for democracy!"

"Really?" Ameena took out a cigarette and lit it, sat back in her seat, and regarded Ali with an interested stare. Ali couldn't recall ever seeing that expression on her face before. "A car rally, hmm?"

"Yes. And they're organizing street theater as well. That's going to start up in a few weeks. You know, to get the message out to the average person."

"That's very interesting. Maybe you could do a piece on it. You know, when we go back on the air."

"Is that going to be anytime soon?"

"I'm not sure. We're working on it . . . let's see. Kazim's going to Islamabad on Monday. I'll go with him. We'll keep you all advised."

Jehangir had stopped pretending to work and was now blatantly staring at the two of them. They'd spent hours telling each other that Ameena was a total bloody monster, *yaar,* who couldn't care less if either of them lived or died. And now here she was paying attention to Ali, and if he wasn't mistaken, leaning forward a little bit and allowing the collar of her shirt to drop open where she'd unhooked a button at her neck. Jehangir was pulling his chair closer, wanting desperately to be involved in the discussion. Ali didn't know why that made him feel so gratified, or why it felt so good to be one up on a person he'd always counted as his friend.

"I didn't think you were all that interested in politics, Ali," said Ameena. "But maybe I've been mistaken."

Jehangir cleared his throat at that moment. Ameena half turned and saw him. "Oh, Jehangir. Do you think Ali's got a future in politics?"

"No, he just goes to all those protests to meet girls," said Jehangir, flashing her a charming grin.

Without thinking, Ali shot back, "You're just jealous, fag."

The moment the words left his mouth, he knew he'd made a terrible mistake. Ameena's face stayed impassive, but there'd been a lens click of comprehension in her eyes—she didn't miss a thing!—as she was processing the stricken look on Jehangir's face, starting to regard him in an entirely new way, at his hair, his slender fingers, the way he wore his shirt tucked into his pants. Evaluating. Putting two and two together. Ali knew he'd murdered his friend more effectively than if he'd picked up a pistol and shot him in the face.

After a silent, nauseating pause that seemed to last forever, Jehangir raised his chin. "Actually, Ali has a great future in politics." His voice was different now, still jokey, but with an undercurrent of poisoned steel. He turned to smile at Ali. "Isn't that right, Ali? Thinking about running for the elections?"

Ali said in a low voice, "I don't know what you're talking

about." Jehangir could be dangerous when slighted, bearing a grudge that lasted weeks or months against even a minor infraction. Ali had seen it happen with other people; girls who'd spurned Jehangir's advances, Jehangir's parents when they refused one of his whims, servants who displeased him with their inefficiency. Ali wished desperately he could take the last five minutes back but there was no turning back time for him now.

"Is your family in politics, Ali? You never said," Ameena said. She looked as though she could put the conversation on a plate and eat it for breakfast, it was so delicious to her.

"No," replied Ali. "We've got nothing to do with any of that." He tried to keep his voice steady, keep up the pretense, even though he knew it was already shattering all around him.

"Oh yes," said Jehangir. "His family's very much into politics. In fact, his father's running for a seat in the National Assembly from—where is it, Ali? Sukkur? Shikarpur? One of those feudal bastions anyway." He waved his hand in a vague direction that seemed to imply everything north of Karachi. His accent tightened and became more clipped, recalling the private school that he'd gone to that required recommendations from heads of foreign banks, ambassadors, even heads of state.

Ali was unable to speak. Two patches of heat burned on his cheeks, and although he was too dark to blush, the blood rushed to his face, then to his stomach, leaving him lightheaded. He wanted to rise and walk away, but he found his legs paralyzed under the table.

Jehangir went on. "What is your father again? A zamindar? A Pir? Or is it both? I can never quite remember."

"I think you've remembered plenty," whispered Ali. His voice barely escaped the confines of his throat.

"But Ali," said Ameena, "I thought you told me your father was—"

"Oh, he's very much alive," said Jehangir. "Owns half of Sukkur, but lives in Bath Island, I think. With his other family. Not Ali's. But then, that's what feudals do, isn't it, Ali? Marry two, three times?"

Ameena's eyes traveled from Jehangir to Ali's face. He thought he could see sympathy in the downcast turn of her mouth—then again, it could be any of a half dozen emotions: disappointment, cynicism, anger, condescension. He could stand to look at her no longer, and bowed his head, defeated. There was no point asking Jehangir how he knew, either. Working at a television station, where information could be bought and sold for the price of a carton of cigarettes, Ali knew Jehangir could find anything out about anyone, and what money or his connections couldn't discover wasn't worth finding out in the first place.

"Don't you think the feudals should be paying income tax like the rest of us, Ali?"

"That's enough, Jehangir," said Ameena softly.

Jehangir shrugged and turned back to his desk, and Ameena made some excuse about having to make a phone call. Before going back to her office, she shot Ali a glance that said, *Are you okay?* It was the concern of the powerful, who could afford to be solicitous in front of those that they pitied.

Ali refused to meet her eyes. Nor did he acknowledge the half-defiant, half-terrified expression on Jehangir's face, the one that said they'd both gone too far. But Ali realized, with the same certainty that told him he'd never see Sunita again, that Jehangir's betrayal was only a part of the self-destruction Ali had brought upon himself with his secrets and lies.

The Game of Kings

C ome, jailer, come and play a game of chess with me."

Ahmed Damani's head jerked up in surprise. These were not the words he was expecting to hear from a man condemned to die in the morning, But then neither had Ahmed expected to find himself working in the Central Jail at Hyderabad, a jailer in the feared Death Cell, where he saw men as they faced their last hours on this earth. And Ahmed had certainly never expected that the British would have ever caught the Surhiya Badshah— the Brave King, tried him in court like a common criminal, and then sentenced him to death by hanging. Or that his would be the cell where the Brave King would spend his last night, smoking and contemplating the full moon that glowed through his tiny window. And yet here was Ahmed, dressed in the black uniform of a death watch jailer, and the Pir Pagaro was inviting him to come into his cell and play a game of chess.

It was an eerily compelling invitation: as a young boy growing up in Hyderabad, Ahmed had dreamt that one day he would become the most famous chess champion in the world. He was from a respectable but poor family that had left their village of Tando Allah Yar and settled in Hyderabad, his father hoping to find better employment than tilling the fields of the Talpur zamindar who owned so much land that if you stood along the banks of the main watercourse and turned slowly in a full circle, everything that you saw belonged to that man.

Ahmed's father, Rahim Damani, decided that a life of labor in the fields, threshing wheat or plowing cotton, sweltering under the unforgiving sun and forever living under the thumb of the zamindar's strict overseer, was not the life that he wanted for himself or his sons. So when Ahmed was barely four years old, his father loaded their few belongings onto a cart, stacked his family on top of the bundles of furniture and clothes, and drove them to a new life in the city, full of prospects and pleasure.

It was a daring move in those days; most men of the country-side feared the city, clung to what was safe and familiar, teaching their sons that leaving the land was tantamount to dying. For in a sense they did die, cutting themselves off from their roots, and having to be reborn in a place where nobody knew who your people were or where you had come from. Even in the cities— Hyderabad, Sukkur, Shikarpur, Karachi—tribesmen sought each other out, associated with each other or those they knew to be their allies, thus protecting themselves from the vagaries of urban life. Adjusting to the crowds, to anonymity, even to the lack of the zamindar's oppressive but all-encompassing security, was a task that few men wanted to undertake in Sindh at the turn of the century.

But Ahmed's father took the risk, and uprooted his small fam-ily—wife, two sons, two daughters—replanting them in city soil and hoping they would bloom there. He found work as a gate-keeper with a well-to-do Sindhi family, sent his sons to school, and worked hard, enjoying the heady taste of self-direction. And to the surprise of everyone, who had predicted a dire fate to repay him for his hubris, they were happy.

Young Ahmed went to school, growing from a chubby child into a tall and lanky teenager who paid the minimal amount of attention to his lessons. He rushed out of the gates each day at noon, and ran to a teahouse not far from his home, where he would spend the next several hours watching the old men play chess. He had discovered them one day shortly after he'd turned fifteen, when he'd taken a detour from his usual route home; the old men were ensconced in front of the *dhabba;* so comfortable were they in their seats that Ahmed half expected to see moss growing over their feet and birds constructing nests in their turbans. Over grimy cups of tea that they could make last for hours, they bent over the board, reenacting the battles of their youth within the confines of the black and white squares on the ancient board that looked as if it would turn into dust if you sneezed on it.

Ahmed was entranced as one old man, Sultan, moved his pawns around the board in wild circles. His opponent, Allah Bachayo, refused to give up a single piece, guarding them as closely as if they were gold coins. The men didn't mind Ahmed's close scrutiny of their game; they even offered to teach him how to play, and he learned quickly, playing against one of them when the other tired of the game. They said he had a gift, but he didn't believe them: he would never be as good as these two, who'd been playing for the last fifty years.

"Harah—I take your rook," Sultan crowed. "With my pawn, no less!"

Allah Bachayo grumbled, "*Gaddha jho phar!* For that I shall have your queen!"

"You cannot—I have protected her with a phalanx of guardsmen—see!"

"But you overlook my knight, who sits in wait for your next step, *so*!"

"Shabash!"

And on and on. Ahmed never tired of their parrying or their verbal jousting. They were like the grandfathers he'd never had—his own grandfathers, maternal and paternal, had died before he was born. He grew immensely fond of these two old men, grizzled bearded Sindhis who wore mirrorwork caps and jackets over their *shalwar kameez* in winter, and turbans made of *ajrak* cloth and simple cotton *lunghis* in the summer. As they fought and argued over the chessboard, they spoke to him of their villages, of the people they'd known and the places they'd traveled, giving him a sense of continuity and connection to the village life that his father had forced them all to leave behind.

They loved to tell him of history, of battles long past, illustrious people who had been born and died centuries ago. Sultan regaled him with tales from Shah Abdul Latif's *Risalo:* the mythical kings, the Seven Queens, the journeys and separations from the Beloved, the deserts of Thar and the waters of the Indus. Allah Bachayo told him about the old days under the British Raj, how the British had gained illegal access to the Indus and used the excuse of bringing a gift of horses to Ranjeet Singh in Lahore as a way of spying on the forts on the river. Ahmed listened, fascinated, as Sultan told him about the Hur rebellion of the last century, and how those fearsome warriors, followers of the Pir Pagaro, roamed up and down the countryside, holding entire villages ransom, proud and unafraid in their devotion to their *murshid.*

"They say," said Sultan, drawing close to Ahmed and whispering in his ear, "that the Hurs are gathering in strength and are preparing for a second uprising."

"*Ssshhhh!*" hissed Allah Bachayo. "Someone will hear you. The *angrez* spies are everywhere!"

"Well, it's true! Ever since they released the Pir Pagaro from jail—not that one, young Ahmed, his grandson, Pir Sibghatullah Shah the Second, the sixth Pir Pagaro—he's become even more bold in his stance. He's had the Hurs released from their settlements, and now he's on tour in Hur country, and I hear that his coffers are full to overflowing with their tributes . . ."

"Nothing like a full pocket to put a fire in your belly, eh?" cackled Allah Bachayo, who was rewarded with a dirty stare from his friend.

"It's not about money, it's about prestige. When they put him in jail, the Hurs went mad at the insult to their Godhead. But jail has only made him stronger. And now he says he can make or break any ministry, so all the politicians, and yes, even the governor of Sindh are groveling at his feet!" said Sultan.

Ahmed sucked in his teeth. This was truly a position of power: to have the great families of Sindh under your control, and to even have the British eager to please you. But the Pir Pagaro commanded such power as his birthright. His was a bloodline that went six generations back; the Pirs of Pir-Jo-Goth could trace their lineage all the way back to the Prophet Mohammed, peace be upon him; Sultan had explained to him that the first Pir Pagaro had defeated all the scholars of Sindh with his own religious knowledge, earning the right to wear their turbans, or *pags*, and his repute had grown from then on. All his followers were devoted to him, but that small subsection of his *murids* who swore allegiance until death had taken the protection of his honor as their blood quest, and his personal army, it was said, now numbered six thousand *ghazis*, soldiers who were ready to fight to the death and become martyrs for the cause.

"And how does Sultan Chacha know all of this?" asked Ahmed, after Sultan had gone home, pleased with having defeated Allah Bachayo in the last game.

"His son's a Hur," muttered the old man, his eyes remaining guarded. For although it was not yet illegal to be a Hur, it was a dangerous business, and to have any association with the Hurs these days, when the Pir was challenging the authority of the British rulers of Sindh, could always be used against you. For the British were suspicious of everyone and everything, with the grumblings of the All-India movement threatening, in 1937, to grow into a roar. Yet they still gave the Pirs of Sindh a long leash, sticking to their policy of allowing them to do whatever they wanted locally, as long as they cooperated with the British when it came to ensuring their *murids'* support of the government.

Ahmed decided not to ask any more questions: his father had always told him to stay away from politics, to concentrate on his studies. The less he knew about politics, the safer it was for a young boy like him. "Do you think I'll ever become a great chess player?" he asked Allah Bachayo instead.

Allah Bachayo grinned, revealing a gap-toothed smile. "Inshallah, son, inshallah! And why not? You have the intelligence, the reasoning, and we've taught you the strategy. Listen to me and Sultan, and you could go far!"

Ahmed treasured the men's encouragement over the next few years, and more so while he was completing his final exams. His father was hoping for good results, so that he could find a good job—a government post, as a clerk or even a very junior secretary, was not out of the question if he scored top marks. Ahmed wanted nothing more than to become a chess champion and travel the world, playing games and defeating men from many countries. While he studied math or geography, he thought about Allah Bachayo and Sultan, how they'd taught him to mount an aggressive attack using bishop and pawns, defend a king with a queen and a rook, checkmate an opponent in merely four moves. But while he studied and dreamt of chess, Ahmed could not help hearing things about the Hurs and the Pir Pagaro. It was what everyone was talking about: how the man who had ascended to the most powerful throne in Sindh at the age of twelve had defied the British, been sent away to jail in far-off Calcutta a youthful brat, and returned a hardened, wily man with the ambition to rule Sindh as an independent king. How the Hurs had managed to stick together in undying unity, to the dismay of the British, who attempted to break them by sending them to guarded settlements and jails in far-off Indian states. And how the Pir was playing a dangerous double game: assuring the British that they had his cooperation, while at the same time intimidating the mullahs who opposed his religious rule and tightening the rope around his political rivals' necks. Everyone whispered about how, when he'd been in jail, he'd smuggled out secret messages between the pages of magazines and the lines of books. The messages were virulently anti-British: they described how the British treated the Indians like donkeys, and how the Indians themselves were cowards for submitting themselves to British occupation.

Ahmed found himself caught up in the thrill of it all: he heard that leaders from all over India came to attend conferences at Pir-jo-Goth, where the Pir's shrine and palace were located; they said it was vital that Hindus and Muslims stayed united against the oppressors. So exciting was the news of his speeches, his orders to his *murids* to wear *khaddar* cloth and give up smoking that Ahmed and his schoolmates, too, began to wear *khaddar* at home and never even touched a cigarette.

Ahmed passed his exams in the summer of 1940 with unremarkable results. Rahim Damani blamed it on Ahmed's daydreaming, his hours wasted playing chess, and the political gossip surrounding them like a swirling desert dust storm. His father's own dreams of Ahmed becoming a clerk or joining the civil service had to take a backseat while he went out and used what little influence he had to try to seek a suitable alternative for his son.

"Central Jail," Rahim Damani announced one evening when he returned from a round of job-seeking among his friends and contacts. The whole family was sitting in the main room while Ahmed's elder sister Marvi pressed their mother's feet and his younger sister Surraya served everyone cups of tea. His youngest brother, Junaid, was fast asleep in the bedroom that he shared with Ahmed.

"What?" said Ahmed, wondering what his father was talking about.

"I've fixed it. You'll start work at the Central Jail."

"As what?" said his mother.

"As a jailer. What else?"

At this, Marvi pinched a nerve in their mother's feet, and the lady let out a scream. "My son, a jailer? You must be mad!"

"Woman, what else do you expect when he's hardly managed to clear his subjects? It was the best I could do, and only because Omar Bachani owes me a favor. He's the superintendent of the jail and the only reason this spot opened up is because the previous man just died, all right?"

"But . . . *jail* . . . he'll be exposed to those criminals, it's dangerous, it's too much!"

"Baba," said Ahmed, "I don't want to be a jailer."

Rahim Damani gave his son a baleful stare. "And why not?"

"Well . . . I don't want to be on their side . . ."

"*Whose* side?"

Ahmed cleared his throat, but the words came out in a whisper. "The British . . . I don't want to be on their—"

At once Rahim Damani took three long strides toward his son and slapped him hard on his face, first with the front of his hand, then the back. Marvi and Surraya both gasped, while Ahmed's mother burst out wailing. Rahim said, "I don't ever want to hear you talking like that again, do you understand? This is serious business, not some kind of crazy dream about being a hero. I know what you and your school friends talk about all day long. Hurs, Hurs, Hurs! Do you know what they're doing to the Hurs and anyone else who's opposing them? Well, do you?"

"Yes, Baba," said Ahmed, hanging his head. He'd heard about the arrests, the deportations, the heavy hand of the British clamping down on them and their families.

"And rightly so. They're criminals, those Hurs. They're creating havoc for poor people like us, they're robbing honest people, they're even catching women and . . ." Rahim Damani glanced at his wife and daughters, realizing that they were listening to the conversation, which was not suitable for female ears. "This isn't about being on anyone's side. This is about earning money, feeding your family. You'll report to Omar Bachani in the morning. Now go to bed."

Perhaps a boy of sixteen could one day think of disobeying his father, but for Ahmed it was unthinkable. He went to bed and woke despondently in the morning, and when he walked with his father to the Central Jail, he could barely lift his head or his feet; both felt as though they were weighed down by rocks. They stopped for a few moments at the shrine of Ghulam Shah on the way, where his father purchased a garland of roses and laid it on the saint's tomb, asking the holy man to help his son be successful in his first job. Ahmed prayed that the dead man whose job he was getting would somehow come back to life and greet them at the gates, telling Rahim Damani there was no vacancy for his son.

When Ahmed saw the black gates of the jail, guards in police uniforms wielding rifles outside, he wanted to cry. Sultan and Allah Bachayo, trying to cheer him up, had told him that it would be a great opportunity, that jailers wielded tremendous power over both their charges and those who wished to be in contact with them, but Ahmed wanted no part of that game. He thought for one wild moment of breaking free of his father's grip, of turning and running away to join the Hurs. He'd happily live in hiding in the Miani Forest, killing and eating the wild animals, give up seeing his family for the freedom a life of crime would bring him. Then they passed through the gates, and Ahmed knew he would be as much a prisoner there as any inhabitant of the jail's miserable, suffocating cells.

And so Ahmed Damani became, at seventeen, the Central Jail's youngest jailer's assistant. Every day he came home from work more and more exhausted; the dark circles grew under his eyes, the lines developed in his face, and he became thin and hollow-cheeked. His mother would cry out and beg him to tell her what ailed him, but how could he talk to her of the things he saw there? The way the men were crowded into cells, eighteen to a room meant for six, iron fetters rubbing sores into their ankles and wrists, the filth, the vermin, the disease . . . she would not be able to bear it. Nor would she be able to hear of the violence that took place between gangs, the unspeakable acts of depravity that the men visited upon each other, the cruelty and sadism of the guards. And the screams when a political prisoner was being tortured . . . No. Better he kept silent, visiting the scenes again and again in his nightmares, than tell his poor mother and frighten her to death with the gruesome reality of his new occupation.

Meanwhile, he continued to visit Sultan and Allah Bachayo when he had time off from work, and from them he heard that the Pir Pagaro was continuing on his path of defiance against the British. They played a game of chess once in a while to pass the time, but both of the old men acknowledged that his talent had surpassed their knowledge a long time ago.

One day in 1941, Ahmed came to the café but found only Allah Bachayo sitting at a table, facing a blank space where his friend should have been sitting in his chair.

"Chacha, where is Sultan?" said Ahmed, hesitating before sitting down opposite the old man.

Allah Bachayo looked as if he was in great pain. He stared off into space, his eyes rheumy and tired, and he sat so still for so long that Ahmed wondered if he had just died in front of him. Presently he spoke.

"His son has been murdered."

Ahmed's arms and legs jerked involuntarily. He'd grown so close to these two men over the years that it was as if he was being told his own brother had been killed. "How . . . When?"

"Yesterday. The British caught them in a raid near the Jamrao Canal. He was shot."

Ahmed bowed his head. It was better than having been captured alive, brought to the jail, and tortured by the British officers and their Indian collaborators to get them to reveal information about Pir Pagaro's activities, or reveal the location of the special camps where he trained the Hurs to fight the British. Ahmed looked down at the chess table in front of Allah Bachayo. The pieces, for once, lay in perfect rows on the edges of the board, the king flanked by his queen, his bishops, and his pawns in front of him. He blinked his eyes slowly and the pieces turned into the Pir Pagaro and his Hurs, the Pir wearing his royal blue robes encrusted with jewels, the Hurs in white with swords and daggers and rifles at the ready, longing to embrace martyrdom for the sake of the Surhiya Badshah, the Brave King. And Ahmed hated life for having turned into a game where all ended in death.

A few months later the Pir Pagaro was arrested, and sent to Seoni in the Central Provinces.

The Hurs lost all reason, and began to enact a war on the British authorities that terrified both British and Sindhis alike. They murdered anyone who was thought to be helping the British, Hindu or Muslim. They sabotaged railway lines and irrigation canals, severed telegraph lines, raided villages, threw mutilated bodies into empty fields. The Central Jail became a main depot where Hurs were herded and locked away before being sent into exile, to Criminal Tribes Settlements in far-flung reaches of India. And Ahmed Damani was exposed to them all, as he walked the halls of the dank and stinking jail, his keys rattling at his belt.

The Hurs in his cells were fierce, silent men who refused food or drink from him at first. They refused to speak. They would not pray even though they were provided with Qurans and water for ablutions. Once in a while Ahmed could hear one of them chanting in a low voice, while others banged on the bars of their cells in time:

> From the North came riding like a black cloud
> The "Pagaro" whose followers are angels,
> Do not oppose this Syed—you devil and infidel,
> You cannot compete with my Beloved. . . .

Ahmed had been told that if he heard anyone singing the songs that praised the Pir and condemned the British, he was to report it to the head of the jail; and that man would be taken and whipped as punishment for his insolence. But Ahmed never told anyone when he heard them sing; nor about the chills that went up and down his spine when he heard their voices, somber and hard like smoky wood after the trees in a forest are burnt down.

He and all the other jailers were ordered to wear cloths wound around their faces, so that they could not be recognized; if they had discovered Ahmed's identity, he and his family would have been killed by any number of Hur men still in hiding from the authorities. Ahmed knew the other jailers resented this but were too afraid to use on the Hurs their own particular methods of control: there was no point withdrawing their food or water because the Hurs would happily starve to death; none of them smoked, out of allegiance to the Pir's old fatwa, so stopping their cigarettes was of no use; and no other prisoners could be persuaded to gang up on a Hur and beat him violently, so terrified were they of that deadly Hur intelligence system that could reach out beyond the walls of the prison and crush a man.

A year passed and the rebellion continued; when news reached Sindh that the Hurs had derailed the Lahore mail train and the son of Sir Ghulam Hidayatullah was killed, martial law was imposed on Sindh. Paratroopers and bombs were used against the bands of Hurs in the lands north of Sanghar and the farthest reaches of the Thar Desert. The British grew desperate in their attempts to contain the struggle, stopping up wells and raiding Hur villages.

The jail continued to fill with prisoners, until the very walls were cracking. And then, in 1943, the unthinkable happened. Ahmed was doing his rounds at three o'clock in the morning, the graveyard shift, when he discovered bodies of prisoners who had committed suicide in the cells. The sound of a tidal wave reached his ears, even though he was in the very depths of the prison. The lights were suddenly extinguished, but he could still feel the rushing wind on his face as dozens of guards and policemen ran down the halls.

"Hurry! Hurry! The colonel is waiting! Guards! Get Cell A ready!"

Ahmed saw one of the other wardens tearing past and grabbed out at his sleeve. "What's happening? What's going on?"

"Don't you know?" the man gabbled as he raced by. "He's here! He's been brought here!"

"Who?"

"The *Surhiya Badshah* . . ."

The month of February was the most terrifying of Ahmed's life. The security in and around the jail was increased a hundred-fold; every day Ahmed woke in fear that the Hurs would try to break into the jail to rescue their leader. The trial began at the court attached to the jail; Ahmed was too lowly to have anything to do with the proceedings, but the news from the courtroom came to him, and everyone who worked or lived at Central Jail, like fire in a forest. He brought that news to Sultan and Allah Bachayo every day, even though all jail officials were sworn to secrecy and if word got out that he worked in the cursed place where Pir Pagaro was imprisoned, his blood would be worth less than the gutter waters that spilled onto the streets from a burst sewer.

All pretense of playing chess was abandoned as the two old men leaned forward and listened hungrily to everything Ahmed had to tell them. "The charge is that he has waged war against the government, but his true crime is wanting to be a king of Sindh. And there is no Jinnah-Sahib to defend him this time. It's a Mr. Dialmal instead. A Hindu man."

"Just as well. Jinnah abandoned him last time!" said Sultan.

"No, he said it was a political case, not a criminal case, so he couldn't defend him," Allah Bachayo said.

"Still," sniffed Sultan. "He's too busy with the Muslim League to help a hero of Sindh . . ."

"And you should see all the people who come to the court," added Ahmed.

"Who?"

"The Junejos, the Narejos, Chatomal, and the Sirhindis are witnesses in his defense. Then there are a great many observers, including many British officers. There is a British colonel, a

Freddie Young, who they say helped his sons escape arrest. He sent them to Aligarh . . ."

"Pah! They want to make Aga Khans out of the sons of Sindh!" spat Allah Bachayo.

"But it will not be a fair trial," added Sultan.

Allah Bachayo scratched his head warily. "How do you know, Bha?"

"It's only for show. They want to stop the Hurs, so they go to the source to cut the cancer out. They will not give him the benefit of any doubt."

"Do you know, the prosecution witnesses speak from behind a curtain?" said Ahmed, shaking his head in wonder.

"The Hurs would hack them to pieces if they saw the faces of those who oppose their king. My son would have not even waited an instant," said Sultan. He looked at Ahmed and Allah Bachayo and smiled. "What, did you think I would mourn my son's death? Don't you know that my son is not dead? Martyrs live forever. That is why they are never afraid to die. Would more people live the way my son did, the British would have more than a revolt on their hands. They would have a catastrophe."

The trial went on. The entire nation came to a standstill; the jail officials had to maintain vigil as the prisoners threatened to riot and burn the jail down. All the while Pir Pagaro spent his days in the court and his nights in his special cell, which was equipped with a small verandah and a bathroom in recognition of his high status. Every morning, when Ahmed had to clear out the Pir's cell and check that there were no hidden messages in his trash, he found a huge pile of ash from the cigarettes that the Pir smoked all night, the only sign that the trial was affecting his nerves. But in a strange sense of loyalty to the man who had dared to become king, Ahmed spoke not a word about this to anyone.

Then one evening, after the last day in court, Ahmed heard the words that chilled his blood and made his heart almost stop beating in his chest.

"Prepare Cell D, Damani. Have it ready by eight o'clock this evening."

Cell D. The Death Cell.

Ahmed unlocked the cell and went in to sweep it and arrange bedding on the simple iron cot. There was one small window near the ceiling and Ahmed stood gazing out at a patch of blue sky intersected by the iron bars. This had been his life for the past three years. He was used to the darkness; his eyes hurt when he went out into strong light. He had grown accustomed to seeing men in chains, bowed down by the weight of their own crimes and the punishment visited upon them. He had seen men come into the jail swaggering and bold, and within weeks grow weak and desiccated, like the husks of grain discarded and thrown into the wind. But how would this small, dank cell hold a man greater than life? By now Ahmed had almost come to believe what the Hurs said about their *murshid:* that he was superhuman, that he moved with the stealth of a panther and the speed of a cheetah. Surely some calamity would fall upon them, for daring to take this man and sending him to his death?

When they brought Pir Pagaro to his cell, a flurry of guards dressed in black with their faces covered by black cloth surrounded him, but he was not in fetters. His white clothes and simple turban made him stand out from his jailers, as if he were already an angel—or a ghost. They brought him through a secret passage so that he would not be seen by the other prisoners, but the word had spread that he was being transported to the Death Cell, and the pressure in the air was as heavy and tense as if a great storm were about to unleash its fury on them.

Ahmed, his own face covered, watched him as he walked by.

There was nothing supernatural about this man, but he was regal and measured in his steps, a king in every sense of the word. He seemed to move in his own dimension of time and space. As he passed each man standing to attention, they all lowered their eyes. Ahmed thought he heard a whispered "Huzoor" from some of the jailers; but Pir Pagaro acknowledged nobody, met no one's eyes. He held a *tasbih* in his right hand and fingered the beads, his lips moving imperceptibly in remembrance of God.

Ya-Majid, Ya-Wajid, Ya-Wahid, Ya-Ahad, Ya-Samad, Ya-Qadir, Ya-Malik, Ya-Rehman, Ya-Rahim.

Ahmed watched from a corner as the Pir was led to his cell and locked inside. The jailers tried to get back to their business, but they wandered around aimlessly, meeting each other with haunted eyes and pale faces. As a low rung in the ladder of the men who ran the jail, Ahmed wasn't even supposed to be in that wing, but recent months had seen several of the other jailers simply refusing to turn up in the morning for fear of the Hurs and their vengeance. Only fear of his father had made Ahmed cling on to his job, but he had never dreamt that he would see this night. Even a man as harsh as Rahim Damani would be terrified of standing where Ahmed was tonight.

Then a cry rang out. "Ahmed! Ahmed Damani! Where are you?"

Ahmed's breath caught in his throat as he tried to make his legs work. He placed one foot in front of the other and dragged himself slowly to where Omar Bachani, the superintendent, was waiting for him outside the Death Cell. Ahmed had not met the man since the day he had started working at the jail. With a shock he saw that the man's hair, jet-black and thick when he'd seen him first, was streaked with white, as if he'd aged thirty years instead of three.

"Do you play chess?"

"Sir?"

"Chess, boy, chess. The prisoner wants to play. You're the only one here that knows how." Ahmed shivered; he knew the jail's spies were everywhere, but he hadn't expected them to waste their time on someone as unimportant as him . . .

And from the depths of the Death Cell, Ahmed heard a man's voice. *Jailer, come and play a game of chess with me.*

Shatranj. The Game of Kings: Ahmed had no choice but to obey. Somehow he felt as though he had turned into one of the Pir's *murids* and had to follow him until the end. The door of the cell was unlocked and hands on his back pushed him through. He stood there, knees knocking, hands trembling, his mouth dry and dull as cotton. The whispers behind him were snakes whipping at his ankles.

The man sat half shrouded in shadows in front of a chess set that had been hurriedly produced from somewhere; the pieces were set up clumsily. Pir Pagaro was slowly aligning them, centering each piece in the middle of each square.

"Come, jailer. Sit down."

Ahmed knew of men who would not sit in this man's presence. They knew the secret codes, the words of obeisance, the proper ways in which to show their devotion to him. But Ahmed was like a huge, clumsy child, all awkward arms and legs, in front of a giant. His heart was beating so hard he could feel it pounding in his throat. And yet somehow he managed to seat himself opposite the man and compose himself.

"Take off your mask, jailer. Let me see your face."

Ahmed's fingers reached up and pulled down his cloth. He felt no fear, no hesitation. There could only be protection in this man's presence.

"So. A young boy doing a man's job. You are not much older than my sons. Let us play."

Ahmed had been told by Sultan and Allah Bachayo that his gift at chess was his ability to play like a virtuoso at his instrument, transcending the immediacy of the moment to think and feel as though he were one with the board and the pieces of war. He had surpassed his masters' abilities long ago, and had synthesized their knowledge with his own talent and intuition. He had beaten scores of men at the café, and people knew him both by name and reputation. And yet for every move he made on the chessboard, Pir Pagaro was three moves ahead of him.

The young man tried to forget his fear as he examined the board more carefully than he had ever studied any schoolbook, calculating the value of the pieces on the board, analyzing the groups of squares, working out strategies to gain control of the game. He knew better than to let the Pir win on this night. Again and again he brought his major pieces to the center of the board, only to have Pir Pagaro entice him away from the vital squares, attacking his positions effortlessly with bishop and knight while keeping his king protected in the corner by his pawns.

The Pir laid traps for Ahmed, fought out of impossible corners with only a few pieces, executed complicated strategies that left Ahmed gasping with admiration. Game after game ended with the same word, softly uttered by the man who had driven the British to despair. *Checkmate. Checkmate. Checkmate.* Ahmed lost track of the number of times he heard that word in that long night, the smoke from the Pir's cigarettes creating a fog around them both, making them appear to Omar Bachani and the other men who spied on them as if they were figures from another world.

The British had spread rumors that the Pir was a monster—they spoke openly of his warped mentality, that he had the vacant stare of a madman. Ahmed knew that they only talked of him in this way because he had gone from being a valuable asset to a dangerous foe. Angel or demon, ally or enemy—Ahmed saw only a man in front of him, utterly absorbed in the game, joyful in victory, fearless in the face of death because he was supreme in the confidence that he could never die.

The game went on, end and beginning losing all meaning; it was one long tournament that seemed to last from sunset to sunrise. As a last resort, Ahmed decided to try the strategy of passed pawns, creating a complicated skeleton across the board, but the Pir created so many holes in the chain that in the end-game, he could bring out his king and move it to the center of the board. From there, it became the strongest piece in the whole game, threatening all Ahmed's other pieces until Ahmed threw up his hands in defeat and the Pir, without a word, began to set the pieces again in their starting positions, a slight glint of amusement illuminating his darkened eyes.

As dawn approached, the Pir's hand did not tremble; his eyes did not grow weary. But he became more and more withdrawn, pulling away from the earth, disengaging from its gravity. Ahmed could see it happening in front of his very eyes; his skin grew more translucent, his breaths longer and less frequent. If Ahmed reached out and placed his fingers on the man's wrist, he was sure the Pir's heartbeat would be the slow beating of a kettledrum, not the brisk beats of tom-tom and cymbals that were crashing in Ahmed's own chest.

They finished the game they were playing; Ahmed losing both rooks and then his queen in rapid succession to the Pir's elusive bishop. And then when the outcome was evident, the Pir, instead of announcing his checkmate, pushed his chair away from the board and slowly stood up. Ahmed could hear the rattling of the bars as Omar Bachani opened the locks, heard the murmurs of the British officers waiting to see the Pir escorted to the gallows. Ahmed wanted to weep, to shout, to rush forward and embrace the Pir, protect him from their bullets and their nooses. But he was paralyzed; he could only watch as the Pir slowly cleared all the chess pieces from the board, leaving it an empty battlefield without even the corpses of war left to keep the ground warm.

Then the Pir extinguished his last cigarette and turned to face the English man, a colonel of the British Army, who had come into the cell.

"Colonel Young," the Pir said, his deep baritone heavy with cigarette smoke.

"Your Excellency," replied the colonel. He, too, was a young man, with sandy blond hair and a sweeping mustache; Ahmed shrank back into a corner of the cell and kept his head bowed, biting hard on his lips to keep them from parting and betraying him to the two men.

"They are safe?"

"I have seen to it. They have been sent on to London. They will be taken care of as wards of the court."

"I thank you for your assistance."

The colonel bowed his head. "It is time."

The Pir glanced back at Ahmed Damani. The faintest hint of a smile appeared at the corners of the Pir's lips, lifting his mustache slightly. He looked like a man who was unafraid, and instead, amused at the vagaries of life, the unexpected destination to which fate had brought him. "A worthy opponent," he said to Ahmed. "A boy, but a worthy opponent." He turned and nodded at the colonel, then walked out of the cell unaided, past the rows of men who flanked the corridors to watch him go. Ahmed brought his sleeve to his eyes and wept then, brokenhearted, until his eyes grew bloodshot and his head grew too heavy to keep it lifted.

The Pir was thirty-four years old.

December 17, 2007

Ali and his friends were gathered outside Aapbara Chowk, shivering a little in the breeze. It was early afternoon, not the coldest time of the day for Islamabad, but the enormity of what they were about to do made them all feel the fear as a chill deep in their chests. He glanced around at Salma, who kept the ends of her shawl wrapped up around her cheeks, and gave her a cheery thumbs-up. She rolled her eyes back at him.

Salma had flown up to Islamabad with the rest of the activists, on this trip that Bilal, Imran, and Ferzana had organized, arranging for the Karachi activists to join the march supporting the deposed chief justice. She'd lied to her parents that she'd been asked to participate in a special medical conference for students. *A great honor,* she'd told them; *you can't let me miss this opportunity.* They'd relented, moved by the sincerity in her voice, she told Ali on the flight up to Islamabad.

"I feel so guilty lying to them . . ." She bit her lip, staring out of the plane window, as if she could see her parents' reproachful faces reflected in the pane of Plexiglas, or in the shapes of the towering clouds beyond.

"You're doing something really important, Salma," said Ali.

"I don't know. I don't know."

"Well, my moth—my parents wouldn't like it, either. So don't feel so bad."

"Really?"

"No way. I didn't even tell my father . . ." The word had come out unbidden; Ali blinked at his own mistake. This was the first time in years he'd spoken of his father truthfully. He looked away, overwhelmed for a moment with the futility of all the lies.

"Wow . . ." Salma's eyes were wide with wonder.

"What?"

"Well, you're so much older than me. I always thought that when I was thirty, nobody would be able to tell me what to do. Or that I wouldn't care what they thought of me by then . . ."

Ali opened his mouth to protest at Salma's having added five years onto his age, but then he saw she was smiling impishly, her cheeks dimpling on both sides. Reminded of his sister Jeandi, he sent up a small prayer that she would grow up one day into a young woman as brave as this one. "At this age, if your parents don't like what you're doing, you're probably doing the right thing."

"I'll take your word for it."

Before coming to Islamabad this time, he'd told his mother his plans; he had to stop being controlled by her disapproval, or her fear. She had looked at him wearily when he said he was flying out to Islamabad to take part in the demonstration. "I suppose you'll be covering it for work," she said.

"No," Ali had said. "I've taken an indefinite leave of absence."

"What does that mean? You've quit?"

Not yet, Ali could have said. Or, *it's only temporary.* "For the time being. I just want to see what my options are." She would not understand that he had to leave City24 because of his desire to be more than just an observer to the events that were taking place around them. He didn't want to chronicle them: he wanted to live them. Nor would she ever appreciate that he had grown weary, after twenty-five years, of being only a participant in his own life. He needed, at last, to be its arbiter.

"And you've got exams to study for," his mother had added, after a long pause in which he looked away while she studied him as though it were the first time she'd ever set eyes on him.

Ali had repeated halfheartedly, "Yes. I've got exams to study for." His exams had finished the day before the demonstration, but he had no idea how he'd done. He'd already failed one class; he'd have to repeat it again the following term. But even the classroom had lost its appeal, compared to what he was learning every time he went out onto the streets to protest with the People's Resistance.

Ali had noticed, as if for the first time, the lines around his mother's eyes and nose, the gray in her hair, the veins bulging from the backs of her thin hands. She'd been through enough, he decided. There were people who derived their strength from being angry all the time, from holding grudges, and nursing grievances. Ali was discovering for himself the possibility that real strength might actually come from generosity and tolerance; he no longer wanted to be the kind of person who thought of compassion as a weakness, forgiveness as foolishness. He wanted to forgive his mother for not being able to understand him. For not being able to talk to him, or listen to him when he was the one who needed to communicate. And even for accepting so passively the treatment she'd received from his father. By putting down the burden of his anger at her for being only what she was, he would be freeing himself.

He had reached forward and hugged her unexpectedly. "What

are you doing, Ali?" she said, bewildered, trying to push him away, then surrendering to the strength of his embrace.

"I don't know, Ama." But he'd been surprised to realize how good it felt; that home would always be the feel of his mother's arms around him.

Ali's thoughts then drifted back to his last day at work. He'd left the City24 News building early in the evening—the first time he'd quit the office before 7 p.m. any time in the last year. He carried his personal belongings in a flimsy box, hoisting it high and stretching his arms underneath to hold it closed. Just as he thought the box would spill all its contents on the road, he'd spotted Jehangir rounding the corner of the building, talking on his mobile phone and gesticulating energetically in the air. Ali set the box down on the ground and waited for Jehangir to approach him.

They hadn't spoken since the day they'd betrayed each other in front of Ameena; they'd avoided each other in the office and maintained no contact outside. Ameena had never mentioned the conversation to either of them, but she had subtly started to pay more attention to Ali, while discounting Jehangir's contributions at work. Every time she called Ali into her office to discuss the People's Resistance movement, Ali wanted to make an excuse and run in the other direction, but he suppressed his discomfort and went to her office, a pleasant smile nailed onto his face. Jehangir always glanced away when Ali came out. Ali often escaped to the bathroom and locked himself in a stall, kneeling in front of the toilet and trying to retch out all the anxiety and stress festering in the pit of his stomach. Finally, it all grew too much, and Ali had walked into Ameena's office that afternoon and resigned.

She'd stared at him, her fingers steepled in front of her face. "Are you sure?"

"Yes."

"Don't be so hasty. I'm not letting you go that easily. Take a leave of absence. Take as much time as you need. But I'm going to call you one of these days, and you have to come back."

Ali had left her office, grateful that at least she hadn't said anything about his father or his family. He hoped he would never have to see her again.

When Jehangir had spotted Ali, he stopped in his tracks and slowly switched his phone off. He came forward, stopped, took another step, then came to a halt a few feet away from Ali, the box between them marking an invisible boundary line. The cars and buses passed on the busy street; the men pouring out of the building's large double glass doors stepped around them like water flowing around a small island in the middle of a river.

"So," said Jehangir.

"So." Ali shook his arms, wringing out his wrists to relieve the tension that was gripping his body.

"You're off, then?"

"Looks like it."

They both glanced away. Ali found a point somewhere in the traffic to focus on, while Jehangir stared down at his shoes. The pause grew longer, heavier with their unspoken words. Ali had considered telling Jehangir that it wasn't what he'd said about Ali's father that had made him decide to leave. Should he have apologized for revealing Jehangir's secret? There must have been things Jehangir wanted to say to Ali as well—they couldn't possibly end their friendship like this, on a busy street, with men staring curiously at them from the tops of buses as they drove by in the evening rush hour.

"*Yaar* . . ." began Jehangir.

Ali had glanced at him, hungry for the reconciliation he hoped Jehangir wanted as well. It didn't matter what Jehangir had said about his father. How long would he have kept his father's second life a secret?

But Jehangir had pointed at the box "What's in there?"

"Just my stuff, you know . . . CDs, a few photographs, books . . . nothing important."

"Are you sure you aren't taking your computer with you?"

"I should. It's the least they owe me. Bastards."

Jehangir's lips twisted in a half grin. "So what are you going to do now?"

"I don't know. I just finished my exams, and then I've got one more semester before I graduate in May, so . . . I'll just concentrate on university for a while, then look for something more serious next summer."

"Yeah."

"Yeah."

Jehangir had scratched his head, fiddled with his mobile phone. Ali was starting to sweat, the fumes from the cars and buses making him feel queasy. He wondered if he should just pick up the box again and start walking to his car. Maybe there really was nothing more to say.

"Heard from Sunita?" Jehangir asked.

"What?"

"I said, have you heard from Sunita?"

"Oh . . ." If Ali heard her name when he wasn't expecting it, then he had to press his fists into his eyes to keep them dry. This was one of those unexpected moments, but he kept his fists down by his sides. "No, I haven't heard from her. It's been a while."

"Sorry, *yaar.*"

Ali had nodded. Another pause, filled with beeping horns and squealing brakes from the stop-and-go traffic. Then he decided to ask anyway. What did he have to lose now? "How did you know about my father?"

Ali could still remember how Jehangir had tensed, as if expecting a blow from Ali. When none came, he dropped his eyes to the ground, then raised them again and met Ali's gaze with half-hidden regret. "You said your father was a bureaucrat but I thought, there's no way you could have gone to study in Dubai on a bureaucrat's pension. I thought he was a tax evader. You could have told me, Ali."

Ali shook his head. "All those things you said about my family . . . that's why I didn't tell you anything. It was exactly what I was trying to avoid."

"I didn't mean . . . I know you're not like that. You're different."

Ali had ignored the usual words that so many meant as a compliment but which always sounded to him like a condemnation. "How long have you known?"

Jehangir had shrugged in his customary way, lips pouting, head bent to the side. "I don't know. Six months, maybe? There was a picture of your father in the newspaper, attending some PPP function in Hyderabad. He looked just like you. It caught my eye, and then I saw that you had the same last name as him. I did some digging. I didn't expect to find any of this out."

Ali knew he had to end the conversation or he would just sink down onto the street and begin to weep. He was tired, so tired of all the pretense, and it hadn't saved him any trouble in the end. Haroon was still dead and Sunita was still gone and his father still lived in the house in Bath Island, a universe away from him.

He put out his hand to Jehangir. "I'll see you around."

Jehangir looked at Ali's hand as if deciding whether or not to take it. Finally, just when Ali was about to withdraw it and walk away, he leaned forward and shook it. "Good luck, Ali." Jehangir's hand was cool and dry, the clasp noncommittal.

"You, too." They might have embraced had the parting been taking place under different circumstances. But there were no promises to keep in touch. No long goodbyes. Just a severing of connections, almost clinical in its efficiency. Ali watched his friend retreat into the building. Then he bent down and picked up the box, relishing the physical pain that overshadowed the sorrow in his heart.

* * *

The police were watching them warily, lined up in ragged ranks on the knolls around the Chowk. The trees behind them formed a second line of defense, casting eerie shadows and filtering the sunlight through branches so that everything appeared somber and gray. Usually traffic would be whizzing by, but they'd cordoned off the roads so that the five hundred protestors had room to gather on the street, their placards and banners at the ready. A few hundred yards away stood the Lal Masjid, an invisible reminder to them all of what the state was capable of doing when its fury was aroused. The state of emergency had been lifted on Saturday night, but they knew that the gesture, aimed at pleasing the Western countries that were pushing Pakistan in the name of democracy, had no real significance.

They were nervously pawing the ground like bulls before the death fight in a Spanish stadium. One of the leaders of the protest, a tall young student from nearby Quaid-e-Azam University, a black band tied around his arm, glanced at his watch, then nodded to the others. On his signal, they raised their placards and began to shout, "Go, Musharraf, go! Go, Musharraf, go!"

Ali, Salma, and the crowd—made up mostly of black-coated lawyers and university students—joined the rising chorus and pushed their fists skyward. The policemen gave them a wide berth, their faces impassive, although their eyes followed the group with suspicion and hostility. There were more than Ali had seen at any demonstration in Karachi. Lined up around the protestors, they were clad in full riot gear, their weapons adding extra tension to the electricity in the air. Some of the students were holding sticks, but Ali and his group had refused the ones they'd been offered. A passing man in a *shalwar kameez* and a thin beard held out a stick to Bilal and nodded at him to take it.

Bilal shook his head. "We don't want to fight with the police. We just want to make our voices heard."

The man snorted. "You'll remember me when the fun starts." He walked off toward another little group and they could see him offering the stick to other people down the line.

"Maybe we should listen to him," muttered Ali, standing on Bilal's left, Salma a few steps behind him, arm in arm with Ferzana.

"He's MI. Military intelligence. They want us to clash with the police. Makes us look bad," replied Bilal.

"Oh shit," said Ali. Then he jerked his head back in Salma's direction. "Don't scare them."

Imran raised an eyebrow. "They're grown-ups, Ali. They know what this is all about."

The protestors stood in the same place for about fifteen minutes, raising their signboards and shouting slogans. Then the men in front shouted, "Release the chief justice!" and Ali's heart began to race.

The crowd took up the cry, a wave that swelled from the beginning of the gathering and rolled powerfully in all directions. And then feet began to follow intention, as the people began to walk. Salma grabbed Ali's arm and shouted in his ear, "Where are they going?"

"The chief justice's house!" he shouted back. "Come on!"

They began to move as one, pressing forward, adrenaline surging as they chanted to the rhythm of their marching feet. Ali saw the excitement on the faces around him: they were laughing, smiling, lips parted to take in huge gulps of air, as if tasting oxygen for the first time in their lives. This was the feeling he loved, his senses sharpened, everything looking and sounding clearer and sharper than he'd ever remembered. Nothing before this moment existed; nothing after it mattered. Here, now, they were only of this time, as excited as children on their first day of school, as filled with potential as newborns in their first day on earth.

He knew the beatings had started when the people in front of him began to move in strange, disjointed jerks, the smooth flow of their march disrupted at the front, then ricocheting back like the carriages of a derailed train flying off the rails, one after another.

The police, who had maintained their distance all along, were now in the midst of the protestors, raising their batons and bringing them down onto the protestors' heads, shoulders, hips, legs. The students tried to raise their sticks in self-defense, but they were no match for the professional fury unleashed upon them. Screams rang out, punctuating the *thwack*ing sounds of metal landing on bone. Ali saw the tall QAU student sinking down under a sweating policeman's quick, brutal blows. He whirled around to look for Salma, but she had disappeared from view. Another policeman had caught Ferzana in a tight grip, her arms pinioned behind her back, her face twisted into a grimace of pain. Ali lunged forward to try to get her out of the policeman's grasp, but the crowds surging around him were a thick wall that he couldn't penetrate.

"Salma! Salma!" Ali screamed. His voice was drowned in the tumult; he desperately scanned the bodies on the ground, but she was nowhere to be seen.

Somehow the crowd gathered strength again and resumed marching toward the chief justice's house. People were limping, clutching limp wrists, holding hands to their bruised heads, but they still continued to walk. *"Release the chief justice!"* The cry thundered from their throats, made all the more powerful for the raggedness of their voices. Ali was jostled forward; even if he tried to fight against the tide, he would have been pushed until he too fell on the ground and was trampled by their moving feet.

The students pushed the policemen back, gaining a little space to regroup and carry on with the march. They made some headway, gaining about twenty yards or so; Ali hoped they might actually reach their destination. They planned to stand outside the chief justice's house and continue the demonstration there for at least an hour. He had to find Salma . . . was that her, over there, in the glasses with a scarf thrown over her head? But the girl who looked like her from a distance turned out to be a lawyer whose black coat had been ripped off by the police.

An armored car drew up alongside the protestors and began to fire tear gas shells. Ali's eyes began to itch, but he was too far away from them to be blinded as yet. The students drew back, screaming, trying to dodge the shells. One landed directly on a lawyer's leg and exploded, throwing him to the ground. He lay there, blood oozing into the shreds of his trousers, staining them dark brown. The police lifted their weapons and began to fire on the crowd: rubber bullets that couldn't kill them but knocked them off their feet and stunned them into submission. Some of the policemen bent down, picked up stones, and hurled them at the protestor's heads.

Chaos had taken over: students ran in all directions, tear gas rising up from the ground in twisted curls like snakes coiling around their legs and waists. Ali's eyes were beginning to blister. He reached for his cloth and bottle of mineral water, but was too disoriented to screw off the cap and pour it onto the cloth. The water bottle dropped from his hands; he wrapped the cloth around his mouth and nose, but without the water it was useless, and he too began to choke and cough and retch.

Through the haze, Ali saw a policeman beating a woman next to him, and when the man had finished with her, she was left kneeling on the ground, her hands covering her face, blood seeping from between her fingers. Two students rushed to her and helped her up, but she fainted in their arms and had to be carried to a waiting ambulance. The police charged, gas masks and black riot gear turning them into strange faceless monsters who rushed at them again and again. The terror that had seized them was a dog snapping at Ali's ankles as he ran from left to right and back again without being able to see where he was going.

Then a strong hand gripped his upper arm, yanking him so hard he thought his shoulder had been dislocated. Ali tried to pull away but was thrown off balance and dragged halfway across the street on the backs of his heels, his arms freewheeling in the air. Strong hands shoved him in all directions; he felt himself being lifted up and launched toward the open doors of a police van. He landed inside, tripping over the legs of the students already rounded up and packed inside like slabs of meat. Policemen screamed into their faces, spraying them with spittle, jeering, calling them foul names. Then the driver started the van, and they were raced away from the street.

Inside the van, people moaned and clutched at their wounds, while others stared straight ahead of them in shocked, terrified silence. Tears streamed from all their eyes. They coughed and choked in agonized whimpers. Ali didn't know whether he wanted to scream or cry, as he felt their humanity ebbing away with every passing second.

The Living Saints

When you travel to the interior, it seems as though you have stepped back in time; the moment you alight from your car or train, you realize that nothing has changed over the last two hundred years, and nothing ever will. This is what Pir Sikandar Hussein thought as he disembarked from the train in Larkana, in June 1979, seven weeks after Zulfikar Ali Bhutto had been hanged by Zia's military regime. Sikandar Hussein had come to Larkana to pay his respects at the prime minister's grave, to meet with his family and offer his condolences. He could not sit still in Karachi and nurse his broken heart; he had to do something, and this seemed the right thing to do.

The entire country was in mourning, as much for their lost son as for their lost freedom; the madman General Zia had stolen from them the idea that ordinary men could have a voice in the destiny of their nation, and murdered its messenger. Democracy is a dangerous beast to those petty men, those tinpot generals, who must draw their weapons and strike it until it is dead, and only then can they sleep peacefully at night, while the rest of humanity suffers, generation after generation.

Sikandar always tried to prepare himself for the heat of the interior, but nothing could truly ready him for the way it slapped him on the face when he emerged from a cool room and out into the sunlight. The sky was white as a furnace, the air dry like the inside of a *tandoor*. You could leave the town, go into the desert, and look into the distance, to the horizon: the line where the sand touched sky shimmered and danced with blue water in the form of a stream or a pool. But there would be no water there; the desert seduced you with false promises, phantom oases. It was the desert's only lie: things were much more duplicitous back in the places where men established their settlements, put down their roots, and tried to bend nature to their will.

The cities were where men learned to cheat each other, out of greed, their immense need to profit from another man's failures. Sikandar knew that greed was the biggest flaw in a man's soul: his *nafs*, his ego, is nourished by greed until it grows so big that it threatens to burst with its own decadence.

Greed and fear was what kept Sikandar's family, a landowning family from outside Sukkur—zamindars, or feudals, as the city men disparagingly called them—in the Dark Ages. And not just his family, but many others like it. For fear of losing their grip on their land during the shaky years after Partition, they clamped down on the peasants who tilled their fields and refused to give them anything more than what it took to stay alive. For fear of progress and change, they refused to educate their sons. (Sikandar still wished his father, Pir Hassan Ahmed Shah, had let him go to school, in that cool white building in the middle of town where sixty wealthy men's sons had learned Sindhi and

English since the days of the British. He, too, longed to clutch a satchel and learn his lessons on a little handheld blackboard, to read books and be taught how to do sums. But his father scoffed at the idea: "He has lands, he will never have to be anyone's servant, why should we send him to school?" Which is why Pir Sikandar Hussein, at the age of forty, could barely read or write. He swore every day by Almighty Allah that when he had sons, they would go to the best schools, the grandest universities. Even if he had to send them to England, or farther away, he would make sure they were educated men who could survive beyond this noble, limited existence.)

Instead of being sent to school, Sikandar lived a life of indolence and pleasure, as did all his brothers and cousins. They went shooting in the winter, traveled to Hyderabad and Karachi looking for the amusement of the cinemas, hotels, and the beach when the summer months lay still and heavy in the interior. In truth it was a fool's life, but they thought themselves living saints by virtue of their bloodline—they could trace their lineage all the way back to the Prophet, peace be upon him—and their possessions.

As they grew older, the boys watched their fathers and uncles conduct the business of their agriculture, and their politics; for a zamindar's survival depended not just on what he raised, but who he knew. The right connections could have your watercourses opened, your taxes overlooked, your rivals squeezed. Anger the wrong person and you would find your canals dry, penalties levied on your lands until you were in debt for the next thirty years. The zamindars therefore always befriended those in power, or sought to be involved in politics in some way or another. Sikandar's family had achieved these goals with some measure of success, because by the late 1960s, his father's name was well known all over Sindh. "Pir Hassan Ahmed Shah," the people would say, "is a great man." And Sikandar himself would speak of his father in tones of reverence and admiration, because *sayeds* and zamindars were always the staunchest believers in their own mythology.

They knew the Bhuttos of Larkana; everyone did, as they were the largest landowners in the area surrounding that town: a man could ride on a horse for three days and still be on Bhutto property. Not only this, but Sir Shahnawaz Bhutto had the ear of all the important officials of the British Raj: the governor of Sindh, the commissioner, and contacts as far away as the Bombay Presidency who ruled Sindh until the 1930s. Sikandar saw him once, when he was a small child, and Sir Shahnawaz had come to visit Pir Hassan Ahmed in Sukkur. Sikandar's father summoned him and his brothers into his drawing room to meet the great man; but Sikandar was shy and could not speak a word when he was introduced to Sir Shahnawaz, a slim, elegant man with dark eyes and an even darker mustache, who sat upright in a leather chair and sipped at a cup of tea served in fine china, for Pir Hassan had last year bought a Wedgwood tea service set from England in order to impress his guests.

"I have a son, Zulfikar, who is a little older than you are," Sir Shahnawaz said to Sikandar kindly—in those days elders hardly acknowledged the young. "He is away, studying in Bombay. And you, little man? What class are you in?"

Sikandar blushed scarlet. To cover up his shame, his father quickly said, "In Bombay? Well, well, well . . ."

"Yes, as the Prophet said, 'Seek education, even if you must go to China.' Well, Zulfikar is not in China, but he has ambitions of going to America, and he is a brilliant boy. Did you know that he was an activist in the Muslim League when he was at the Cathedral School?"

"I didn't know that," grunted Pir Hassan.

"Our children must be educated," continued Sir Shahnawaz, thumping at the arm of his leather chair. "They are our greatest treasures! And only then, when they are men of knowledge, will they be able to look after the poor. It is our duty to care for those less privileged than ourselves."

"Of course, of course," Pir Hassan murmured. Sikandar was not sure whether his father gave a moment's thought to the poor, apart from how hard they worked on his lands. But he was not confident enough to argue with Sir Shahnawaz, who was so eloquent that he had earned a position of power in the court at Junagardh, in neighboring Gujarat. Neither did Pir Hassan share Sir Shahnawaz's sense of obligation to the poor—born of his marriage to an honest but impoverished Hindu lady, Lakhi Bai. Pir Hassan, in contrast, was married to his cousin when he was fourteen and she was sixteen, in order to keep her inheritance within the family. So bound by tradition and *purdah* was she that her name did not even appear on the wedding invitations. This nameless, faceless lady was Sikandar's mother; none of them was any match for the revolutionary way in which Sir Shahnawaz chose to nurture his own family.

So Sikandar lived the life of a young Pir in Sindh, while Zulfikar Bhutto rose to power like a comet streaking through the sky, a tail of brilliance and accomplishment stretching out far behind him. Sikandar and his cousins gathered around the radio and listened in envious admiration as he spoke to the United Nations in 1957, as the youngest member of Pakistan's delegation. They knew this was a tremendous honor, though if you asked them, they would have been hard-pressed to tell you where the United Nations was, or what it stood for. The next year, Sikandar's younger brother Imtiaz burst into his bedroom door clutching a newspaper in his hand. "Look, look, Adda Saeen! Bhutto has been made energy minister!"

Sikandar could only look at the photograph and make out some of the words: General Ayub had taken over in a coup earlier that year, and now that he'd formed his cabinet, Bhutto was included, again as the youngest minister. Only thirty years old, and he was treading a path that men ten, twenty years older could only dream of walking. Sikandar was half Bhutto's age, but he could no more dream of becoming a government minister than he could dream of becoming a space traveler.

"How does he do it?" Sikandar said, sitting up in bed, pulling the *rilli* around him.

"It's the way he talks. He makes everyone fall in love with him the moment he opens his mouth," replied Imtiaz.

"Maybe it's his destiny," said Sikandar.

"Adda Saeen, you're always talking about destiny. You're beginning to sound like a holy man!"

"Well, we *are* Pirs . . ." But in honesty Sikandar was confused about that as well. Yes, they were the descendants of a saint whose tomb lay not far from their home, and they were meant to be its guardians and overseers. Pir Hassan's men made sure the walls of the shrine were strong, that they did not crack and fall on the heads of the people of the nearby villages who flocked to the shrine every day, bringing their woes and problems to the saint, begging him for his help in their everyday affairs. Pir Hassan organized feedings of the poor every Thursday night, arranging for huge pots of *biryani* to be cooked and given to the hungry who waited patiently for their free meal and dedicated their prayers to them and our progeny. And he accepted tribute from those families of the area who were rich and wealthy, and needed his prayers in return.

But if they were meant to be the keepers of the spiritual world, why were they so concerned with the affairs of this earth? Pir Hassan went over his accounts every morning with his *munshi*, who sat in front of him with the ledger books spread out on the table: the numbers written in neat rows of Sindhi, forming a picture of incomings and outgoings in the farm kitty. If the numbers were good, the *munshi* received a nod of approval; if they were bad, Sikandar's father spent the whole morning shouting and raving at the simple man, who clutched his accounts nervously and tried to make the Pir see reason, that the failures were not his fault, but acts of God: the wheat crop had been cut down in the recent storms; the bananas had been stricken by worms. The man contracted to take the onions had run away before making the final payment. The sharecroppers on the far landholding had vanished overnight, leaving mangos that needed to be harvested but were now rotting on the trees.

It wasn't just money that occupied Pir Hassan's time: he spent most of his evenings hobnobbing with important government officials; he spent lavishly on dinners and parties where big men came to drink his whiskey and eat his food. Sometimes he would take them out for grand *shikar*, and they would stay out camping for days in the desert and mountains, returning with trophies of deer and ibex and wild sheep piled high in their convoy of jeeps. The villagers would watch in awe as they passed, bowing and clasping their hands in salute to the zamindars and their honored guests. They must have been the only people to walk the earth who were not just living saints, but kings as well. Sikandar's brothers and cousins accepted this as the natural order of things, but Sikandar wondered if this was really what they were put on this earth to do, and be.

"You don't understand," Pir Hassan would always tell his son. "We have to live this way. If we didn't have all this show, all this influence, do you think my rivals would wait one day to take over our lands, gobble up your inheritance? We don't live in the dream world of Gandhi and Jinnah. We live in dangerous times. We have to be strong, now more than ever."

There was one matter on which Sikandar tried to defy his father: he engaged a private tutor to teach him the rudiments of reading and writing. Over the months of his sixteenth year, he learned the alphabet from the Sindhi *qaida* that seven-year-olds used in school. By this time Zulfikar Bhutto was helping President Ayub to negotiate the Indus Water Treaty, which gave the waters of the Sutlej, Beas, and Ravi to India, while Pakistan received the waters of the Jhelum, Chenab, and Indus. By this time Sikandar understood that India had received more than Pakistan, because the eastern waters were far more powerful than the western ones. But Bhutto had impressed Ayub, who appointed him foreign minister two years later, and if his star had begun to shine when Sikandar was a child, by the time he became a man, it had burst into full glory, and was now a powerful sun that gave them all warmth and light in which to blossom.

In contrast to Bhutto's life, Sikandar's milestones were few and far between: each birthday brought with it a gift of some sort from his father—his twenty-first birthday in 1965 was significant because his father bought him his first car, a stately white Cadillac, and it was the year war broke out between Pakistan and India, barely twenty years after they'd separated. Bhutto negotiated a peace treaty with the Indian prime minister, which was so conciliatory to India that the prime minister died—"of happiness," according to Bhutto—the day after the treaty was signed. Sikandar drove his jealous cousins up and down the streets of Sukkur in his Cadillac while people rioted in the streets against the exchange of prisoners and the shame of having to go back to Pakistan's prewar boundaries. Sikandar and his cousins felt far removed from those disturbances; on the lands, watching the wheat grow tall and the mangoes heavy on the trees, they felt that no matter what happened in the outside world, here they would rule forever.

Two years later, Bhutto had split from President Ayub over

the acrimony generated by the 1965 war. He began to travel up and down the country giving political speeches. Without telling anyone in his family, Sikandar went to hear a speech in October 1966. He watched as Bhutto stood at a podium and enthralled the masses of poor people with his rhetoric, his powerful words. He was tall and handsome, full of charisma. Sikandar could not take his eyes off Bhutto as he raised his hands in the air and clapped them above his head, shouting, "Islam is our faith, democracy is our policy, socialism is our economy. Power to the people!" The crowds swelling in front of him raised their hands, taking up his cry with one voice. His face glowed with their adulation. Sikandar felt he was witnessing the beginning of a revolution, and shivered, because he did not know what it would mean for his family.

Bhutto became so popular that in 1967 he formed his own party, the Pakistan People's Party; entranced by his message of people power, men and women from all over joined, whether they were Sindhi, Punjabi, or Muhajir. In that same year Pir Hassan arranged Sikandar's marriage with his cousin, Pir Hassan's brother's daughter. The young couple was married in Sukkur in December, but their wedding guests, arriving in Sukkur from all parts of Sindh, faced erratic trains and roads blocked by PPP activists who were holding protest strikes and marches all over the country against Ayub's dictatorship.

Sikandar's wife became pregnant, and he ignored Bhutto's metamorphosis, concentrating instead on the transformation of his own life. He began to prepare a portion of the family house for his wife and unborn child, and already inquired about the best schools in Hyderabad and Karachi for when his son would take his first steps toward his future as a learned man.

But as Bhutto's star climbed ever higher, disaster struck Sikandar. His wife died in childbirth and took with her their child, a daughter. Sikandar was himself unable to recall most of that terrible day, when he waited outside the *haveli*, the women's quarters, but he did remember standing against a wall, kicking at the dirt with his shoes, when a mangy little kitten came walking in front of him. Sikandar looked at its thin face, its ribs straining against its meager chest, and went to the kitchen to fetch a plate of milk.

As he passed by the chamber where his wife lay in her childbed, he strained for any sound, any sign of what was going on inside. But there was only a deadly silence. Then suddenly the air was cut by the wails of the women who were attending her, shrieks and howls of grief and horror.

Sikandar dropped the saucer on the floor. The milk splashed onto his legs and puddled around his feet. Before anyone could find him to tell what had happened, he ran outside. The kitten was still squirming in the dust. He picked it up and walked slowly to the nearest well. He leaned over the sides, smelling the dank, blackened water, his eyes blinded by the shadows inside. It must have been a type of madness that made him take the kitten and suddenly fling it into the depths of the well. He still begged Allah for forgiveness for that evil deed, and knew he would carry the sin of it to his grave.

After that, he put aside all thoughts of family and children, even though his mother pleaded with him to remarry within the year. But he could not bear the thought of embarking upon that exercise so soon. Instead, he threw himself into *zamindari*, taking over from his father much of the day-to-day running of the farm. He rose before dawn, reciting his prayers before going out to inspect the fields and take accounts from the overseers. He did not return until noon, when the heat was so strong that a grown man could faint if he spent half an hour in an unshaded place. It was a punishing schedule, but he did not feel he deserved anything better.

Sikandar began again to follow Zulfikar Bhutto's path to power, as the People's Party won a huge number of parliament seats in the 1970 elections. He listened to the radio into the dark long hours of the night, the whine of the shortwave comforting him in his loneliness, and learned that the Bengali Sheikh Mujib, leader of a rival party, had won the majority in East Pakistan. Bhutto refused to allow him to become the prime minister of Pakistan. The night that President Yahya had Mujib arrested and the Pakistani army embarked upon a genocide that saw the streets of Dhaka run black with innocent blood, Sikandar was haunted by dreams in which faceless dead Bengalis knocked on his door and cried and asked him, *For what crimes have we been killed?*

By the end of 1971, they were plunged into war. Bangladesh was a place that nobody in the interior had ever seen, but the war reached out beyond its borders to strangle everyone who laid claims to that far-off land. At night Indian Air Force jets whined over Sindh, bombing army installations, the cold clear desert sky lit up by the flashes of incendiary weapons, which hazed the air with phosphorescence and drowned out the stars. Women wept under the stairs and in makeshift bomb shelters, while children eagerly put up black paper on the windows and practiced marching to air-raid sirens. Everyone in Sindh, including Sikandar, believed that Pakistan would win in the end; patriotism was a tide that swept everyone along with it, inflating their egos and convincing them they could beat the Indians simply because Allah was on their side.

Ya Fattah, called all the *maulvis* in their Friday sermons. Sikandar sat among the congregation and listened to their speeches, as incendiary as the bombs that were falling all over Pakistan. *He is the Victorious One, He will grant us Victory over our enemies!*

And then they lost.

Yahya resigned and turned power over to Bhutto, and while

the rest of Pakistan mourned, all of Sindh was enthralled with the ascent of a fellow son of the soil to the most powerful position in Pakistan.

"We should join the People's Party," Imtiaz, Sikandar's brother, told Sikandar one evening as they sat smoking after dinner in the verandah.

"Why?"

"A Sindhi prime minister, Saeen! We must show our support."

"You care for nationalization? And labor reform?" said Sikandar, who by now could read well and was following the debate in the newspapers and on the radio. "Do you know he's been talking about land reform?"

Imtiaz's face darkened. "I know, I've heard it, too, but if we don't show our loyalty, it will be worse for us when it actually happens."

Sikandar shook his head. "You join if you want to. Leave me out of it."

"But Saeen! We have to show our unity as a family . . ."

"Leave me out of it."

Imtiaz fell silent, hurt by Sikandar's offhanded dismissals. By the next morning, he seemed to have forgotten about his idea of joining the party. It was a relief to Sikandar; politics had never interested him, despite his father's and uncle's endless appetite for the petty machinations of rural governance. He preferred the daily rhythms of agriculture, which never varied or wavered, no matter who was in office or out of it.

But in early 1973, when Sikandar's friends in the district government whispered in his ear that the government planned to take over a million acres and give them to the landless peasants of the province, Sikandar summoned his father, brothers, and cousins to a series of discussions to devise a rational strategy to deal with the coming storm.

Imtiaz, his voice trembling with indignation, began to shout even before he sat down in the leather chair where Sir Shahnawaz Bhutto had talked to Sikandar all those years ago. "How can he do this to us? Bhutto is one of us. His father was one of the biggest zamindars in all of Sindh. How can he betray us like this?"

"It's his Hindu mother," their cousin Akbar spat. "She's the one that filled his head with ridiculous ideas. Because she came from nothing, so he thinks that he owes the poor a debt that *we* have to pay on his behalf. It's preposterous!"

"Don't speak like that about a lady," Imtiaz said.

"All right, but it's still her fault!"

"But what should we do?" This was Pir Hassan, whose voice quavered—Sikandar glanced at him and took in at a glance how white his hair had become, how he had lost inches in height, pounds in weight. He had placed the turban on Sikandar's head last year in the *dastarbandi* ceremony that conferred upon him the title of *sardar*, head of the clan, but for all intents and purposes Sikandar had been leading the family for the last three or four years now. Responsibility had made Pir Hassan old, and now it was Sikandar's turn to become aged and haggard through its demands. Just this morning he had noticed the first strands of white in his hair when he combed it. He should have had a wife to show her, so that she could coo and fuss and assure him that he was not getting old, just wise. He should have had a child who could sit on his knee and pull his beard with both fists, so that he knew that when he became as old as his father, someone else would wear the turban and look after all their concerns. But Allah had decreed something else for him, and he had no choice but to fight for the future of their family, such as it was.

"I've devised a plan," Sikandar said. "You'll all transfer some of your land to your children and wives. I've worked out the numbers, the amounts, and the notaries who are willing to file the papers.

Come here on Friday after the prayers and we'll start the process. But we have to act fast. The reforms will come soon, I'm told."

"And you, my son?" said his father. "In whose name will you put your land?"

"I will transfer my land to anonymous holders. *Khatedars*."

"Are they trustworthy people?"

"Very."

"Good, my son. What else?"

"We'll sell off our unproductive land, get rid of the useless pieces. Consolidate our holdings and distribute across the family so that none of us exceeds the allowed amount. Don't you worry, Father. We'll be all right."

Sikandar's brothers and cousins were looking at him in admiration, at his unshakable confidence. They had always thought of him as somewhat of a fool, discounting him while they rushed around in their pursuits, which they deemed more important than his interests and activities. But now that the time had come where they needed a brother to look up to, a son to trust, they all came back to Sikandar. The power in his hands was like a strong horse that could buck and throw him at any moment. But they were sure that he had learned, over the past ten years, how to ride.

"Don't worry," Sikandar repeated. "Bhutto cannot defeat us. He has been prime minister for three years. We have been zamindars for three centuries. We will survive."

* * *

Bhutto was now buried in his family graveyard at Gahri Khuda Baksh, next to his father. Sikandar had made the shorter journey from Larkana to Naudero, the Bhutto ancestral village, and now stood at his tomb, jostled by the crowds in the morning sun, watching as they pushed and shoved each other, men, women, children, the elderly—Sindhis of all ages and classes, come to pay homage to their slain martyr. Most were weeping openly. Others read from Qurans and little prayer booklets, while those who could not read simply fingered prayer beads and whispered the names of God. People held green cloths and strings of roses and marigolds to lay on his grave. The wound was still open, their loss still bleeding and raw. Their grief was a live animal that lay stretched out on the ground and howled its loss to the world.

"They've taken our son, our son . . ."

"Our father . . . stolen him from us . . ."

"May Allah Saeen bring a painful death on that traitor, that tyrant, General Zia!"

"Ameen!"

"May he burn in hell for the ignominy he's heaped on Shaheed Bhutto's head!"

"Ameen!"

"Hanging him in the middle of the night like a common criminal!"

"Not even giving him the chance to say goodbye to his family . . ."

"His poor sons, in London, couldn't even come back to see their father buried . . ."

"Those poor daughters . . . orphaned, all orphaned . . ."

As Sikandar pushed his way to the front and stood in front of the stone marker of his grave, the scent of thousands of rose petals rising up in a heavy, intoxicating perfume, he was reminded for some reason of that Greek myth his tutor told him about a man who lived thousands of years ago and dreamt every day of flying like a bird. He'd made wings and glued them to his shoulders. But he flew too close to the sun, and its heat melted his wings, sending him plummeting to earth, to his death. The same thing had happened to this man, who'd had such dreams for Pakistan.

Had God punished him for forgetting that he was only a mortal?

Sikandar looked around at the other graves in the tomb. All the members of the Bhutto family were buried here: Sir Shahnawaz, Lady Khurshid (née Lakhi Bai), Sikandar Bhutto, Imdad Ali . . . A space in his own family graveyard lay in wait for Sikandar, the bones of his wife and daughter crumbling into the dust, patiently awaiting the day when his body would meet theirs. Their bones would mingle with the soil, nourishing it as it had nourished them for so many generations, so repaying the debt of fertility and affluence with their deaths. This was what it meant to be a zamindar. This was what it meant to be a Sindhi.

Sikandar raised his hands in prayer and recited the *Fateha* for Bhutto under his breath:

> In the name of Allah, Most Gracious, Most Merciful.
> Praise be to Allah, the Cherisher and Sustainer of the worlds;
> Most Gracious, Most Merciful;
> Master of the Day of Judgment.
> Thee do we worship, and Thine aid we seek.
> Show us the straight way,
> The way of those on whom Thou hast bestowed Thy Grace,
> those whose portion is not wrath, and who go not astray.

He took one last glance at the tomb. Where Bhutto's grave had once been a simple mound of earth covered with rose garlands, it was now reinforced with concrete; the concrete would be replaced by marble, and turned into an elaborate structure where people for generations would come to pay obeisance. The simple ancestral graveyard would grow into an opulent mausoleum, a massive shrine to which the devoted would flock. The people, the poor and disenfranchised of Sindh, to whom Bhutto had wanted to give equality and justice, *roti, kapra aur makan*, would say prayers for him and worship him as a martyr. He would be transformed from a man into a living saint. This, too, was the way of Sindh, and it would never change.

"Goodbye, Bhutto Saeen," Sikandar said, before he turned and walked away. "Fi Amanullah."

* * *

There was one more thing Sikandar had to do before returning to Sukkur: go to the house of the Bhuttos and condole with the family to express his sorrow. Bhutto's sons were not in the country; they had been sent by Bhutto to London. Only his widow Nusrat and daughters Benazir and Sanam remained. Nusrat and Benazir had been kept in detention for months, and just recently been released. They had come straight to Larkana to visit Bhutto's grave, then stayed at the house to meet with PPP leaders and supporters, which they had not been permitted to do since Bhutto's death.

Bhutto's pride and joy were his children. Sikandar had heard rumors that he was not entirely constant when it came to his wife, but in his children he pinned all his hopes, lavished all his love and affection. Especially the eldest, Benazir, whom he had sent to the finest universities in the United States and England—an unheard-of thing for a Sindhi girl, the daughter of a feudal.

Tongues had wagged in Sikandar's family, as in all Sindhi families, at the ridiculous plans Bhutto had for his firstborn. "Is he crazy—sending her that far away? It isn't safe to leave a girl alone like that, in America, of all the places . . ." said Sikandar's father.

"She'll get up to all sorts of mischief, she'll mix with boys and—" said his mother.

"Don't talk like that about a lady!" Imtiaz, ever the defender of the honor of women, spoke up.

"All right, but still . . . Educating girls? He's sending her to

Harvard? I've never even heard of the place. The man's been possessed by the devil, I tell you . . ."

"She'll go wild, disgrace the family. Bhutto will rue the day he put her on the plane; he'll wish he'd kept her in *purdah* like all honorable women!"

Sikandar sat and listened to the conversation, unsure which side to take. He wondered, if his daughter had lived, whether he would even consider letting her go abroad to study. He was not as averse to the idea as the rest of them. In this, as in so many other things, Bhutto had been a revolutionary, and had not listened to people he considered backward and foolish—and the family of Pir Hassan Sikandar, affluent as they might be, were certainly counted among their numbers.

But the daughter Bhutto sent as a gawky child had come back a polished, educated woman, with a backbone of steel. Now even Sikandar's family spoke admiringly of her; they all knew how she had led the struggle against General Zia after her father had been imprisoned; Zia had sent her and her mother to detention in Rawalpindi, and house arrest in Karachi and in Naudero. It was only by some miracle of God that the harsh conditions of jail did not break her, accustomed as she was to privilege and luxury. Why, she could hardly even speak Sindhi, her own mother tongue!

Sikandar was curious to see this girl, as were so many others, and everyone had, at some point, tried to meet with her. The Pirs and zamindars who were his contemporaries spoke of her in hushed, reverent tones, and all the young men could not help but fall a little in love with the idea of her, although they never would have shown disrespect to her or her father by approaching him for her hand in marriage. To them she was a mixture of several things: sister, daughter, heroine, queen. She was like the Seven Queens of Shah Abdul Latif Bhitai, that Sufi poet who wrote so movingly of the women of Sindh who'd fought oppressors, led wars, lost their lives for their lovers. Benazir had lost her beloved father, but she would not accept death or exile. She pitched herself in full tilt against General Zia and the might of the army: she was braver than most men Sikandar had ever known.

Sikandar approached the house in the early evening. Al-Murtaza, the ancestral home, which Zia turned into a sub-jail so that Benazir and her mother could be incarcerated there, was a grand structure with blue and white tiles all along the doorways, depicting in curious hieroglyphics the lives of the men and women that lived in Mohenjodaro, the City of the Dead located not too far away. Soldiers in khaki uniforms stood guard outside the gates, keeping a wary eye on all men who passed in and out of the house. Plainclothes policemen must have been mingling with the crowds, too, taking note of the names of PPP big shots who arrived in their convoys of jeeps and cars with darkened windows.

There were no women who came to meet the Bhutto ladies; they would not have been comfortable leaving their homes to travel so far, nor would they have been permitted to come out of *purdah* and walk among so many strange men. But Benazir did not observe *purdah*. Now that the official period of detention was over and the telephones restored, meetings with visitors allowed, they were making up for all those months when they had been cut off from the rest of the world, their names excised from the newspapers, their efforts to publicize Bhutto's plight struck down by the paranoid, shame-faced general.

Sikandar was directed by some of the Bhutto servants to go to the garden, and as he joined the men who thronged there, he noticed bushes of beautiful roses growing along the boundary walls. Their colors enticed him; tangerine, lavender, golden. He bent down to admire them, to stroke the petals of one that looked so perfect it could have been molded out of clay. One of the servants, a young boy in a Sindhi cap, saw him, and saluted, then spoke to him in the soft buttery tones of Seraiki-accented Sindhi.

"These were Bhutto Saeen's favorites. He brought them from all over the world."

"Did he?"

"Yes. And Bibi looked after them while he was in jail. She comes down here every morning at seven and helps the gardener water them. She tends to them as if they were her children. It is sad to watch. It makes me want to cry."

Sikandar touched the boy on his head and gave him a ten-rupee note. He already looked as if he had been crying for days, his eyes swollen, his nose red and chafed. No older than fourteen, he could not understand why his master had been taken and murdered. He had never been to school, could not understand the grand designs of the men who wanted to rule the country. But he would have taken comfort from the fact that his loyalty to the Bhutto family was something he could understand, and rely on. Until now.

Suddenly, a buzz rose up from the men gathered in the garden: "She is coming. She is coming. Bibi is coming."

"Stand here, Saeen," said the boy to Sikandar. "She will be sure to come near her father's roses. She loves them so."

He did as he was told, keeping a distance from the other men who were pressing to catch a glimpse of the tall, chador-clad figure as she stepped from the confines of the house and into the garden. The air was still heavy and hot from the day, though the scent of *raat-ki-raani* heralded the approaching coolness of night, and Sikandar thought he saw her flinch when the warmth hit her; it had not been long since she'd been released from those claustrophobic rooms where sunlight and fresh air were hard to come by.

He strained for a look at her; from this spot he could see a gaunt face, with great shadows under her eyes and cheekbones. But she held herself straight and proud, her chin lifted, glancing down her long, proud nose at the men who stumbled forward and greeted her, their hands pressed to their chest in respect. A small space was cleared in front of her so she could walk with dignity, speaking to each man and nodding her head slowly. She did not lower her head or look away, as most Sindhi women would have done; she faced each man and looked him straight in the eye, speaking in a strong, steady voice, despite her flawed Urdu.

Ten minutes passed, fifteen, thirty . . . an hour later, Benazir broke through the crowds and came toward the rosebushes, just as the young boy had said she would. Sikandar waited behind one of the hedges so that she did not see him at first, and he could watch her as she stood next to the roses, straightening her chador and closing her eyes. Only when she was close to him could he see how very young she looked. Her skin was translucent, the veins underneath her pale skin blue and fine like small rivers. Her eyes were huge, the eyebrows arched above, giving her an intelligent, intense expression. And though she was a tall woman, she looked delicate, the chador heaped over her thin shoulders, her hands clutching at its edges bony and thin.

Sikandar cleared his throat, and she glanced in his direction. She was tired, so tired, he could see it in the depths of her eyes, in the lines above her forehead. Even her clothes and shoes looked tired, worn-out and faded in the dusty heat. He stepped forward and began to speak.

"Lady, I am Pir Sikandar Hussein Ahmed Shah, from Sukkur. I have come to tell you how pained my family and I are by your loss. Truly, the nation has been robbed of a great man."

She did not smile, but she pressed her hand to her heart. "Thank you. You are very kind. Did you know my father well?"

"I did not know him, but I admired him greatly, as we all did." As he spoke, Sikandar realized he was telling the truth. Few zamindars agreed with Bhutto's ideas about liberating the poor, pandering to their greed. It would have upset the natural order of things. And he was ashamed to say that in earlier days, he had shared the view that if they, the nobility of Sindh, were not educated men, why should peasants and their children go to school so that they could leave the farms for the cities, believing themselves better than the zamindars and worthy of more than the life of servitude offered to them?

Disappointment flashed across her face. She was about to make her excuses and leave, Sikandar could tell. It hurt him more than he was expecting, to let her down, when she was so hungry for anyone who might have spent a little time with her father. He could not say that he completely understood that feeling, but he, too, knew what it felt like to lose his flesh and blood.

"But I know something about him that I must relate to you, Lady," Sikandar quickly continued. She flicked her great, dark eyes back to him and gave him her attention once more.

"On the day of his hearing before the Supreme Court, back in December, he was taken from jail and brought to the court in a very weak condition. He had not eaten, had not had fresh water for days. He was ill . . ." Benazir nodded in recognition and painful remembrance. "When he stood before the judge, ready to speak, many people did not think he would be strong enough. But then he gripped the sides of the dock and called out for help to Saeen Lal Shahbaz Qalandar, the great saint of Sehwan . . ."

Her hand was at her throat, and for a moment it seemed as if they were the only two people in the garden. "And then?" she whispered.

"The whole room began to grow bright, and your father's face was illuminated, as if the light of God was shining on his face. And then he regained his strength, and he was able to speak, and he spoke eloquently, for four days after that."

Her face too was shining, even though grief was an ever-present color on the skin of her thin cheeks. "He did not even need notes, you know?"

"Yes, Bibi. He was a brilliant man, even when he was standing with one foot in his grave."

Then her face shifted into a frown, and she looked away. "But how do you know it really happened like that?" She was so desolate, so devastated despite her outward show of strength, that Sikandar, in that moment, would have cut his own heart out of his chest to give to her.

He said, gently, "I was there, Lady. I went to his trial. I sat in the benches and watched your father defend himself against the charges."

Her eyes widened. Sikandar could see her heart had begun to resume beating again, a triumphant drumbeat that could never be stilled. The color came back to her face. Someone called her name from the far side of the garden then, and as she walked away, she said, "I will not forget your kindness, Pir Sikandar Hussein. Come to me in Karachi. We will see what can be done for you."

Just for the gift of those precious moments, he was grateful that he had told her such a great lie. For of course Sikandar had not been to Bhutto's trial. The story had only been told to him by someone who had actually been there, and it would pass into legend, as would all the tales and myths surrounding his mysterious death—that Bhutto had not been hanged, but beaten to death, that he was a living saint, a martyr, and that martyrs never died.

In truth, on the day that they tried and hanged Bhutto, they tried and hanged all of Sindh. Therefore, Sikandar's being present in spirit was something that could never be doubted, and his not being there in body was not important.

December 18, 2007 (ii)

After leaving them, Sikandar Hussein only ever called Ali to tell him to do something for him.

"We need to file our taxes. Find the papers for the house, Ali."

"Bring my case, the one with the black handle. It's in the storage room, on top of the other suitcases. I'm leaving for Islamabad on the evening flight."

"I need the electricity bills for the last year. Send them in the morning so that I can get them to the KESC office by noon."

Ali always listened, asked for clarification to his instructions. Sometimes he took notes. But would it have been so difficult for Sikandar to ask about any of them on one of those phone calls, even as an afterthought?

"And how are you doing, Ali? What's happening in school?"

"Did you find the answer to that algebra problem? See, you're a smart boy. I knew you could figure it out."

"So you want to study business? That's a very good idea. You can

help me manage the lands, after you graduate. You'll learn things I could never even imagine."

Ali gave up on his father after five years of his cold distance, trying to be stoic about his father's attitude. But it hurt Ali to see his mother age before their eyes; the burden of bringing them up alone wore her out until there were days when Ali would catch her reflection in a mirror and almost mistake her for his grandmother.

The only one who still carried any illusions about their father was Jeandi, barely seven when he left. At twelve, she remained in love with him as only a young girl could, and flew into a rage if any one of them dared say anything negative about him. "Don't talk like that about him! He's our Baba! He's given us everything!"

Listening to her mantra, uttered in a trembling, tearful tone, seeing her small chin wobbling, Ali only felt the deepest sorrow for both her and Haris, who was only twelve when their father left.

Ali's father paid for everything; his children's upkeep, education, a few trips to Dubai, and a few years ago, a new car—let it never be said that Pir Sikandar Hussein was irresponsible when it came to looking after his family. He was only on the other side of town, but it might as well have been the other side of the universe. Sometimes when Ali spoke to him on the phone he could hear the crackling of static, intergalactic line noise, other conversations cutting into the line in a million alien languages, and an eerie delay and echo, as if their voices were bouncing off satellites deep in space.

After Pir Sikandar's first wife died, he had become involved in politics and the PPP. It was the stuff of family jokes, how impressed their father was by Zulfikar Bhutto while he was alive, and traumatized by his death when he was hanged. He'd even gone to his trial in Rawalpindi, and to Naudero to condole with the Bhutto family back in 1979. It was in the Bhutto house,

Al-Murtaza, that he'd promised his allegiance to Bhutto's daughter Benazir. She had given him a bouquet of flowers from among the prized roses in her father's garden; Ali found one pressed between the pages of his Quran, papery brown, a few pieces broken off and ground into a fine dust.

The years of Zia had been difficult: Benazir was jailed again and again, and then finally she went into exile, but Ali's father had worked with the PPP and the MRD, the Movement for the Restoration of Democracy, to prepare the ground for her return in 1986. The details were vague—Ali was hardly four or five years old, but he somehow remembered the secret phone calls, the meetings, the times when Ali's father would come home drunk, his face a blazing blustery red, and he would pace the corridors of the house, shouting that his beloved Sindh would never succumb to the imperialist invaders.

But there was hardly anything left of the Sindh that Pir Sikandar dreamt about. Land reforms instigated by Bhutto had cut everyone's landholdings dramatically, and few in the interior could get an education or find employment because there weren't enough schools or jobs. So Ali's father had moved the entire family to Karachi; even though their income was assured from the lands (he'd been clever about the reforms, managing to put his lands into various family members' names while pretending to agree with Bhutto that reforms were necessary for Sindh's progress), he'd wanted his sons to go to good schools—proof, perhaps, of his love for them.

He was so crazy about Sindh that he didn't even consider the Balochi Sindhis, who'd been settled in the province for the last three hundred years, to be true Sindhis. "Legharis, Jatois, Chandios, pah! Even the Zardaris are not Sindhi!" he'd shout. When Benazir married Asif Zardari in 1987, he'd gotten drunk and stayed drunk for three days. He'd attended their wedding at the racecourse legless. Ali pictured him lurching toward the platform where Benazir and Zardari were sitting, laying his hand on his heart to tell Benazir that her father would have been so happy to see this moment. Then he'd turned to climb back down the three steps, but he'd fallen off the platform and broken his ankle, and had had to be in a cast for three months.

It was always just automatically assumed that Ali would follow in his father's footsteps: inherit his lands and his title, and continue where he left off when he was too old to look after the farm or his other interests. As the eldest son, Ali knew he would one day be the *sardar* of the extended family. His religious duties would not be heavy: like most Pirs of today, Ali's father knew little about religion beyond the daily prayers and a few verses of the Quran, which they dispensed like aspirin to the few men who came to him for religious advice. Learning about agriculture was more complicated, but Ali had wanted to study business management and come back from Dubai to help his father shift into a more progressive way of doing things. He would build a school and a hospital for the poor, improve the road system, get sanitation installed in the village.

"It will all cost more money than you'll be able to afford," his father had told him when Ali talked to him about his plans. Sikandar was settled in his chair, a whiskey and water by his hand, and he was watching Benazir on the nine o'clock state news as she addressed Parliament, the country's first female prime minister, the world's youngest Muslim woman to lead a nation. The sound was turned down low so that Jeandi wouldn't wake up, but Ali's father was mesmerized by the expressions on her face—animated and proud, those imperious cheekbones and arching eyebrows screaming privilege and entitlement even as her huge Persian eyes shone with intelligence and determination.

Ali had eagerly turned away from his books and toward his father. "It won't be that bad. We have to try, don't we?"

Sikandar nodded at the television. "That's what her father wanted to do. Give the peasants and serfs power. *Power to the people!*" For a moment, a bitter, wry look crossed his face, but then he shook his head as if clearing it of treacherous thoughts. "*Roti, kapra, aur makan.* Made him popular with the masses. Not a bad idea, but done in the wrong way."

"You mean the land reforms?" Ali had asked. "They weren't a good idea, were they?"

"Not for us."

"So why did you go along with them? Support him so much?"

"We had no choice. We had to do it to survive."

Ali was too young to know the word *hypocrisy*, and even if he had known it, he wouldn't have dared apply it to his father. He had believed everything Sikandar told him about politics, Bhutto, Benazir, the way the world worked. He was the ruler of Ali's world back then; through the filter of his eyes, Ali could take politics, history, economics piece by piece, absorb them, digest the knowledge in morsels until he was ready for the next bite. There was so much more he wanted to talk with his father about; He needed Sikandar to approve of the way his mind worked, to tell him that he would be a prime minister himself one day.

But his silence had intimidated Ali, and the weary way in which Pir Sikandar raised his drink to his lips, the ice rattling inside the glass. Then the news finished, and he switched off the television with a deft flick of his wrist on the remote control, and stood up to go out for the evening.

Looking back, Ali realized now that for all his grand ancestry, his noble traditions, for all that he had been taught how to be a zamindar and a Pir, none of his forefathers had taught Pir Sikandar how to be a father.

* * *

The police beat them even after they locked them in the van, taking some sort of sadistic pleasure at having them all trapped in one place, unable to escape their wrath. Everyone else in the van was just like Ali, young and afraid. Ali didn't recognize anyone, but he felt as though he knew them all. There were no girls in the van; they'd been taken away by women constables in charcoal-gray uniforms, sneers of disdain contorting their faces as they pulled at their hair and ripped their clothes. Ali had no idea what had happened to Salma or Ferzana, but he'd seen Imran writhing on the ground, being clubbed viciously as he clutched at his eyes, one hand flung out in front of him in a mute cry for mercy.

One of the younger men sat quietly sobbing in a corner but the rest were too stunned to even cry. The van sped through the streets of Islamabad, sirens wailing, until it stopped with a jerk that threw them on their hands and knees onto the floor. The doors were wrenched open and men started shouting at them to come out as rough hands reached inside to yank them out, blinking like bats in daylight too strong for their teargassed eyes. They were shoved into the police station at Aabpara where it had all begun.

No matter how macho everyone pretended to be in Pakistan, even the biggest muscle-bound buffoon was frightened of being taken to a police *thana*. It was the stuff of nightmares for couples caught on illicit dates, or women who were raped and stupid enough to report it at a police station. All that happened was that men got thrashed and women got raped again. Through his work at the station, Ali had heard of street children being taken to the police stations and being made to have sex with policemen so that they were allowed to sell flowers on street corners. There was a news item back in January, a report from some human rights organization that made its way to their fax machine, that they'd tortured a man accused of stealing in Larkana, beating him severely, cutting off his penis and leaving him in a cell in a pool of blood. Ali watched Ameena's face as she read the fax: it drained of all color, leaving her skin looking like cottage cheese, and she hurriedly threw down the piece of paper and ran to the bathroom.

Jehangir picked up the fax, read it, and whistled, then tossed it to Ali. "I guess we're not going to be running this on the evening bulletin . . ."

Their knees were knocking as they were herded into the police station and made to stand in front of the desk, bruised and bleeding, while policemen swarmed all around them, shouting and screaming and hurling abuse. They stripped everyone of their cell phones and wallets, and Ali knew he would never see either again. He stared at the dingy cracked walls and the concrete floor, where a puddle of blood trickled past his legs—but when he blinked his eyes, it was only water from a leaking faucet at a filthy sink in a corner of the room. There was a smell like burst sewers emanating from somewhere outside the room, curling into Ali's nostrils and making him want to vomit.

Two hours passed like this, as they sweated and tried to clean their eyes and begged for a glass of water or to be allowed to use the toilet, requests that were all ignored. Finally a Station House officer showed up and instructed a constable to take down their details while he stood close by, his hand caressing the pistol holstered on his hip, and scrutinized each person with deep-set, shadowed eyes. Each person was registered, fingerprinted, photographed. Abuses were hurled at them and their family members, and if anyone protested, he was caught by the collar and slapped hard on the face.

Then one by one they were taken down the hall to the jail cells. Ali wondered if they would be beaten more in the cells, or just left to sit or stand or lie on the floor until someone figured out what to do with them.

One young man started to gasp and panic when it was his turn to be led away. "Oh my God, oh my God," he moaned. "My father's going to kill me! My father's going to kill me!" It was an odd thing for a grown man to say, but Ali felt an answering spasm in his own chest. Before he'd broken ties with his father, Pir Sikandar's approval or disapproval was the most important thing in the world to him: he waited for it like a mariner consulting the weather before deciding to take a trip out onto the sea. Since they'd stopped speaking, Ali had learned how to trust his own judgment, checking his own compass instead of someone else's all the time. But that young man's fear resonated with something inside him. He reminded Ali of himself when he was seventeen, before he knew the shape of his father's perfidy.

Suddenly, the officer at the desk was shouting at Ali. "You! You, come here."

Before the man standing guard could push him, Ali stumbled forward, eyes still smarting. His fingers burned where the baton caught him against the edge of the van door. The SHO cast a glance over Ali's sorry appearance, his dirtied clothes and swollen, defiant scowl. The register on the desk was filled with the names and details of at least thirty different people. The officer's pen hovered over the page, ready to add Ali's name to the list.

"Name?"

"Sayed Mohammed Ali Sikandar." He scratched it down painstakingly, each stroke of the pen another jab in Ali's throbbing eyeballs.

"Address?"

Ali mumbled it out. The officer remained impassive when Ali said he was from Karachi.

"Father's name?"

"Pir Sikandar Hussein Shah." It came out automatically, as it always did when Ali was asked for his father's name in a hundred different bureaucratic situations: filling out school forms or applying for a passport, opening a bank account or buying a SIM card for a mobile phone. And even more so in social situations: people always asked Ali who his father was as a way of identifying him on the tree of society. Among Sindhis, Ali was the apple growing off one of the topmost branches, deriving an elevated status from his father's high position.

The police officer's pen kept scratching on the paper. But the SHO cocked his head, peered at Ali from underneath bushy eyebrows. Close up, his eyes were not the usual brown of most Pakistanis, but rather a hazel that didn't match the somber tone of his oak-brown face.

"Wait," the SHO said to the officer, whose pen froze a millimeter above the page. The SHO beckoned Ali to follow him. Ali strumbled behind him, his legs trembling with weakness. They went to an office, a tiny room just off the main hall fitted out with a wooden desk and two chairs. A ceiling fan whirred uselessly overhead. The SHO clasped his hands behind his back and stared out the window onto a small grassy patch of ground outside. He didn't invite Ali to sit down.

"Your father is Pir Sikandar Hussein? Of Sukkur?"

"Yes." Ali's heart pounded harder than before; his mouth was dry. He wanted to ask for a glass of water but he was too afraid of being shouted at, or worse.

"You are sure?"

"Yes, I'm sure."

Abruptly, he reached for his pocket, and for one crazy moment Ali was certain the man was going to take out his gun and shoot him, point-blank, right here in this room. But instead, he passed Ali his cell phone with a grunt. "Call your father."

"What?"

"You heard me. Call your father. If you can get him to come up here, I'll release you without charge, on his recognizance."

I don't want to do this. Ali longed to tell the SHO that he couldn't call his father, that he hadn't spoken to him on his own initiative in two years. He wanted to break down in tears, tell the SHO how his father left them all, found a woman who wasn't Ali's mother and slept with her and now Ali had a half-sister whom he'd never seen but who apparently looked just like his sister Jeandi. There was something about this man's eyes that told Ali he might just understand.

But the man stared at Ali, his hazel eyes with their slightly raised eyebrows expressing the tiniest bit of impatience, and Ali knew that if he didn't make the call, he'd be stuck in this jail cell and probably beaten up by any police officer who'd had a fight because his wife wouldn't make love to him, or who didn't have enough money to get his daughter married and needed to take it out on a rich, spoiled brat like him.

The phone rang a few times, and then that familiar, raspy voice, mellowed by years of whiskey and cigarettes, came down the line and into Ali's ear, going straight to his heart. "Hello?"

"Baba?"

A pause. "Ali?"

"Baba, it's me."

"What is it, Ali?" If he was surprised, he didn't let it show in his voice.

"Baba, I'm in trouble."

Another pause.

"Where are you? Have you had an accident?" Ali could hear the breaks where he stopped to light a cigarette, breathe it in, expel the smoke in short strong puffs. Ali's mother used to beg him to stop smoking, saying that it was terrible for his health, but he never listened to her about anything. Ali glanced at the SHO, who'd turned his face away again, as if to give Ali some privacy, a symbolic gesture Ali was too shaken to appreciate right now. "I've been arrested."

"What?"

"I'm in the Aapbara Police Station. The SHO let me call you." Ali spoke in Sindhi but he knew the SHO could understand every word he was saying.

"You're in Islamabad?"

"Yes, Baba." Ali's voice caught on his name. "I was . . . I was in a march."

"A march?" It was to his father's credit that he didn't sound shocked, but Pir Sikandar had not always been a man who could stay in control of his reactions.

"For the judges."

A long pause this time, a deep exhale and inhale. "I saw that on the news. It looked bad. Are you all right?"

"I'm all right. A little bumped about, but . . ."

"Let me talk to him."

Ali handed the phone over to the SHO. Ali was on autopilot now, relieved to have two grown-ups to whom he could turn the situation over. They spoke to each other, but Ali wasn't listening to the SHO's responses. He closed his eyes, wishing he could sink down into the chair, even though its seat was torn and one leg was shorter than all the others.

At last the conversation ended, and the SHO handed his

phone back to Ali. Ali pressed his ear to it, enjoying the warmth against his bruised skin. "Ali? Just stay there. I'm coming on the seven o'clock flight. Don't worry."

Ali nodded even though his father couldn't see him doing it. Then he switched off the phone and handed it back to the SHO. The man pocketed it, then pulled out the chair and told him to sit.

"You can stay in here until he comes for you."

"Thank you."

Ali was so tired he could have fallen asleep for a thousand years. He lowered himself down gingerly; no position felt good with aching ribs and fingers, and an assortment of bumps and bruises that ran all the way up and down his spine. He had never been in this much pain in his life.

His head was starting to fill with fog, and although he was wondering why the SHO was giving him special treatment, instead of leaving Ali to rot in the cells with the others, he knew that it was because of Pir Sikandar Hussein Shah of Sukkur. That was the way it always went in Pakistan: you could get into any kind of trouble—you could even kill a man—and as long as your father knew the right people, you'd never have to pay the price. Maybe Pir Sikandar promised the SHO a nice little sum of fifty thousand rupees to make sure that his son didn't have to endure the ignominy of jail, shaming him and bringing him down from the treetops, onto the ground where the ordinary people had to live and survive.

The SHO glanced toward the door to make sure it was shut, and then he sat down at the desk, opposite Ali. He leaned forward and started talking in a soft voice, and Ali realized he wasn't hearing Urdu or even Punjabi, but Seraiki, that sweet language spoken by people from the lands on the border of Sindh and Punjab. If an artist drew a map of Pakistan not in solid inks but in watercolor, you'd see a soft melting line between the provinces, blurred and seeping onto the page, and that was the way Seraiki people lived, between the spaces where Punjab and Sindh knock into each other.

"My village is in southern Punjab," the SHO was telling Ali, who understood him perfectly, as all Sindhi speakers could. "We've been devotees of Khwaja Khizr for six generations. We've been many times to his shrine, where your village is. The Sufi poetry written in his honor is sung in our village. Some in my family are followers of Pir Sikandar Hussein. I cannot have his son in my jail, even for a single day. It would be a matter of great shame for me."

He got up, left Ali alone with his thoughts. Ali closed his eyes. Would it be too hypocritical to offer a prayer of thanks to the saint, who saved Ali's neck, even though he never asked for the favor? Ali had been maybe five times in his life to the shrine. He said it anyway, hoping that the saint wouldn't think him a hypocrite. And then he drifted away.

* * *

The last flight from Islamabad to Karachi left at one in the morning, and it was a rush to get out of the jail and into the airport in time to make the plane. Somehow they managed it, though. The SHO offered them dinner but Pir Sikandar refused, saying that he didn't want to put the man through any more trouble. Father and son ate, instead, at a little roadside restaurant on the way to the airport that served fresh barbecued food. Ali was ravenous, but when he tried to eat the chicken tikka his jaw throbbed and he was forced to mouth down the food half chewed. It saved him from having to say anything to the man sitting across from him at the table, who, despite all the DNA they shared, was a stranger to him.

It was not until they were both sitting in the plane, strapped into their seats, that Ali was able to relax. Everything was swirling through his mind like a parade of scenes from a movie montage, but he was just too drained to do anything more than watch them and then let them go. He wanted to worry for Imran, Ferzana, Bilal, and most of all Salma, but the relief that he was not in jail was much greater in comparison. These were days in which thousands of people had disappeared, or been arrested by the government for engaging in "terrorist" activities. The army had practically been waging war against the people of the Frontier and Balochistan, thanks to George Bush's influence on Musharraf. Ali knew he had come close to becoming one of its victims. He was not ready to die for his country yet, but if he'd been one of those nameless victims, shot or bombed or jailed or simply disappeared, nobody would call him a *shaheed,* or put him in a martyr's grave.

He leaned his head back in the seat, although any way in which he tried to twist his body caused more pain. The lights in the cabin were dimmed and the plane began to taxi down the runway. His father was sitting with his eyes closed, his hands resting on his knees. He was whispering a small prayer under his breath; Ali suddenly remembered that Pir Sikandar had always been afraid of flying.

With a bump and a thrust, they were airborne, and Ali looked out at the lights of Islamabad dropping away beneath them, the darkened line of the Margalla Hills standing guard over the city. The plane tilted sharply and pointed one wing toward earth, pivoting to make the turn southward to Karachi. Sikandar gripped his knees a little bit tighter, and Ali could see his knuckles start to grow white. He patted his father's hand awkwardly. "It's all right, Baba. We're in the air, look, we're practically home already."

Sikandar squinted one eye open, then quickly shut it again. He murmured, "I don't know what you're talking about. Go to sleep."

Ali resisted smiling. His father was too proud to admit that he was terrified of going down in a great big fireball of death. Ali had no such fears; planes relaxed him, put him to sleep. His eyelids were being tugged downward, so he leaned back in his seat, trying to find a comfortable place for his arms to rest, and thought about Sunita.

Suddenly, Ali was shaken awake by a pocket of turbulence. The whole cabin began to rattle, dishes in the galley clattering in their trays, the luggage in the overhead bins banging around against the doors of the compartments. The flight was not full, and some people still slept through the racket, but Sikandar sat bolt upright, his eyes open wide, glimmering with fear. He looked around from side to side, trying to see what was going on. The seat belt sign flicked on, and Ali glanced down to make sure his father was wearing his, then gazed back up at his face and tried to breathe slowly for him. Sikandar's teeth were clenched, his jaw tense.

"It's okay, it's okay, Baba," Ali said softly.

The shaking got worse and Sikandar grimaced. "Where's the air hostess? Why isn't anyone telling us what's going on?"

"It's just turbulence. An air pocket. Don't worry. It's like bumps on a road, when you're in a car." Ali's first instinct was to soothe him, to reach out and grip his arm, give him some sort of comfort. It confused him; he'd hated him for so long that he felt he should be enjoying watching him frightened and uncomfortable. He hadn't even talked to Ali about the march, or what he was doing there. Yes, he'd dropped everything to come up and get Ali out of jail, but wasn't that more out of a need to save face than it was to save his son? Appearances had always been more important to Pir Sikandar Hussein than anything else.

But maybe it was up to Ali to talk.

The prospect of having this conversation with his father made him recoil in fear. It was scarier than facing the police in the march, seeing their faces with their teeth bared and their batons lifted in the air, ready to bring them down on the protestors' heads. The last time Ali was this scared was in the moments after the explosion at the rally for Benazir, when he raised his head and realized he was still alive, but others around him were dead. It was his only chance, though. They were no longer in Karachi, where normal rules applied. On the ground, Sikandar was strong and Ali weak. In this metal tube going at six hundred miles an hour, twenty thousand feet in the air, Ali could dare to take the first step, freed from gravity and of the pain of the last five years.

He took a breath, swallowed hard. "It was terrible, today, at the march. They teargassed us. They were beating up girls. I never saw anything like that before." He spoke slowly, his voice low, trying hard to control his nerves.

"What were you doing up there?" Sikandar muttered through clenched teeth.

"I joined the People's Resistance Movement. We made a plan to go together and show our support for the judges."

Sikandar let out a snort. "Those corrupt bastards? They're not coming back. Don't waste your time."

He was not telling Ali directly that he didn't want him involved, but Ali could sense it. He replied, "I don't think it's a waste of time. I want to be a part of it; I want to make a difference. We're all tired of the way this country's leaders have been plundering the nation. We want a change."

Sikandar turned his head to stare at Ali, who tried to meet his father's eyes, although turning his neck sent a spasm of pain all the way down his spine and into his hips. He felt braver, though. And he came out with what he'd been dying to say since the beginning of all of this. Or maybe even further back: for all of his adult life.

"Baba, every government since Bhutto has been corrupt down to the core. Bhutto talked about socialism and equality but he acted like the worst kind of dictator when he was in power. General Zia turned the whole country into a bunch of raving fundos. Nawaz Sharif made a fortune out of selling every state asset off to his cronies . . ."

Dare he say it? Dare he talk about his father's beloved Benazir? Another bump hit the plane, sending them up and then down in a sickening lurch, and Sikandar flinched. Ali could stop now, turn back down this path, and subside into sullen indifference, but something had been cut loose inside him and he went on, his words gaining momentum. "And Bibi? Marrying Asif Zardari? Look at what they've done. Mansions in Surrey, the South of France. She lives like a queen in Dubai. Every taxi driver in Dubai knows about her palace in Emirates Hills. What has she done for this country?"

"You don't understand—"

"You're right, I don't understand how you just sat there and went along with all of them, even when you knew they were wrong. How? Why?" His voice still cracked on the last word.

Even in the dimmed lights of the cabin Ali could see the familiar angry flush creeping across his father's cheeks, although there was no whiskey in his hand to help it along. Sikandar started to push himself out of his seat, but the seat belt clamped over his stomach kept him trapped in the chair. The veins in his neck bulged and for one second Ali feared he would have a heart attack and die right there next to him. Then he realized that this man who had endured the last fifty years, associated with political goons and racketeers of the worst kind, been married three times and buried a wife and child, was strong enough to deal with his son, even in the midst of the turbulence that was his worst fear.

"We had to. I had to. It was a matter of our survival. You can't be a zamindar and make enemies out of people in power. It just doesn't work that way. It's the way it's always been done. Your grandfather, your great-grandfather, do you think they could fight people who could cut off their water, seize their lands?" Sikandar glared straight ahead, one wary eye still looking for trouble, a wing on fire, an exploding engine; he still couldn't face Ali. But at least he hadn't lapsed into stinging silence, which always made Ali feel foolish and small. At least this time he was trying to explain. "The British, the Talpurs—they would have crushed us. They only cared about power. We had to play the game that way. At least we zamindars care about Sindh."

"I care about Sindh!"

"No, you don't. If you did, you'd take interest in the lands, in politics. You'd work with me to make sure that we're strong, you'd be by my side. But you don't want to be a feudal like me. I can see it. You haven't wanted anything to do with me for the last five years. I've lost you."

"Everyone hates the feudals," Ali began. "They always say it's our fault Pakistan is the way it is."

Sikandar shook his head. "They're wrong. The feudals are a dying breed. We died years ago. We killed ourselves with our own stupidity."

He sank back and pressed his forehead against his fist. For the first time, Ali realized his father was old. And sad. And tired. His day, for all intents and purposes, was over. Ali's had just begun.

"You do what you like," Sikandar said. "You're old enough to know your own mind. I can't stop you from doing what you want to do. Just don't forget about where you came from. Don't forget about your history."

Ali couldn't understand what had just happened. He was so lightheaded that he could float away like a balloon released into the air, the hand that was holding on to it so tightly letting go and allowing the string to slip through its fingers. A terrible sadness flooded through him. He sat back in his seat, breathing deeply,

tasting a bittersweet liberty mixed in with the stale air-condition-
ing and scents of frying food from the galley. Not exactly freedom, but a turning point between him and his father. But where
would he and Sikandar go from here?

And then, just like that, the turbulence stopped. A moment
later, the pilot's voice crackled through the loudspeaker, telling
them that they had started the descent to Karachi.

The Eighth Queen

KARACHI, 1961

When Pinky was a little girl, she had always wanted to visit the Shrine of the Crocodiles at Manghopir. She didn't know when she'd first heard of the place, which was famous for its hot sulfur springs that could cure a sick person of any ailment, and the crocodiles that swam in its murky green waters, who were said to be sacred disciples of the Sufi saint Pir Mangho. But from the moment she heard the tale of the saint and his reptilian pets, she longed desperately to go there and see them for herself, commune with the crocodiles and offer them a few morsels of meat in return for their blessings.

Perhaps she'd heard the servants talking about it as she went into the kitchen in search of her favorite chocolates that Papa had brought back from Paris. Pinky loved chocolate. It was her true passion: one day she would turn to romance novels to satisfy her dreams of everlasting love and happiness, but as a seven-year-old child whose father was still her first love, chocolate warmed her stomach and filled her heart.

When she lay sleeping in her bed, wearing her pink princess nightgown and being watched over by a faithful old *ayah* from the village, she dreamt of chocolate, great big bars of it growing all around like a forest, and rivers of chocolate on which she would sail a boat that was made of more chocolate, and her mother and father would watch from the banks of the chocolate river, and when she reached the shore and ran to them, they would give her even more chocolate, just because they loved her so. Lulled by her chocolate world, Pinky smiled in her sleep, which the old *ayah* took as a sign of the little girl having been sent straight from heaven by the angels. *Just look at the child's pink cheeks, like apples and roses,* the old woman thought to herself, and leaned forward to chuck the child's chin. In the daytime the child was given over to an English governess, who taught her how to speak and act like a little *mem,* but at night, Pinky belonged to the faithful old village woman, who sang her Sindhi lullabies and kneaded her arms and legs affectionately with her gnarled brown hands.

Besides chocolate and her father, her other great love was to sneak away from her room in the middle of the afternoon and go to the kitchen in the hopes that the servants would share with her the remnants of their lunch. Pinky was made to eat proper food: potato and leek soup, roast chicken with potatoes and carrots, and mounds and mounds of boiled beans and spinach. She hated all of these foods, even though she was told by her governess, Miss Lucy, that they would make her strong. But she longed for the spicy bite and greasy welcome of *daal* and *salaan* and *muttur pulao* on her tongue, not the bland English food that her mother ordered cooked for Pinky and her brother Mir and sister Sunny. Her baby brother Shah was the most unfortunate of all: he only got to eat ground-up apples and rice from a plastic bowl, not a china dish like the rest of them.

Pinky would pretend to eat her food (hiding most of it under her fork and knife, or sneaking it onto her brother's plate when Miss Lucy's back was turned—her brother didn't mind; he had the appetite of a horse and would happily eat two or three servings of any food that was offered to him, English or otherwise). Then she would wait until everyone was taking a nap after lunch, and run downstairs to the kitchen in a pair of rubber *chappals* that only squeaked a little bit. She would burst into the kitchen and imperiously demand from Aftab the Cook a plate of chicken *karahi* with naan hot from the marketplace *tandoor;* she would sit on a small stool, hunched over her illicit meal, and slurp the mouthfuls down delightedly, wiping her mouth with the back of her hand and even letting out a small burp or two, something Miss Lucy would never have allowed at her table.

It was during one of these secret feasts that she heard Aftab talking about his son to one of the other housemen.

"The doctor calls it epli—epil—*epilseppy*," Aftab said mournfully. He was a short, squat man, who was said to have cooked for the governor-general of Sindh back in the days before Partition, which Pinky knew from listening to her father talk with his guests was something to do with parting your hair so that there was as much hair on the left side of your head as there was on the right. She listened to them curiously, as she chewed slowly, her eyes fixed firmly on her plate so that they would not suspect she was eavesdropping.

"What is that, brother?" said the majordomo, Babu, a loyal and longtime servant of the household.

"Oh, it's a terrible affliction: my son suffers fits, his eyes roll back in his head, he falls to the floor and shakes for ages, and foams at the mouth. I'm so afraid that one day he will swallow his own tongue and die, brother."

"Tauba, tauba!" Babu stroked his ears and nose in fear. Pinky, too, touched her own nose and ears, then frowned when she realized she'd dirtied them with her greasy fingers.

"Is there no cure?" breathed Yusuf, another houseman who was Sindhi like the others who all hailed from Papa's village in Naudero, but was Sheedi, with dark African features and a powerful, muscled body. Pinky had observed him with his shirt off once as he washed Papa's car, and he looked to her like the photo of a boxer she'd seen in the newspaper. But Yusuf was not very intelligent; once Mir had come in with an ice cream cone and said to Yusuf, "I don't think this is very good, will you smell it for me?" Yusuf dipped his head obligingly to the ice cream, and Mir thrust his hand up quickly so that Yusuf had ice cream all over his nose. The other servants laughed and jeered, and Yusuf joined in good-naturedly, but Pinky, who had seen Mir play this joke a dozen times before, would never have fallen for it herself.

Aftab sighed. Pinky felt her own heart do a somersault of sadness with him, her plate of food long forgotten. "There are medicines, but we've tried them—Saeen has been very kind and given me extra money to pay for his treatment. Still, they don't seem to be doing anything for him; he just gets worse with each year. I've taken him to a Pir in our neighborhood but he hasn't been able to do anything, either. It must be the will of Allah that my son must suffer so. We are cursed—cursed!"

Babu patted him consolingly on the back. "Don't say that, brother. There is always a way. You just have to have faith."

"But I have!" wailed Aftab. "God has forsaken me!"

But Pinky was watching Yusuf's face, which had begun to shine as if the man knew a beautiful, dazzling secret. He said, "Brother Cook, there is something you must try. You should take your son to Manghopir. He will be cured there!"

"To *Manghopir?*"

"Yes, yes." Yusuf nodded vigorously. "Pir Mangho will cure your son."

"He's right, you know," said Babu. "They say if you take a bath in the water of the hot spring, your disease will be cured."

Aftab looked bewildered. "But that's only for skin diseases! My son has a disease of the brain. How on earth will going to Manghopir help him?"

"Of course it will help him!" replied Yusuf. "Pir Mangho can cure any disease. Not just skin diseases. That's what he's most famous for, of course. Even the leprosy hospitals bring their patients there because they get cured of their leprosy."

"Their what?"

"Leprosy. You know, the disease that makes people's hands and legs fall off."

"Are you sure the crocodiles at Manghopir don't bite them off?" Babu said grinning.

Yusuf scowled. "Don't be stupid! The crocodiles never harm the saint's *murids*!"

At this, Pinky leapt off her seat. "Where are the crocodiles?" she demanded. "I want to see them."

The three servants turned to Pinky with a single look of dismay on their faces. They had forgotten she was sitting there, and they knew now that she would never cease to torture them until she got her own way. Saeen and Jiji, her parents, spoilt Pinky-bibi without limit; if she cried, the servants were the ones that got slapped for making her upset. The only person who was not afraid of her tantrums was that ridiculous Miss Lussi, with her high starched collars and her glasses perched high on her nose, through which her cold blue eyes blinked sternly at Pinky: three blinks was enough to make Pinky calm down and go calmly upstairs at bedtime, even if she wanted to stay up to listen to the grown-ups' talk, as they nursed their brandies and curls of cigar smoke wafted up to the high ceilings of the formal drawing room where Saeen entertained his important guests late into the night.

"Pinky-bibi, you can't see the crocodiles," said Babu. "They are very far away, all the way to the north of Karachi."

"I don't care," replied Pinky. "Papa took us last year to London, which is *much* farther away than Mango—Mangy—Mangawhatsit—and, he took us to the zoo in Regent's Park and we saw crocodiles there, so I want to go."

"But the crocodiles are dangerous," said Aftab, shaking his head forbiddingly at the child.

"Yusuf just said that they never harm the Pir's followers." Pinky could be stubborn when she wanted to; she never gave up on something if it was what she truly wanted. And she was too clever for them all, much cleverer than all three of them put together.

"They aren't dangerous at all," said Yusuf, his eyes shining, "and during the Sheedi Jat we sing so many songs to them and they come out of the water, they love listening to the one about the Sheedi Basha, our king from Africa, and they also dance; oh, what dancers they are! And we give them fresh meat, and the Gaddi Nashin comes and puts a garland of roses around the neck of the chief of the crocodiles, Old Mor Sahib, and then—"

"*Will you shut up!*" hissed Babu, elbowing Yusuf in the ribs.

"I want to see the crocodiles dancing!" bellowed Pinky.

Aftab moaned, "Bibi, you can't! Jiji would never let us!"

"She would!"

"She wouldn't!" said Babu. "And Saeen would send us back to the village and we'd have to become peasants and . . ."

"Arré, Babu, would you shut up? Do you realize what you're saying?" Aftab was almost hysterical by now. If Pinky began to cry and caused a scene, Saeen would come in and take her away, sobbing; and then later he would summon them to the back of the house and have them whipped by one of his guards. He had had that done before, to a hapless *chowkidar* who had dared to stare at Jiji as she was getting out of her car; the screams and howls of that man still echoed in all their ears.

"Listen, Pinky-bibi." Yusuf knelt down in front of the child and was looking beseechingly into her eyes.

She pouted but hesitated, as though trying to decide whether or not to throw a fit. "What?" she said sulkily. Aftab and Babu muttered a silent prayer that Yusuf wouldn't say something stupid, like the time he'd told Pinky that her cat had died when in actual fact it had only run away, just because he hadn't wanted to be made to look for it.

"You can't go to see the crocodiles because it's a place only for sick people, all right? A healthy little girl like you . . . you should let the truly needy, the very poor, the desperate people go see the crocodiles. They need them more than you do. Do you think you can do that?"

A slow nod of the head. "Dadi says we should always look after the poor."

"Your Dadi-jiji is a very wise lady."

Aftab and Babu were staring at each other in amazement. For once, Yusuf hadn't ruined everything! Could the fool be finally learning how to think like a normal person, instead of a stupid Sheedi?

"And because you're so good, I'm going to take you to somewhere much more fun and exciting than the stupid old crocodiles, who are dirty and smelly and have mostly lost all their teeth by now anyway."

"Where? What?" Pinky was standing up now, her fists clenched by her sides, breathing noisily through her parted lips.

"I'll take you to Abdullah Shah Ghazi's Mazaar, which is nearby, and you can have a parrot pick out your fortune. The Tota-Fal is never wrong."

Pinky clapped her hands in glee, and a wide smile turned her apple cheeks into blooming roses. "Really? When? When can we go? Can we take Sunny and Miss Lucy with us? Should I go upstairs and get ready now?"

Yusuf turned to grin triumphantly at Babu and Aftab, expecting extravagant praise for his cleverness, and couldn't understand why Aftab sagged against the kitchen counter, his hand pressed against his forehead, or why Babu's eyes were already closed in despair.

* * *

Sneaking Pinky-bibi out of the house was not as simple a task as it might seem. It was easy enough to choose a day when Saeen and Jiji were away, on a trip to America where Saeen was sent often on important government business. Getting money for the Parrot Oracle was no problem either: Jiji always charged Pinky-bibi with looking after the house, giving her a small sum of money that Pinky turned over to Babu, and stood next to him while he wrote down the accounts in a small black notebook. The day before the planned outing, she turned to Yusuf, who was lolling against the fridge and watching the transaction with curious eyes, and asked him, "How much does the Tota-Fal cost?"

"Two rupees," replied Yusuf.

Pinky carefully counted out four rupees and gave the rest to Babu. "Here, Babu. I'm keeping this much for the parrots. One turn for me and one for Yusuf, because he's taking me. You can have the rest. Mama gave me fifteen rupees, and I know it only costs ten to get food for the whole house. There's one extra rupee for you, to buy your special medicine."

"How clever you are, Bibi!" said Babu, knowing he would have to go without his cigarettes for that day.

"I know," smiled Pinky. "Papa tells me so all the time."

Yusuf planned that he, Babu, and the driver would take Pinky to the shrine of Abdullah Shah Ghazi, which was only two minutes up the road from their house at 70 Clifton, while the *ayah* and Aftab the cook would stay behind to look after the other children. The parrot masters set up their stalls on the pavement outside the shrine, enticing devotees of the saint to try their luck and see what fate had in store for them, and Yusuf was as curious as Pinky to learn his own future.

"But what about Miss Lussi?" said Babu. "She'll tell everything to Saeen when he comes back from Amreeka."

"You leave her to me," Yusuf said with a smile. He felt around in his pocket and produced something that Babu and Aftab both leaned forward to see: a tiny, greasy ball of opium, which, dropped in Miss Lussi's cup of tea, would make her sleep for three hours and have the most beautiful dreams while she was gently snoring the afternoon away.

Babu sucked in his teeth in horror. "You can't give her that!"

"Why not? Don't we give this to babies in the villages so that they will sleep through the night? It's perfectly safe. My mother gave it to me all the time and there's nothing wrong with me at all!"

"Yes, just look at you," muttered Aftab.

Pinky could hardly eat her lunch; roast mutton with cauliflower was her least favorite meal of all on normal days, and today the excitement almost choked her. But Miss Lucy had told Mama that a good roast lamb on Sundays was what all the children in England were brought up on; lamb was not commonly eaten in Karachi, the smelly meat adored only by the wild men of Kashmir, but Mama considered goat's meat, lean and tough, a good enough substitute. Pinky made sure to gulp down each and every bite on her plate, earning a rare glance of approval from

Miss Lucy, and she could hardly wait for Miss Lucy to have her tea, served to her in a china cup reserved for Papa's most important visitors by the obsequious Yusuf. The Englishwoman's daily half-hour nap would surely be enough time for Pinky to go to the shrine and have her fate told by the parrots. She wasn't quite sure what they would tell her, but she hoped it had something to do with castles and ponies, and chocolate—a huge amount of chocolate. Maybe even a castle made of chocolate! Or a chocolate pony that could somehow walk around in the sun all day without melting. You never knew . . .

Mir finished his lunch and ran off, and Sunny toddled away, too, but Pinky sat and stared at her plate with its fork and knife neatly crossed together, until she heard Miss Lucy yawn loudly, one, two, three times. The governess was rubbing her thumb and forefinger in the corners of her eyes, and it looked like she was having a hard time holding her head straight. "Oh, my dear . . ." Miss Lucy began, then yawned again. "I think I shall have a little lie-down. I'm suddenly very tired . . . Do you think you could play quietly for a half hour, my dear, while I take some rest? Read the books that your papa brought you from London. There's a good girl."

"Yes, Miss Lucy," said Pinky primly. But as soon as the governess climbed the stairs to her room, Pinky raced into the kitchen. "She's gone, she's gone, Yusuf! Let's go. Quickly, before she wakes up again!"

They ran to the car, where the driver and Babu already waited in the front seats. Yusuf's teeth gleamed white and straight in his dark face, and Pinky smiled so hard that her cheeks hurt, and Babu, hearing her infectious laughter, could not help but allow the corners of his mouth to be pulled out of their downward droop. In a few moments they swept out of the driveway and were driving up the street to the seafront, where a simple left turn took them to the Mazaar, the shrine of Abdullah Shah Ghazi, the patron saint of Karachi.

Pinky gawped at the green building, set on a high hill, connected to the ground by means of a long, thin staircase that looked to her as if it might go all the way up to the sky. A few figures were climbing up the stairs; it was Sunday afternoon, too early for the crowds of people that usually visited the saint and thronged the street beneath the tomb, buying green cloths and garlands of roses and other religious knickknacks to take back to their families after their day of pilgrimage. She wondered what the tomb looked like on the inside: she imagined a very cold room, with stalactites growing from the ceilings, dripping cold drops of ice water onto the floor, like a cave Papa had once visited in China. But she would never be allowed to see it for herself: her mother told her, as they drove by the shrine, that bad people visited it and bad things happened in its basement, so she was a little afraid, and she turned her head away and looked instead for the parrot-master sitting on the sidewalk. And sure enough, she saw him immediately, an old man who crouched next to a large cage shrouded by a white cloth turned gray with grime, and a placard next to that that showed a picture of a bright green parrot with an envelope in its beak.

The driver parked the car a safe distance away from the Parrot-Master—it would never do for Saeen's Buick to be recognized standing in front of a common Tota-Fal stall. He jogged back to find the little group standing around the old man as he explained that for two rupees his parrot would choose an envelope whose contents would reveal the future to the lucky customer. The man was tiny and wizened; he spoke a type of coarse Sindhi that suggested he might have been a fisherman from the coast in a previous life. When he smiled at all of them, there were gaps where his teeth should have been, and Pinky stared at them, astonished: she had never seen a toothless man before.

"Who wants to go first?" said the Parrot-Master.

"I will," said Yusuf, clutching two rupees in his fist.

"Let me pay!" said Pinky, pushing back his hand and offering her money to the Parrot-Master instead.

Yusuf shook his head. "No, *bibi*. I have to pay for my own fortune. You keep your money."

"Then I'll pay for Babu!"

Babu put up his hands in protest. "*Na, baba!* I don't want to know the future! My present is confusing enough, thank you!"

"All right, then." The Parrot-Master drew the cloth off his cage and revealed a gleaming green parakeet, large-breasted and long-tailed, which dipped its head back and forth and let out a happy whistle when the sunlight hit its cage. Pinky clapped her hands in delight as the Parrot-Master opened the cage door: the parrot didn't fly away immediately, as Pinky would have done if she were a bird trapped in a cage. It merely hopped out and stood with its head cocked, waiting obediently for its master's command. "What is your name?"

"Yusuf Sheedi."

The Parrot-Master leaned forward and repeated Yusuf's name three times to the parrot, who nodded and squawked, and slowly began to pace up and down the row of long envelopes spread out at the old man's feet. On the third round, the parrot stopped and plucked out an envelope, then fluttered up and perched on the Parrot-Master's shoulder. Pinky waited with bated breath and Yusuf's face grew more and more fearful as the Parrot-Master opened the envelope and began to read. Babu's eyes narrowed at the idea that this simple man was literate, but he too listened carefully to the man's words.

"You are a simple man, without cares or worries. But you must be careful not to fall into bad ways, especially gambling and fighting. Otherwise there could be a bad end waiting for you. Seek refuge in Allah, and be kind to your mother."

Yusuf scratched his head in confusion. "My mother is dead," he ventured.

"Do you want another try? Two rupees, only."

Babu glanced at Pinky, who was dancing from one foot to the other with impatience. He nudged Yusuf, who looked as though he might be willing to hand over another two rupees on the spot. "Let Pinky-bibi go. She's why we're here in the first place, remember?" He gently pushed the child forward. "Do hers, Parrot-Master, so that we can be on our way."

Pinky held out her fist to the Parrot-Master, dropping the coins in his hand, old and seasoned as the wood of a forty-year-old fishing boat. He nodded, showed her money to the parrot, then said, "And what is your name?"

"Pinky."

"That is not your real name. It won't work unless I know your real name."

The child hesitated and looked at Babu—she'd been taught not to reveal her real name to strangers, but she was torn between wanting to obey her parents and having her fortune told. Babu smiled reassuringly, then bent forward and whispered it in the Parrot-Master's ear, along with a threat that if he revealed the child's identity to anyone, Babu would see to it that the Parrot-Master's legs would be broken and the head of his parrot wrenched off its neck by nightfall. The Parrot-Master's face remained blank as he said to his parrot, "Pinky, Pinky, Pinky. The young lady's name is Pinky. Find her fate, with the help of the blessed saint, Abdullah Shah Ghazi!"

The parrot, instead of pacing up and down, this time flew

directly to a card at the end of the row, picked it up, and flew straight back to the Parrot-Master's shoulder. Babu registered the look of surprise in the old man's raised eyebrows, the tremble in his fingers as he opened the card and stared at it. For a few minutes, he did not speak.

"What is it?" said Pinky fearfully. "What does it say?"

The Parrot-Master said nothing. He turned the card around and showed it to all of them: no lettering, but the picture of a gold crown.

"What does it mean?" said Yusuf.

"She is a queen," said the Parrot-Master slowly. "She is a queen."

Yusuf and Babu looked at each other and shrugged. That much was already obvious: a child arriving with a battalion of servants in a car that most people would never be able to afford even if they saved up the money they earned in a lifetime— what else could she be but a queen? And of course the Parrot-Master knew whose daughter she was; that much was obvious, too. *A waste of money,* Babu was already thinking, *but if it makes Pinky-bibi happy and we can get her home quickly, no harm done.*

Yusuf, too, was disappointed that the Parrot-Master had said nothing of any value to him or Pinky-bibi; what if he was wrong about the ability of the waters of Manghopir to be able to cure Aftab's son? Yusuf could feel the walls that held up the sky of his simple world begin to sway, as if being shaken by an earthquake.

Pinky simply looked confused.

Then the Parrot-Master spoke again. "She is a queen, but not just any queen . . . she is the Eighth Queen, which Shah Abdul Latif wrote about on his final trip to Thar . . ."

Babu frowned deeply, sharp lines cutting a path into his face that showed what he would look like when he too was as ancient as this man one day. "What are you talking about, Parrot-Man?"

"In the *Risalo*, Saeen Shah Abdul Latif of Bhit wrote about the Seven Queens, Marvi, Sassi, Sohni, Leelu . . ."

"Yes, yes, we know about all that." Babu was irritated. He knew his Sindhi folklore as well as any other man of Sindh! Did the Parrot-Master think he was a fool like Yusuf, or an *angrez,* like Pinky-bibi, who, for all intents and purposes, was being raised like a memsahib in a Sindhi girl's body? "But I've never heard of an Eighth Queen. You're talking nonsense!"

The Parrot-Master gazed at Babu with a wounded expression in his rheumy eyes, turned blue with cataract and age. "Shah Abdul Latif was one day upset with his beloved wife, so he took a long journey and went into the desert of Thar. The Tharis welcomed him and shared their meals with him, and he wandered with them for many months, learning their ways. And when at last he came back, he started to write the epic poem of the Eighth Queen, whose name he never revealed. Like the others before her, she would fight for love, for freedom, for truth. She would be separated from her beloved, and pine for it all her days in a foreign land. And she would return, and lead her people to victory from the oppressors . . . This is that queen, she is standing right here in front of me, I know it."

"There's no such tale. You're mad, old man!" said Babu. Pinky's shoulders were starting to shake, and her chin was beginning to wobble. The child was clearly being upset by the rantings of this old charlatan. Best to get her out of here, and pretend this day had never happened. "Don't listen to him, Pinky-bibi. He's just an old man. He doesn't know what he's talking about. Take Pinky-bibi to the car," he said to the driver. "I'll be there in a minute."

"Yes, I'm mad!" shouted the Parrot-Master. "Mad with love for my beloved! My queen! I throw myself at her mercy! You have my allegiance forever, my queen!"

Pinky was crying now, as the driver and Yusuf quickly hustled her away and into the waiting car. Babu glared at the old man, drawing his foot back to kick the wrinkled old body as hard as he could. But a figure like this, old, destitute, raving like a lunatic, could only be pitied. Violence and anger were wasted on those too weak to give you a good fight.

He set his foot down again and watched as the Parrot-Master shoved the parrot back into its cage and covered it up with the shroud, gathering up his envelopes and packing them away into another filthy cloth. The old man panted like a thirsty dog with the effort of jerking himself up off the ground, and slung his parrot cage onto his back; Babu felt a sudden sharp pang of fear as the Parrot-Master trotted away toward the shrine, still ranting. "My queen! My beloved! She has come to save Sindh! She will live forever! Martyrs never die!" Then Babu blinked his eyes and when he opened them again, the Parrot-Master had vanished, as if he had existed only in Babu's mind.

By the time Babu walked slowly back to the car, Pinky had been cajoled into good humor by Yusuf, who was pulling a variety of foolish faces and telling her silly jokes that even she, with her limited Sindhi, could understand. She was giggling, her hand in front of her mouth, the pink cheeks and sweet dark eyes showing no trace of the unhappiness and fright the Parrot-Master had induced in her only a few minutes before.

"Let's go, Pinky-bibi," said Babu, wiping his hand across his forehead and feeling as though he had aged ten years in the last ten minutes. "Miss Lucy will be wondering where we are."

"I want some chocolate first, Babu," said Pinky. "Can we go to the store and buy some before we go home?"

December 26, 2007

I will bring you food!"
   The crowd cheered.
   "And clothing!"
   Another cheer.
   "Housing that you can afford!"
   Applause swelled up like the tide that was beating against the shore a few feet away.
   "Health, prosperity, and jobs . . . But most of all, I will give you *khushali*—well-being—for you and your children and for generations to come!" Men cheered and clapped and whistled and hooted, wide smiles on all their faces. Ali clapped, too, allowing himself to be carried away by their enthusiasm.
   The speaker raised his hands, until the noise died down. "All you have to do is let me into your home and your heart. I promise I will never let you down. I am a simple man, not the great magician that everyone says I am, but if you do not forget me, I will never forget you . . ."

The street theater was proving to be a great success: a few members of the People's Resistance were performing a skit they'd written called *Jadugar*, about a magician who persuaded a poor family to let him stay in their house, eating all their food in return for a few extravagant promises. This was the third performance they'd put on that afternoon on the long Seaview road, which ran all the way down Clifton Beach. After receiving a text message about the show, Ali made his way to the beach at five in the evening, and was standing in the audience now, enjoying the crisp winter air, the caressing breeze of the Arabian Sea, the water flat and blue like a mirror laid on the sand, reflecting only milky wisps of clouds scattered here and there in the sky.

Ali turned away from the impromptu stage to observe the people who'd gathered around: young men in *shalwar kameezes*, cheap shirts and trousers and baseball caps; five or six women; and a dozen giggling children standing in the front row with their hands in their mouths. The actor playing the magician wore a black *shalwar kameez* and a cape, with an impressive head of long hair and a matching beard; when he came close, the children drew back, eyes wide, fearful that he might actually cast a spell on them. The men, who knew better, went along with the spirit of the performance, calling out to the poor family, warning them that the magician was up to no good, while the few women in the audience said nothing with their mouths but everything with their eyes, lively and amused in their otherwise serious faces.

It didn't hurt so much to turn his head anymore; Ali's bruises were healing nicely, although his fingers still hurt when he tried to pick up even the lightest object in his hands, refusing to bend and paining him during the night, especially when it was cold. On landing in Karachi, Ali's father had taken him straight to the emergency room at the Aga Khan Hospital, where a sleepy intern examined Ali and ordered a few X-rays to find out the extent of the damage.

Ali and his father sat in silence, side by side on a row of hard plastic chairs in the waiting room. The bumping of the plane's wheels on the runway had ended their brief interlude; now again they fell into a companionable silence. Ali's father stretched out his legs and leaned his head back against the wall, closing his eyes: it was three o'clock in the morning. But Ali's mind began to stir, like a restless dog, and was soon flooded with thoughts of Salma, here in the clinic that she'd described so often to him, where she underwent the torture of her lectures and rotations. He rang her phone several times, then Ferzana, Bilal, and Imran: no reply. Frantically, he began to send out text messages with his good hand.

"Who are you messaging?" Ali's father asked.

"A few friends who were with me at the march."

"Ah."

Just then the intern reappeared with Ali's X-rays: he summoned them into the examining room to tell them that there was no permanent damage, but two fingers were broken and had to be padded in a splint, and Ali needed bandaging around a cracked rib and a stitch just under his eye, which would leave a small scar. "It will make you more attractive to the ladies," the intern said, as he poked around with a needle and surgical thread, while Ali's father watched with a frown as Ali tried not to wince at the doctor's ministrations.

The car ride from the hospital to Ali's house took less than ten minutes. The driver navigated the darkened streets, while they sat in the back, each encased in his own world of private thoughts and silent regret. Ali knew by now that his father held many sorrows about the events of the past. And he was just like his father: suspended in the amber of his mistakes, nursing the wounds he had sustained in the trauma of separation. All this time, Ali and his father had been longing for each other, hurt and grieving in isolation. That they had reconnected now, and managed to show each other the depth of their pain, was a possibility too momentous for Ali to contemplate.

Suddenly, Ali's mobile phone beeped. He glanced at the screen: it was a message from Ferzana.

Released just now. Coming home tomorrow. Salma with me. Imran & Bilal still in jail.

Ali quickly sent back a reply: *Thank God. R u ok?*

After a minute, the phone beeped another affirmation. *We r ok.*

He let out a long, shuddering sigh, and then the tears broke through the fog in his mind that had been holding them back all day. He wanted to press his fingers in the corners of his eyes to stop them, but the stitches were in the way, so he let them pour out over the wound on his eye, stinging him as the salt seeped into the stitches, and he raised his arm and wiped his sleeve on his face.

Ali's father was alarmed. "*Khariyat?*"

"It's . . . it's okay. They're all right. I was really worried . . . there's this girl, a friend, really young, and . . . she got arrested, and I was scared about what might have happened to her." He could hardly get the words out. The sobs caught in his throat and he had to swallow hard to push them back down. And then, to his surprise, he felt his father pat his arm gently.

"*Bas, put* . . . Enough, son. Don't cry. Come on, everything is all right."

Ali resisted the urge to lean into his father's embrace. But he managed, somehow, to stop crying, and when his father offered him a clean starched handkerchief from somewhere in his pocket, Ali took it gratefully and wiped his face, dabbing carefully around the cut beneath his eye, before giving it back to his father. "Here . . . thanks."

"Keep it."

They were outside Ali's house now, and the driver was holding the car door open for him. Ali put one foot on the ground; half in and half out of the car, he tried to turn back to look at his father, but the movement sent a wrenching pain around his waist and up his back. With difficulty he planted his other foot outside and heaved himself up to a standing position. Like a man in a suit of armor, he turned so that his whole body faced his father, still seated in the car. "I'm going now."

"I'll call you tomorrow."

"You don't have to." The response was automatic, proof that his defenses were still active, still second nature. He already needed to ward off the rejection that he was sure would come tomorrow. He had spent too many years of his life waiting by the phone, looking down the driveway, standing trembling in the doorway of his father's room, his childish schoolwork in his hands. He was almost superstitious about it by now: *think no thoughts of your father, push his image from your mind, because he'll know you want him, and then he won't come.*

A shrug of the shoulders, a hand through the hair that had once been generous but was now receding and grayed. "Well, you know where I am. If you need anything."

Ali nodded. *I don't need anything,* he wanted to say to his father. *I haven't needed anything for years.* And then he closed his eyes and saw Haroon's face, his friend, his brother, who had died without being able to say goodbye to his father. The pain in Haroon's father's eyes when he'd come to the office, searching for the remains—the remnants—of the boy in whom he'd invested his hopes, his dreams.

"Thank you, Baba Saeen." Until the other day, he hadn't uttered the endearment in years, but now he was using it as he always had when he was young. Was there love behind the name anymore? Or just respect, an acknowledgment of what his father had done for Ali tonight? He didn't know. He would never know. But he would remember what there had been, once upon a time. Ali would know forever, because of what his father had done for him tonight, that once, a long time ago, he had been loved.

And just maybe there was still some of that love left for him. He didn't want to dwell on the thought, but if the chance was there, then he'd have something to hold on to when he had to face the next day, and the next, and all the difficult ones after that.

As the driver closed the car door, Ali thought he heard Sikandar say one last thing before the engine started and the car pulled away into the night.

"Give my *salaams* to your mother."

* * *

The magician had by now moved into the poor family's home, but was eating up all their food, taking up their valuable space. He wore a green cap and a comfortable brown housecoat and lolled on a chair, reading a newspaper upside down, while the family members squatted on the ground in front of him.

The head of the family said, "We've done everything you asked. You said we'd have more food, better housing, better jobs if we let you stay. Now it's your turn!"

The magician put down his newspaper and looked down his nose at the man and his wife and daughter. "You still need to do more. You must keep some fierce dogs to protect yourself, and make the walls of your house higher. Only then can I bring richness into your house, because then it will be properly protected!"

"We can't afford that. You've been here for months, my

mother has died, and my young son is still unemployed! It's time for you to deliver on your promises!"

The actors playing the family looked into the audience, holding their hands up helplessly. "What should we do, friends?"

The crowd began to call out: "Kick him out! Get rid of him! Send him away!" Nobody was naïve enough to believe that the play was only about a magician and a poor family, even the children. Some of the men in the crowd were muttering to each other about the president and other unpopular politicians who had also outstayed their welcome. Ali grinned at the curses heaped upon their heads. After eight years of dictatorship, they had gained nothing, despite the extravagant promises, the dreams of a prosperous future that the power-mongers had guaranteed would someday turn into reality. Their leaders were like an artist standing in front of a blank canvas and telling them the beautiful painting he would create, if only they supplied him with the right kind of paint; they knew full well that they had been duped, and that the masterpiece would never be completed.

"Throw him out!"

"We've had enough of these looters, these plunderers!"

"They can go to hell!"

Ali, too, called out, enjoying the feeling of being able to vocalize his displeasure. Frustration and anger were written large on everyone's faces; why else did people misbehave the way they did on the streets of Karachi, driving like maniacs, littering the streets, defacing property? Because nobody cared. The country and its people were a whore to be used violently and greedily until the users were spent and exhausted and could grab and take no more. And they would be forced to give and give and give, for generations, not able to lift their heads or think of anything beyond daily survival. It was the quickest and surest way to destroy a nation, poison its people, shatter a land into pieces that could never be put together again.

Ali's mobile phone beeped in his hand. He looked down; he didn't recognize the number. He put his free hand over his ear and pressed the phone to the other ear.

"Hello?"

"Where are you?" It was a female voice, a soft voice that made his heart hammer frantically inside his chest like a moth beating against a lit window.

"Sunita?"

"It's me, Ali. Where are you?"

"Uh . . . I'm at Seaview . . . where are you?" His hands grew clammy, even though the day was cool and dry. "Are you at college?"

"Put your hand up and wave so I can see you. I'm in the crowd, I just can't see where you are."

Ali turned around, but his vision failed him, and the faces surrounding him melted and blurred into one indecipherable mass. He blinked his eyes over and over again, trying to find the one face that he'd been looking for, all these days and weeks. He put his hand up in the air and searched desperately for that dark hair, those doe eyes, the tea-colored skin that he missed as much as the gentle laugh, the teasing smile, and the generous warmth of the girl he loved.

Sunita.

She was standing there, having somehow materialized behind him. She wore a dress in a wine-red color, one that he hadn't seen before. It gave her skin an added luster, brought out new highlights in her hair. Weeks had gone by since he'd seen her last; perhaps she had a whole new wardrobe by now, a new boyfriend, a new life. She looked healthy and well, but there was surprise on her face. She reached out for him and touched the scar under his eye. "Does it hurt?"

"No." He knew she'd want to know how it happened. "It's a long story . . ."

"Did they do that to you on the march?"

It was his turn to be shocked. "How did you know?"

She smiled crookedly, then moved her hand from his face to cover her mouth. "Don't you know? You're a TV star. It was on the news. I didn't see it, but Jehangir called me and said that you'd been arrested." He held up his hand for her, and her eyes widened at the bandage around the two fingers of his left hand. "Are you all right?"

"Let's go sit down over there." He led her to a bench, away from the crowd. She followed him, and they sat side by side. Ali wanted to stare at her, to fill his eyes with her beauty. But he was suddenly embarrassed, and instead gazed out to the sea, where a trawler was crossing the horizon, just west of Manora Island. He'd been to that island once on a navy boat, a long-forgotten picnic from his childhood, where he and his brother and their friends for that day had played around the lighthouse and watched the boats ferrying people to and from their jobs on the mainland. Karachi from that distance looked like a different place, the white buildings stretching on the gentle curve all the way from the West Wharf to Seaview, where they were now. Maybe some children right at this moment were on that island, looking at the city that had morphed and grown into something gigantic, something beyond anyone's control.

"My father took us to Manora once, on a picnic," Ali said. He'd never been able to tell her the truth about his father; she thought he had died five years ago. She'd believed the lies he'd told her, just like everyone else. He took a deep breath. "My father . . . he came to get me out of jail after the march. I got arrested. Beaten up. I don't know what they would have done to me if he hadn't come. Two of my friends are still in detention up there."

Sunita was silent, but Ali could hear the fresh hurt in the way she breathed out in a long exhalation that was midway between a sigh and a gasp. A smattering of applause burst out; the play had ended and the crowd was dispersing, leaving the actors to stand together in a little band, smiling and shaking hands with a few supporters who'd hung back to talk to them. There'd be a discussion; they'd talk about whether or not the play affected them, related to their lives. Ali would have liked to take part, but the person whom he'd affected was sitting right next to him, and he had to make things right with her before he could think of fixing the rest of the world.

"I know what you're thinking," he said quickly. "That I've lied to you about everything. And you're right. I have. I've been a coward."

Sunita was twisting her hands in her lap. Ali reached forward and took one of her hands in his own. He massaged her palm lightly with his thumb, stroked her fingers, felt her warm skin and the beat of her pulse in the web of skin between thumb and forefinger. "My father's a Pir. He's a zamindar. He has two wives. I have a half sister I've never seen. I thought you wouldn't love me if you knew all of this . . ." His voice trailed off before he could confess that he hoped she would love him still. He would make no excuses for his deception. Perhaps she would sense his earnestness like she sensed so many things about him: his insecurity, his fears, his weaknesses. And most of all, his shame, through the nights when he was unable to sleep and lay awake in bed, smoking and talking to her for hours on the phone. "Don't say anything," he said. "Just tell me you forgive me."

"I don't know . . ."

"I'm sorry. I'm so sorry I hurt you."

Sunita shook her head. He knew she wanted to say more, and waited for it. She swallowed instead, and he watched as her delicate throat moved with effort. "I don't even know you."

"Then why did you come?" He asked the question gently, but a knife edge of desperation lay underneath his soft tone. Her answer would tell him whether he had a chance at redemption or whether he should give up now and never hope for her again.

She looked down. "I missed you." Her lips were trembling, and she pulled her hand away from his, but he couldn't help the slow spread of joy that started at the base of his spine and moved up his back, gooseflesh rising on his arms, a warmth that lifted the hair off the nape of his neck and caused his cheeks to burn. This was not the moment for the arrogance of the victor, the triumph of the conqueror. In losing Sunita, he had very nearly lost himself. In humility he had to kneel at her feet, hope that her compassion would grow into forgiveness, that forgiveness would once again blossom into love.

They sat together, side by side. He breathed with her and mirrored the movements of her limbs, crossing his arms when she crossed hers, stretching out his legs when she stamped her feet and shook her sleeping foot up and down to wake it up. He had never felt so peaceful, so whole. The sun began its descent toward the horizon, and a chill embraced them both. She shivered; he would have put his arm around her, but they were in a public place and it was still Pakistan. He leaned into her and willed his blood to warm her just as her words had warmed his soul.

Half an hour passed, and then his phone rang again. It would be his mother, asking where he was. "I'm sorry. I have to take this."

Sunita nodded. He smiled at her as he flipped open the phone and held it to his ear.

"Hello?"

"Ali, it's Ameena."

"Ameena? Is everything okay?" She must be calling him about his last paycheck, he thought. He still hadn't received it; there had been some question about Ali not having given proper notice when he'd quit. He didn't care much, but he appreciated her following through. He'd heard enough horror stories at other offices of people who didn't get paid for months, or who had to come every day to finance departments and beg for the money owed them.

"Ali, glad I caught you. Listen, I know you're on leave, but there's something I want you to do."

He frowned. "What is it?"

"I want you to cover a political rally for me. Benazir Bhutto's going to be speaking tomorrow."

"Where?"

"In Rawalpindi. Liaquat National Bagh. I know it's short notice, you'd have to take the first plane out tomorrow morning, but you'd be there in time. The rally starts at three p.m. Can you do it?"

"Ameena, I'm not supposed to be working right now . . ."

"What can I say, Ali? I want you to come back to us. In my mind you're still on the payroll. You're a damned good reporter. If you say yes, I'll make sure you host your own youth show in six months. And I'll make you an anchor after you graduate from university."

"Hold on." He put his hand over the phone, quickly related everything to Sunita. In Sindhi, which he knew Ameena could not understand, he asked her, "Should I do it?"

"Ask for twice as much money as you were being paid before."

Ali grinned. "You are a genius." He spoke into the phone once again. "All right, Ameena. I'll do it."

"Come to the office in the morning. There'll be a plane ticket waiting for you."

"I'll be there." He didn't realize, until he heard Ameena's tones of command even while begging him for a favor, how much he'd missed being at the channel. It made him feel good to know that his absence had been felt, that Ameena wasn't ready to reject him because of his true background.

He shut the phone and put it in his pocket. Then he took Sunita's hand again. This time, he wanted to talk to her until the sky turned the color of crushed dark velvet and the stars came out, first the North Star and then the other constellations, winking out their silvery Morse code above the heads of the Sindhi fishermen in their boats on the Arabian Sea. He wanted to be with her until the moon followed the path of the sun toward the flat line of the ocean, and the sun rose up again in the east, bringing the new day, and with it, a new start for both of them, with no more interruptions.

Signs

When the world was still to be born
When Adam was still to receive his form
Then my relationship began

When I heard the Lord's voice
A voice sweet and clear
I said "yes" with all my heart
And formed a bond with the land I love

* * *

Rawalpindi had always made her nervous. In this garrison town lived the army in their fortified barracks; GHQ was not half an hour from where she was right now, in her Islamabad home. She had spent months in detention here, waiting for her father to die. He had been hanged in the Rawalpindi Central Jail on April 4, 1979, a date emblazoned in her mind, always taking precedence over the birthdays of her children, the anniversary of her sister's marriage, her own anniversary. Not a single happy day could pass without her thinking of him, weakened and ill, dying a martyr's death when he should have been living a king's life.

Her father's birthday and his death day were separated only by four short months. He had been a Capricorn, like Muhammed Ali Jinnah, who died on September 11, 1948. A disaster for Pakistan sixty years ago; a disaster for the world sixty years later. April 4, 1979, had turned out to be a disaster for Pakistan thirty years ago; what disaster would befall her country on April 4 in 2008, thirty years later? She had always been suspicious, superstitious, that way; everywhere she turned, she saw signs, and they chilled her. She consulted holy men and oracles, Pirs and sheikhs, to try to find consolation, but her heart was always fluttering like a trapped bird beating its wings against her rib cage.

Rawalpindi was the scene of yet another disaster for Pakistan: the assassination in October 1951 of Liaquat Ali Khan, the country's first prime minister. An Afghan from the Zadran tribe had shot him twice in the chest as he was about to make an announcement at the Municipal Park. It had been renamed Liaquat Bagh Park in the murdered prime minister's honor, and it was here that she was to address a political rally that afternoon.

She had told everyone that she wasn't afraid for her life. The long poems she had composed during those days in exile were her heart's honest outpourings, testimony to what she felt about herself, her life. When you have buried a father and two brothers, what else is there left to fear from death?

From Marvi I learnt
From past mystic saints
From my dear brother Shah I learnt
That handsome youth who fought another tyrant

That
Were I to breathe my last, living
Away from the home I loved
My body won't imprison me.

Still, she wished for a moment that she was not in her house in Islamabad, but back home in Larkana. She always felt strongest in her ancestral home, not far from where her father was buried. It was as if his bones had leached into the sand and given her strength; as long as she could be connected to the earth, through her feet and legs, she would not lose him. And yet, as Shah Abdul Latif had written in the epic poetry she adored (and tried to emulate in her own humble attempts at poetry), life was about separation and loss; she had been through the cycle time and time again, exiled from her beautiful Sindh, forced to wander for years, away from the love of her life.

Larkana, loved one, I remember
The sweet scent of roses
Of fresh rain on desert sand
Of trees washed by nature's hand.

She could not bear it if she were to never see Sindh again. But then she shook her head and pushed away the gloomy thoughts: of course she'd get through this, as she had, by the grace of God, got through all the other days. She'd learned something from the terrible night back in October: not to trust the government's assurances of safety, not to rely on their promises. Her security people had made arrangements for jammers, for strong floodlights; she'd talked to the Americans and the Israelis for private security contractors to protect her. The Israelis were still considering her request, but the Americans had provided her with some men, and she had faith in God.

And then there were her children: handsome Bilawal, with his first term at Oxford nearly over—how proud she'd been to take him there herself, show him the lawns where she'd studied, the halls where she'd debated, the rooms where she'd talked politics and movies and life, late into the night. Her daughter Bakhtawar, who wanted to be a punk musician—she'd even asked that rapper, what was his name? Puffy, Puff Daddy, Diddy, something like that, to help Bakhtawar out when it came time to try to enter the music industry. *The things one has to do for one's children,* she thought to herself with a wry smile. And Asifa, whose skin had begun to grow patchy, sending mother and daughter fleeing to the best dermatologist in London, the Dubai sun no good for her condition.

She had so much to do for all of them; she thought constantly of them when she was away. A mother's heart, pulled in so many directions; but her husband could never accuse her of *not* thinking of the children.

The meeting that morning with the EU election observers had gone well. She'd informed them of the preparations the president's party had been making for weeks: the plans to stuff the ballot boxes, the ghost polling stations, the intimidation of the voters that was by now a vital part of the playbook of Pakistani elections. The American lawmakers would be given another full dossier, when she met with them after the rally. She'd prepared her documents, working late into the night, hunched over her laptop computer with her glasses perched on her nose, a green pen in her hand to mark the printouts wherever she saw an error or a place where an amendment could be made.

Nobody knew where she found the stamina to keep working the long hours after everyone else had fallen nodding into bed, but she knew she had to be note-perfect when she spoke to Senators Specter and Kennedy, after they'd been wined and dined by the president, and he'd sung his song of fair elections and honorable intentions to them. She would not let them be hoodwinked by him.

She could hear muffled words, urgent whispers coming from outside the door where she was working, and she called out to them, "What is it? Tell me now . . ."

A reluctant aide approached her, and stood in front of her, shuffling from one foot to the other. Finally, he spoke up: "Bad news: four Nawaz supporters were killed. Someone fired upon them from a rooftop. The PML is blaming the Musharraf group. Violence to scare opponents away from the polls."

"Nothing new," she said. "Send a message of condolence through the official channels. Tell them that no dictator can stop the democratic process. It is what the people want."

> *Away I live in a mansion grand*
> *But I long to campaign*
> *On rocky roads*
> *In bumpy jeep rides*
> *With flags and banners*
> *With selfless zeal to change*
> *The sad present*
> *Into a smiling future.*

At two o'clock, she called out, "What's for lunch?"

"*Aloo salaan*, and chapati . . . sorry it's so plain."

"Don't be silly. It's my favorite!" She had always tried to watch her weight, what with her propensity for sweets, ice cream, and chocolate, but had given in when she realized that she would never regain the slim, willowy figure of her youth. She'd been interviewed by BBC reporters when she'd been prime minister, and one of them had asked her if she was pregnant again, after Bilawal's birth.

"No," she smiled, coolly umoved by the man's intrusiveness. "I am not pregnant. I am fat. And, as the prime minister, it is my right to be fat if I want to." That had shut him up, she thought to herself with glee, watching the reporter open and close his mouth several times. She giggled behind her hand when she was alone and thinking what a fool he looked.

They settled down to the meal, she and her closest circle of friends and colleagues, the inner circle, as they were called. Everyone seemed tense: she looked at the drawn, white faces, the hands that were only pushing the food around on their plates as they scanned her face for signs of a sudden loss of nerve. She felt calm, even concerned for those of her party who'd been traveling with her for months now, staying up nights in long vigils. "Please, Adda, relax and eat," she told the man who was her right hand, a top official in the PPP, and he blushed like a schoolboy being told by his mother to clean his plate.

"Do you want to go over the speech again?" he asked her, trying to cover his embarrassment.

"No, let's just enjoy the moment," she said. "It's a beautiful day, isn't it?" But after the meal was over, she took her notes over to the window that overlooked the serene Margalla Hills, and she sat quietly in a large chair, reading them over and over again. *I call on my homeland of Pakistan to come out and fight for Pakistan's future. I'm not afraid. We cannot be afraid.*

There was still time for the post-noon prayer; she got up from her chair, leaving the notes on the table, and went to her bedroom, where she gathered her prayer mat and her *dupatta*. She stood on the mat, *dupatta* draped primly over her head, and began the cycle of prayers, the four *sunnat*, four *farz*, two *sunnat*, two *nafl*, prescribed by the Prophet, peace be upon him. Then she lifted her hands in *dua* and asked God to look after her children, her husband, her ailing mother, her country. Finally, she prayed for her own safety. And for her father's soul.

I raise both my hands
And ask my children
To raise their little hands
Marvi, of Maru and Malir
In the mists of time
She raised her hands
While the world slept
To God
Full of hope
Praying to see her homeland.

Three o'clock: time to get dressed.

She looked at herself in the mirror. She hated having to wear the bulletproof vest, but her husband and children insisted, as did her head of security. "But it makes me look so fat!" she'd wailed, the first time she'd put it on. She'd grown used to it, eventually, although she couldn't bear the weight of it, or how much it made her sweat. But when she was out there, in front of her people, listening to their cheers of *Jiye Bhutto! Jiye Bhutto!* and smelling the sweet scent of the rose petals they threw on her path, she forgot everything: physical discomfort, fear, thirst, hunger, heat, and fatigue. She only remembered her father, telling her to be strong.

Opening her closet, she took out the *shalwar kameez* to wear on top of the vest. She'd chosen a peacock-blue tunic: it offset the white *dupatta* perfectly and the silk material brought out the stark contrast of her pale face to her dark hair. The day she'd returned to Pakistan after those eight long years of exile, she'd worn a green one: green for Pakistan, green for Islam, green for the verdant farmland of Sindh. Today she'd chosen blue: honor, dignity, loyalty, serenity. She was no longer as young as she used to be, but she loved herself more: her confidence, her wisdom, the way she carried herself in the world. She smiled, reminded of the feminist diatribes in which she and her friends were so well versed, back in those heady days at Radcliffe when young women were just beginning to get a sense of their own potential. *A woman's worth is not in her looks, but in her personality, her mind! It's not youth that matters, but confidence, inner strength, wisdom!* What she would tell those raw, eager girls, if she could go back in time, share with them all the things she'd learned in the thirty-odd years since she'd been a student. But she could share them with her daughters—there were so many things her girls needed to hear from her.

"Time to go, Lady," said an aide, when she emerged from her bedroom into the drawing room once again. "It's three forty-five. Your car is ready."

She looked around the room, at the sweeping view of the hills, the afternoon sun sending rays of light that slanted from heaven to earth, illuminating spots of land with the precision of a laser beam. How beautiful! As if God Himself had painted the scene, just for her. It had to be a sign. She was a firm believer in signs: it was all over the Quran, that God had littered the universe with signs of His existence, His power, His mercy. *Verily, in all this there are messages indeed for those who can read the signs.*

She closed her eyes, thought once more of her children, said a small prayer. Then Benazir Bhutto gathered up her notes in her hands and called to no one in particular: "Come, let's go. I don't want to be late."

Children: Hear the desert wind
Hear it whisper
Have faith
We will win.

December 27, 2007

D ammit, I can't see her."

The press pit was in the wrong place: Ali craned his neck to get a view of the podium, but it was impossible from behind the crowds, a great sea that stretched from one end of the public park to the other. They wouldn't stand still; they surged up and down, heads rising, lowering, arms stretched out, people rising to their feet en masse, making Ali feel as though he were on the deck of a ship being tossed on endless waves. "Let's move around this way." He urged the cameraman to follow him, and they pushed and shoved their way through the gaps in the crowd till they found a space in which they could not only breathe, but also see Benazir Bhutto as she stood at the podium, waiting to begin her speech.

They were a hundred yards away from the stage, but Ali's vantage point was better now. He stood on top of a chair and directed the cameraman to start shooting even before she had begun to speak. The podium came midway up her chest, hiding most of her body, but they could see her white *dupatta* slipping from her head, and she had already begun to pull it up with her hands. She would have to perform this trademark maneuver at least two dozen times in the course of her speech, Ali knew from watching previous footage of her: she was too vain to pin it down, preferring to let it slip and slide around her face like a restless sea, while her carefully arranged hair remained visible underneath.

She was watching the crowd with a pleased look, waiting for them to quiet down. Ali thought she looked nervous, a young schoolgirl waiting to give her first speech in the school assembly. There was a sweet smile on her face, and she waved her hands excitedly above her head, stirring up the crowd, who began to cheer and whistle and stamp their feet in approval. Banners bearing the colors of the PPP fluttered in the wind, party workers clutched even more flags and posters in the audience, and the red chairs and red-carpeted stage made it look as though they'd all gathered for the biggest birthday party anyone had ever seen. All that was missing was a gigantic cake and the sound of "Happy Birthday" playing on the PA system, he thought to himself wryly.

She was speaking now, but all they could hear was a muffled whine from the speakers. "Shit," said Ali to his cameraman, Rasool, who doubled as driver and cameraman for the channel's Islamabad bureau. Rasool had collected him from the airport at one, then brought him straight here to get in position for the rally. "Can't hear a thing. Are you picking anything up?"

Rasool strained to hear through his headset, then shook his head. "Let's go back to the press pit."

"No way, then we won't see. Just wait . . . Ah, that's better." Someone had reached forward and adjusted Benazir's microphone and her voice rang out from all four corners of the park, strong and strident.

"I am happy to be here, to address you, at Liaquat Bagh . . .

Rawalpindi is the home of the brave, of the simple people who are ready to sacrifice their lives for the cause of democracy . . . I used to live in Rawalpindi and I consider it my second home. When Bhutto Sahib was a minister, I lived here and went to school here. I have seen great happiness, and also great pain . . ."

"She's speaking well," muttered Rasool.

"At least she doesn't make so many mistakes anymore." Her lack of Urdu or Sindhi had been a running joke in Pakistan for years, but to Ali it seemed she'd finally conquered her linguistic failings, and had found a working compromise between the heavy political phrases and the simple speech of her heart.

As she went on, Ali faced the camera and addressed a short commentary to its opaque eye. The feed would be sent to Ameena in Karachi; they'd edit it there and package it for the six o'clock news. "We're here at Liaquat Bagh Park, where Benazir Bhutto is addressing a political rally consisting of her loyal party workers. She's talking about how Rawalpindi has been the site of many brave sacrifices in the face of dictatorship and authoritarianism. She's naming some of the prominent party workers who took up the struggle for democracy: Abdul Majeed, Idress Baig, and of course, her father, Zulfikar Ali Bhutto, who was hanged almost thirty years ago here in Rawalpindi, the scene of many difficult memories for Ms. Bhutto."

Rasool cut back to filming Benazir; Ali knew that the sight of the woman, in her dark blue tunic, garlands of jasmine and roses around her neck, would make for an arresting visual. She had always been photogenic, but today it seemed as though something else emanated from her: a depth and solidity that he'd never recognized in her before, a gravitas that had little to do with her statuesque frame, but everything to do with her squared shoulders and her strong hands firmly gripping the podium. He wrapped up his remarks for the camera, then stood back and let out a long breath. He took out his phone, shot a text message to his father: *In Islamabad. Benazir rally.* He paused, then pressed the buttons to type out: *She's speaking very well.*

The phone beeped back, almost instantly: *Ok. Take care.*

Ali listened to Benazir's speech carefully, taking each word and measuring it in his mind, trying to regard her as if he'd never seen her or heard of her before. Everyone deserved a fair trial, after all. This was hers, in his mind: her chance to convince him that she was sincere, in this, her third attempt to seek the seat of power.

He heard her description of the travails of the people of Rawalpindi, of her father's attempts to establish the PPP in the name of the poor, the disenfranchised. And then she said, "Even in the face of all this, you have never left your sister alone . . . Bhutto Sahib recognized the importance of Rawalpindi. It is the heart of the Punjab, and Punjab is the heart of Pakistan."

Yes, thought Ali to himself. *She's right.* But there was something that she wasn't saying, and he wanted more than anything to tell her the all-important truth that everyone had forgotten about Pakistan: if Punjab was the heart of Pakistan, then Sindh was its soul.

Benazir put down her notes and stared intently into the crowd. Ali could feel the shiver starting from the top of his head and moving down his arms. He was too far away to be able to meet her eyes, but her intensity reached out and pushed into them all, as if she were alone in a room with each one of them, and taking them into her confidence. The connection between her and them began to sing and hum, as if wires were sparking and growing hot with energy.

"Wake up, my brothers! This country faces great dangers. This is your country. My country! We have to save it."

The men roared as if they had received an electric shock. To his astonishment, Ali found himself clapping, nodding his head. Even Rasool had put down his camera and was raising his fist in the air.

Benazir continued: "We have to have hope, no matter what. And never surrender."

The passion was irresistible. The crowd erupted in chants. *Jiye, Bhutto! Jiye Bhutto!* She surveyed the crowd, with an expression that Ali could not begin to recognize, filled with elation, fury, confidence, power. And yet he could see the sadness, like a dab of paint dropped into the clear water that slowly changed it from neutral to a different hue, start to wash from her eyes and color the other emotions struggling on her face.

The speech had ended. She was accepting congratulations from the party workers that surrounded her on the stage. Her smile chased away the clouds on her face, and Ali thought that he had only imagined the wistful look. She began to climb down from the stage, and Rasool was prodding him with his microphone, which he had unknowingly dropped on the ground.

"Ali? Ali, let's go. Let's finish up here. Come on. Let's go!"

"No. No, wait." Ali rubbed his forehead with his hand. The moments were passing; he might never have this opportunity again. "Let's follow her. Come on, let's just get a shot of her leaving."

"But . . ." Rasool was looking at him strangely, but Ali had already climbed down from his chair and begun walking toward the gates to the park, where Benazir and her entourage were pushing through, the security men and police officers keeping the crowds a good distance away from them.

Ali somehow managed to squeeze by and now he stood outside the park, blinking at the crush of people around Benazir's vehicle: a big white Land Cruiser, a ship waiting to ferry her through the crowds and back to the safety of her house in Islamabad. He wondered whether or not he should turn back, but then he caught a glimpse of Benazir's white veil, and it beckoned him on like a flag to come closer.

"Ali, Ali!" shouted Rasool. "I'm right here behind you!"

But Ali heard nothing he said. Benazir was in the Land Cruiser, standing in the front seat, her body halfway through the sunroof. She was smiling and waving, and people all around cheered and reached out to her.

Ali took slow, deep breaths to try to still the erratic drumbeat of his heart, but another, more primal part of him wanted to run straight to her, to tell her he had been wrong about her before, that he agreed with everything she was saying. She deserved a second chance, and a third, and a fourth, just like he did, just like everyone else did. Her whole life had been about struggle and about perseverance, and who could have gotten things right the first time round? Just by standing here today, she had done more than most leaders had achieved after a lifetime of power. But more than that, he longed to tell her his story: that he knew what it was like to lose a father, to be lost and adrift and struggling at sea, and then, finally, to see the shore and begin swimming toward it with all one's might.

He began to walk; then he broke into a run, until he reached the side of her vehicle. She was standing tall above him, smiling and waving. In a moment she would turn his way, and he would be able to call out her name. He was not nervous or afraid, even in the presence of this woman who had seen all that power had to offer.

All he could think of was how much he wanted to tell her that not only had he found his beloved, but his beloved had also found him. Of all the people in the world at that moment, he knew, as he stepped forward to reach for her hand, that she was the one person in the world who would really understand.

Acknowledgments

In order to write this book I had to fall into a trancelike state, somewhere halfway between a dream and a long hallucination into the past of this beautiful province. While dreams have their place, though, there are many people I need to thank, because without their help, the dream would never have become a reality.

Sincere thanks to my very first readers. My father, Shafqat Ali Shah, and my brother, Reza Ali Shah, encouraged me every step of the way, provided invaluable advice about the workings of the agricultural system in Sindh, and shared tales and myths from its rich history and the annals of our own family. Aamer Hussein, who believed in this novel from the very start and nicknamed it GSN, or "The Great Sindhi Novel," gave me a critical, writer's opinion as well as a more emotional reaction as someone with rich Sindhi heritage himself.

Dr. Javaid Leghari told me many stories about Benazir Bhutto's abilities and qualities as a leader—the two were close friends and he ran the Shaheed Zulfikar Ali Bhutto Institute of Science and Technology with excellence and professionalism, earning Bhutto's respect, and later mine, when I taught writing there for four years. Thanks to him, I was able to see a precious copy of the PPP manifesto with Bhutto's handwritten notes on it, in green ink, as written in my story. And it was with his permission that I used Benazir Bhutto's own poetry in the chapter titled "Signs." A big thank-you to my students and colleagues at SZABIST: they provided me with inspiration and educated me as much as I educated them. I must also thank Tariq Islam, who shared with me the tale of Zulfikar Ali Bhutto's trial and other insights into Benazir Bhutto's personality and character.

Sabeen Mahmud and Awab Alvi helped me immensely in writing the chapters on Ali's involvement with "smart protesting." Thank you to Sabeen for allowing me to put the Second Floor in the novel, a real-life establishment where many of the People's Resistance meetings actually did take place, and where the Constitution was actually "suspended" from the rafters. Awab Alvi shared information about the resistance movement with me and explained the organization's aims to me. I salute their courage and their principles: today's Sindh is a stronger place because of them.

This book would not have been written without the groundbreaking research and writing done by others before me, and so I must acknowledge these authors and their works here. Professor Sarah F. D. Ansari wrote *Sufi Saints and State Power,* which helped me to understand how the descendants of the saints became power brokers in Sindh. Her book was the inspiration for the chapters "The Gift," "Outlaws," and "The Game of Kings," providing the historical framework over which I was able to layer the freely imagined, fictional events in those sections. The books of H. T. Lambrick, including *The Terrorist* and *The History of Sindh in Two Volumes,* also provided background material and history. Khadim Hussain Soomro's *Freedom at the Gallows: The Life and Times of Sayed Sibghatullah Shah Pir Pagaro, The Brit-*

ish in Sindh: Immoral Entry and Exit, and *The Path Not Taken: G.M. Sayed: Vision and Valour in Politics*, were three more fantastic resources. *The Races That Inhabit the Valley of the Indus*, by Richard F. Burton, and *A Voyage on the Indus: Travels into Bokhara*, by Sir Alexander Burnes, helped me fill in historical details in "The Gift," "Outlaws," and "The Game of Kings." Articles that helped me a great deal: Griff Witte and Emily Wax, "Bhutto's Last Day, in Keeping with Her Driven Life," from the *Washington Post;* David Pinault, "Fortune-Telling Parrots of Pakistan and Singapore," in the *Pakistan Studies News;* and Ananda K. Coomaraswamy, "Khwaja Khadir and the Fountain of Life in the Tradition of Persian and Mughal Art," in *What Is Civilization and Other Essays*.

The poetry of Shah Abdul Latif Bhitai plays a central role in this novel, and I must acknowledge the translators of these verses: the late Annemarie Schimmel and Elsa Kazi, two German scholars who showed their great love of Sindh and of the Sufi poet by devoting themselves to his work and creating such beautiful English versions. H. T. Sorely's *Shah Abdul Latif of Bhit: His Poetry, Life, and Times* provided the historical background I needed to envision the poet's life in Bhit Shah. I owe a great debt to the poet himself, as he is my ancestor and the great guiding spirit of this novel.

Many thanks to Anne-Marie Doulton at the Ampersand Agency and Rosie Buckman at the Buckman Agency for all their work on the Italian edition. I'm very grateful to Hannah Ferguson and Jessica Woollard at the Marsh Agency for their encouragement and help in bringing this, the original English-language version, into being. I owe my biggest debt to Joseph Olshan, my editor at Delphinium Books, who read the book when it was in a far more confused shape, and fell in love with it despite its weaknesses and flaws. His insight, instincts, and brilliance as both an editor and a writer as well as his generosity as a reader have proven him to be a true champion of this book.

Finally, thank you to my friends and family for all their support and encouragement. It isn't easy living with a writer and the concomitant mood swings, grouchiness, absentmindedness, and temporary insanity that take over when a book's on the way. I'm sorry you had to hear me going on and on about the novel, and I appreciate your patience, your sense of humor, and the occasional kick in the ass I needed to remain grounded. I can't do any of this without you, and I promise I'll be better next time.

Thank you to Alina Hasanain Shah for her excellent reading of the manuscript.

The poems of Benazir Bhutto, which are included in "Signs," come from Benazir's book of poems *From Marvi of Malir and Shah Latif.* They are reproduced with permission from SZA-BIST University Press.

The poem about Pir Pagaro in "Game of Kings" comes from Sarah Ansari's *Sufi Saints and State Power* and is reproduced with permission from Cambridge University Press.